The

Christmas
Gathering

The Christmas Gathering

Shelley Shepard Gray

Lenora Worth

Rachel J. Good

KENSINGTON
PUBLISHING CORP.

www.kensingtonbooks.com

KENSINGTON BOOKS are published by

Kensington Publishing Corp.
900 Third Avenue
New York, NY 10022

ISBN: 978-1-4967-5030-3 (ebook)
ISBN: 978-1-4967-5029-7

First Kensington Trade Paperback Printing: October 2024

10 9 8 7 6 5 4 3 2 1

Printed in the United States of America

Contents

A Christmas Reunion

SHELLEY SHEPARD GRAY

For Alicia Condon,
a wonderful editor with a very kind heart

Acknowledgments

I absolutely love working on these Christmas novellas for Kensington. I'm so grateful for the editorial team for the opportunities they've given me. Thank you to Alicia, Elizabeth, Carly, and everyone else who works so hard to make my stories shine.

A big thanks also goes out to Lynne Stroup, who literally drops whatever she is doing to quickly read the first drafts of my work. Finally, I'm sincerely grateful for the chance to be "novella buddies" with authors Lenora Worth and Rachel J. Good. It's an honor to be in such amazing company.

Clap your hands, all you people. Shout to God with joy.

—Psalm 47:1

Pleasant days are just ordinary days made better
by good people.

—Amish proverb

Chapter 1

December 23

Once again, the Troyer homestead looked pristine and bare compared to its brightly lit and festooned neighbors' homes just outside of Wooster. The only signs that Christmas was approaching were the numerous pine boughs decorating the fence line, barn door, and front porch railing. Each of the evergreen branches was attached with a piece of burlap tied in a bow at regular intervals.

Though Brandt Holden imagined some of the Amish family's stricter neighbors and friends might find fault with even this small amount of decorating, he thought it was perfect. The freshly cut pine smelled wonderful and the burlap bows lent a homespun charm to the sprawling farm.

It also made the white farmhouse look especially welcoming.

After parking his truck in the designated area west of the barn, Brandt grabbed his duffel bag. Not bothering to lock the truck, he headed toward the house along the gravel path that was lightly covered with snow.

The closer he got to the house, the more Brandt felt his shoulders relax. He'd made it back.

This wasn't his home. It wasn't even his extended family's home. In addition, he wasn't Amish and he didn't actually know much about the Amish faith—except that the Amish didn't use electricity and drove horses and buggies. He was an Englischer—the usual Amish way of referring to anyone not Amish through and through.

None of those things mattered, though. This farm was where he wanted to spend Christmas. In spite of their many differences, this large, unwieldy, extended family made him feel like he belonged.

He hadn't felt that way in a long time.

The front door opened before he'd made it to the porch's first step.

"Brandt! You're here!" Abel Troyer called out as he quickly shut the door behind him to keep out the cold. As he stepped forward in his overalls, thick green shirt, and worn Red Wing boots, the middle-aged man's blue eyes, faded blond hair and beard were a welcome sight. From the first time they'd met, Brandt had liked the father of his Amish friend Mark. Abel was a larger-than-life presence. In short, he was a force to be reckoned with.

He was also tall and had a deep, bullfrog voice.

As far as Brandt was concerned, the man's name suited him perfectly. Abel could do almost anything—and did. He managed a four-hundred-acre farm, four children, a menagerie of animals, and was even a partner in a number of businesses in the area. Somehow, the man made it all look easy, too. To top that off, his talents included greeting wayward friends who had nowhere else to go for the holiday.

Even his son's friends.

Stomping down the stairs, the burly man grinned brightly. "I'm mighty glad to see ya again." Looking Brandt over, he added, "You are looking fit as ever, son. The weight you've put on suits you."

Even though Brandt was a little worried that maybe Abel thought he was looking a little thick around the waistline, he decided to take his words as a compliment. "Thank you."

Holding out his hand, he continued. "It's good to see you too, sir. Thank you for allowing me to join your family again." Sure, he sounded awkward, but what could he do? It might not be easy for him to display the warmth and affection that Abel and his wife Annie did, but he hadn't been raised by animals. His parents had taught him good manners.

Not that Abel noticed. His eyes glowered above his fluffy beard. "What did I tell ya last year when you began with all that foolishness?"

"Not to call you *sir*."

"You've either got rocks in that big brain of yours or you're of a mind to be stubborn." Still not cracking a smile, he propped his hands on his hips for good measure. "Which is it?"

Still not used to the Amish man's way of joking around about almost everything, Brandt froze as he debated the right way to respond.

"Leave him alone, Daed," Mark said as he joined his father. "You know Brandt isn't sure how to respond to your teasing."

Abel wrinkled his nose. "I don't know that I was teasing him."

"*Daed. Halt*, or I'll tell Mamm."

Immediately, Mark's father looked sheepish. "I apologize, son," he said to Brandt. "I promised my *kinner* I'd try not to be quite so loud and pushy this year. Elizabeth, especially, has said she's had enough of me frightening her friends."

Though Brandt privately thought that Mark's oldest sister was a bit of a spoilsport, he reckoned she might have a point.

"It's okay," he said quickly. "I'll do my best to leave off that *sir* the rest of this weekend . . . as long as you don't tell my mother if your paths happen to cross."

"That's a deal I can agree to." He shook Brandt's hand at last, clapped Mark on the back, and then continued on his way to the barn.

Brandt grinned at Mark. "It's good to see you," he said, taking in Mark's dark red hair, the spattering of freckles on his nose, and his thick canvas pants, blue shirt, and sweatshirt. "It's been too long."

Mark grinned widely, revealing a gap between his two front teeth. "It sure has. I couldn't believe it when our plans to get together over the summer fell through."

"That was a bummer, but it couldn't be helped." They'd both had too many obligations to get away to Brandt's parents' summer cottage on Lake Erie.

"No worries. All that matters is that you got here. At last."

"At last?"

"*Jah.* Most everyone else arrived two days ago. You shouldn't have waited so long. And don't even try to tell me that you had work. I know you've been on break."

Brandt was a guidance counselor at his local high school. While it was true that the students had two whole weeks off, he usually worked a few extra days, especially since a lot of students were in the middle of college applications or applying for summer internships or extracurricular courses.

So he had been busy.

But that wasn't the reason he'd waited. He hadn't wanted to get in the way. "I'm already interloping."

"You aren't. Not at all. Everyone has been asking about you."

"Better that than wondering when I'm going to leave, huh?"

Mark shook his head. "You are nothing if not modest." After eyeing Brandt's duffel bag, he glanced at his friend's truck. "Where's the rest of your stuff?"

"I've got a coat, my cooler, and a box of gifts in the back of the cab."

"Let's get 'em now." Mark pulled open the passenger door, reached for the cooler, and hefted it out. "This is actually the real reason we were looking for you, buddy."

"Don't worry, I didn't think you invited me here for any other reason than to support your soda addiction."

"So, you did bring me some Dew?"

"Yep." Inside the large cooler was a twelve-pack of Mountain Dew—Mark's favorite vice. Also inside was a large box of See's Candies for Mark's mother, and a plastic container of chocolate eclairs for Tricia. He'd gone to the bakery just that morning to pick them up.

Just thinking about Mark's cousin Tricia made his insides warm. Unable to stop himself, he asked, "Is Tricia here yet?"

"She is. Why?"

"Oh, no reason. I, um, just was curious," he said in what he hoped was a cool and collected tone.

"Uh-huh."

Since Mark was smirking, it was obvious that he'd sounded anything but cool. "Guess I can't fool you, huh?"

Picking up the cooler while Brandt grabbed hold of his duffel and coat, Mark chuckled. "Not even for a second. You might be here because we've been friends forever, but there's only one reason you wouldn't miss this reunion for the world, Brandt Holden. And that reason has brown hair, brown eyes . . . and has been eager to see you too."

Brandt didn't attempt to hide the grin that no doubt spread across his face. It would have been impossible to do, anyway.

Chapter 2

Her great-grandmother used to say that Christmas was a time of kindness, faith, and moments of wonder. Tricia liked her description, but to be honest, she'd always taken her great-grandmother's words with a grain of salt. After all, most of December was occupied with preparations for the big day, and that involved being stressed and tired. It was nearly impossible to help her mother address and send out three hundred Christmas cards, make gifts for loved ones, and bake dozens and dozens of cookies without sometimes yearning for a break.

They always did the same things, too. She helped her sister Rachel, her mother, and her Aunt Annie prepare baskets for the needy, stitch Christmas quilts for two or three families, and bake and bake and bake for their neighbors, friends, and even for the bake sale they put on in the middle of the month.

In addition, they went to her aunt and uncle's farm on December twentieth to help clean guest rooms and prepare for all the events included in the annual family reunion.

All that busyness was why she was still trying to finish the dress she wanted to wear on Christmas Eve. Glad for the bit of light reflected by the sun outside her window, she did her best to concentrate on neatly stitching the hem of the cranberry-colored fabric. "It's almost done," she whispered to herself. "And even though making it has been a pain, you'll be glad to have a new dress that fits well and is flattering."

She bit her lip. She knew better than to be worried about her looks, but she was only human. Besides, it wasn't as if she yearned for everyone at the gathering to think she looked nice . . . there was only one person whose opinion she cared about.

A nervous shiver skittered up her spine as she allowed her mind to drift back to the one man she couldn't seem to banish from her thoughts for more than a few hours at a time. Brandt Holden. Handsome, kind, smart, perfect Brandt. Who was also as Englisch as could be—and therefore completely unsuitable for her.

Her heart didn't seem to care about that, though.

Once again she attempted to push her wayward thoughts away and sew the never-ending hem of the dress.

Until she heard a burst of laughter drift up the stairs. Mark, her favorite cousin.

Eager to see what her cousin was laughing about—and for a break from stitching—Tricia hurried out of the guest room she was sharing with her sister and rushed down the stairs. And practically ran right into the man who'd been at the forefront of her mind for almost twelve months.

"Brandt!"

Reaching out, he somehow was able to gently settle her into place so she didn't tumble into his arms. "Hey, Tiger," he said with a grin.

And just like that, her cheeks heated. No doubt she was beet red. The first night they'd ever spent any time together was the next-to-last night of her family's reunion last year. Mark had invited Brandt over when he'd learned that his friend didn't have any plans. When someone had decided to start a Monopoly game, they'd both joined in. Brandt had been given the shoe and she the dog to mark their places.

She'd reacted a bit like a spoiled child, complaining that instead of a dog she wished there was a tiny tiger to mark her progress.

Brandt thought that was hysterical and had immediately begun calling her "Tiger" instead of Tricia.

She'd pretended to hate the new nickname but had secretly liked it, especially when Rachel looked a little jealous.

But how could she not be flattered? Usually, Rachel was the one who got all the attention because of her pleasing looks and modest demeanor. She, on the other hand, had always been a bit too loud and a bit too big for most of the men in their circle.

Tricia figured she shouldn't be surprised by that fact either. She was at least forty pounds heavier than Rachel and two inches shorter. Her hair wasn't a soft, sleek brown like her sister's either. Instead, it was a strange shade between brown and blond. There was a bit of curl to it, too. No matter how hard she tried to tame it, she thought it always looked a bit wiry.

Last but not least, Tricia also had an unfortunate competitive spirit. She not only liked to play games and join in group sports, but she also liked to win.

Her mother often remarked that she would fare better if she didn't overthink things so much. Tricia agreed. Unfortunately, common sense didn't always direct her thoughts.

But she was not going to make a fool of herself this year with Brandt. She was going to be cordial and friendly, but not overly enthusiastic about winning or him.

Jah. That was right. She was going to be cool and collected this Christmas. She was not going to embarrass herself again.

Taking a calming breath, she summoned a less exuberant smile. "I'm glad you arrived safe and sound. How are you?"

"I'm good." He smiled down at her. "You are looking well."

He still had his hands wrapped around her upper arms. She wasn't sure if he was attempting to hold her in place so she wouldn't get any closer or if he simply hadn't noticed he was still touching her.

Tricia wasn't aware of anything else. His hands were big and strong. And though his fingers were digging into her skin a bit, she felt safe and contained in his grip. As if she wasn't going to be able to do anything without his assistance.

Which was completely inaccurate and more than a little silly.

But maybe that's who she was now, a silly girl. Because she remained in his grip, as if she didn't notice his hands on her either. "*Danke.* You are looking well, too."

He raised one eyebrow. "Listen to you. So proper."

She glanced at Mark, who was talking with someone down the hall. "I'm the same as I always am, Brandt."

"I hope so," he murmured in a low, soft voice. "I liked the woman I met last year."

And . . . there she went. Practically melting in his arms. "*Jah?*"

His lips twitched. "*Jah.*"

"Brandt, why are you still holding on to my cousin?" Mark asked, verbally splashing the moment with cold water.

Immediately Brandt's hands dropped. "Sorry. I hadn't realized I was still holding on to you."

There was her answer—if she'd ever needed one. He didn't even notice whether he was touching her or not. So much for his being as attracted to her as she was to him.

"I hadn't noticed either," she said quickly. Because a girl had to hold on to her pride—at least where men were concerned. "Well, I'll see you later." She had a lot of things to do. Like a dress's hem to finish.

"*Nee*. Wait, Tricia!" While Mark looked on, Brandt strode toward her. "Don't run off. Not yet. What are you doing now?"

Now? "Nothing too exciting," she declared. "Just, um, some chores for the gathering."

"We have a lot to catch up on. Is there anything I could help you with?"

"Well . . . I have to collect pine cones in the woods." When she heard Mark grunt, she added quickly, "I'm sure you have other things to do though."

"Are you sure about that?" He grinned. "Or did you just mention the pine cones as an excuse?" He lowered his voice again. "Is this the Amish equivalent of you needing to go wash your hair?"

Getting the gist of his question, she shook her head. "Not at all. I'm going to spray-paint them gold. They'll serve as holders for place cards at the dinner table on Christmas Eve."

"There are going to be a lot of people here. Weren't there almost fifty last year?"

"*Jah*. There will be that many again."

"No one ever turns down an invitation to this reunion," Mark joked.

"If there are fifty people to make place-card holders for, then you're going to need a lot of pine cones. I'll help you carry them."

It went without saying that pine cones weren't heavy or all that bulky. Especially when they were contained in an old pillowcase. But that wasn't the point. Brandt wanted to be with her—and she wanted to spend some time with him as well. "Shall I meet you by the front door in fifteen minutes?"

"I'll be there." Turning to Mark, he said, "Where does your mother have me staying?"

"We have two new guest rooms in the back of the barn. You can have one of those."

Surprised, Tricia turned to Mark. "I thought Brandt was staying in the basement."

He shook his head. "There's no room. My parents' good friends from northern Kentucky are coming up. They're bringing their two teenagers."

She didn't like the idea of Brandt being sent out to the barn. "What about one of the spare rooms on the second floor of the dawdi house? Or the attic?"

Brandt stepped closer. "Tricia, don't worry. I'm glad that I was invited to your family's gathering again. Where I sleep doesn't matter."

"Maybe I should go with you to make sure there are bedding and towels."

"There are," Mark said quickly. "Besides, you and I need to talk for a moment, Trish." Looking at Brandt, he added, "I left your cooler outside on the porch. You can find your way to the barn, I trust?"

"Of course." He gave Mark a long look, and then his expression lightened. "I'll see you in the entryway in a few, Tricia," Brandt said before grabbing his duffel bag and heading toward the barn.

When he was out of earshot, Tricia glared at her cousin. "What in the world are you doing, Mark? I know your *mamm* wouldn't have put Brandt in the barn."

"There's nothing wrong with him staying there."

She didn't agree but she wasn't about to argue the point much further. "Fine. I'll see you later."

"Oh, no. Wait a moment." When she turned to face Mark, he said, "What is going on with you two?"

"Nothing."

"Tricia, that's not true. It's like you two know each other well. Like, real well."

"We do."

He narrowed his eyes. "How can that be? You only met him at last year's reunion."

"We've been writing to each other."

"Writing? Like, letters?"

Sometimes Mark could be so obtuse. "*Jah, letters.* What else would we be writing?"

"I don't know." He pulled off his dark felt hat and ran his fingers through his hair. "I don't understand it, though. I mean, what could you two possibly have to say to each other?"

"What is that supposed to mean?"

"You're Amish. He is not." He shot her a meaningful look, as if this proclamation was going to be news to her or something.

It was not.

But the point wasn't that she was Amish and Brandt attended an Episcopal church. The point was that they were friends and genuinely liked each other. She didn't appreciate Mark's acting as if that wasn't possible. "Mark, you're Amish and the two of you are *gut* friends."

"That's different."

"How so?"

"Don't play games with me. You are a sheltered Amish girl intending to one day marry a sheltered Amish boy."

"You are making my life sound like a storybook. A very boring storybook." When Mark's eyebrows rose, she quickly added, "I'm not sure who I'll marry. Don't make assumptions."

"All I'm saying is that you two don't have a future."

That stung. Somewhere in between his words, it felt as if he was secretly saying that she wasn't good enough or interesting enough for Brandt. "I have to go."

"*Nee*, wait—"

"Mark, just to be clear, we are going to the woods to pick up pine cones. Not have some dark and secret assignation."

"What does that even mean?"

"If you don't know, perhaps you should be writing letters to someone, too. At the very least, it would broaden your vocabulary."

And with that, she turned away and headed into the house.

Chapter 3

It turned out that the pair of bedrooms in the back of the barn were just as nicely appointed as any of the ones in the sprawling main house. The floor was rough-hewn wood, the walls were painted a creamy white, and the bed and bedside table were solid oak and stained a dark honey-walnut color. There was also a simple white ladder-back chair next to a small cabinet with doors across the front. Inside were a pair of towels, a washcloth, soap, and two bottles of water.

The focal point of the room, however, was a gorgeous quilt in a Texas star pattern. It just happened to be sewn in shades of red and green. The room looked festive and yet perfectly plain and neat all at the same time. His grandparents would have loved it.

"Knock, knock."

Brandt turned to find a man of about forty-five dressed like a model out of an L.L. Bean catalog. Thick khaki pants, flannel shirt, rag wool socks and Bean boots. "Hey."

"Hi. I just wanted to introduce myself." Striding forward, he held out a hand. "Carter Winscott."

"Hi. I'm Brandt Holden."

"Since you look as much a part of the outside world as I do, I'll ask the obvious question. How do you know the Troyers?"

"I'm a friend of Mark's. He's their youngest son."

"I know Mark. I played ball with Abel's older cousin Doug."

It took a second, but Brandt was able to place Doug. While a few of the Troyers' extended family were Englisch, he was pretty sure Doug was Old Order Amish. "Ball?"

"Yeah." He grinned. "We played baseball together in high school."

He still didn't understand. "Doug didn't grow up Amish?"

"He did, but he was also a wicked good first baseman." Looking nostalgic, Carter added, "He had the best instincts of anyone I've ever seen play the position. He could tag a kid out faster than David Ortiz and seemed to have eyes in the back of his head." He shook his head, looking fond. "If he'd had the mind to do it, he could've gone far. I know he could've played Double-A ball at the very least."

Brandt knew he was staring at the guy, but he was shocked. "I had no idea."

"That Doug was so talented or that an Amish kid would play ball in high school?"

"Both."

"I've never heard of another boy doing it either, but at the time I don't recall its seeming so strange. He asked his parents to let him continue his schooling, with a promise to decide about getting baptized when he graduated."

"I guess that's what he did?"

"Yep." Looking thoughtful, Carter folded his arms over his chest. "I remember when Doug made the decision. His grandfather talked to him about faith and pride and family and community. Next thing I knew, he was finishing the season with us but ignoring all the recruiters from college and even some minor league talent scouts."

"It must have been hard for him to give all that up."

"I must admit that I thought so, but I've seen him from time to time over the years, and he's never acted as if he's had a regret. He told me once that he was grateful the Lord gave him that experience but is glad that he's gotten to spend the rest of his life looking after his family and living the life he leads."

"I'll look forward to talking to him this weekend."

"I'm sure you'll get a chance if things aren't too different from two years ago."

"I don't think I remember seeing you here last year. It was my first time to attend the gathering."

Looking a little pensive, Carter said, "I spent last Christmas with a cousin's family. It wasn't the same as being here."

"The Troyer family is wonderful." Realizing that his fifteen minutes were almost up, he said, "Excuse me. I promised a friend I'd help her hunt for pine cones."

Carter laughed. "Sounds like an important task if I ever heard one. Have a good time."

"Thanks. And thanks for sharing that story about Doug. I hope to hear more about the two of you playing ball in high school."

"I'm here for the full two nights. You?"

"The same." Though if things were going well with Tricia, he might try to stay one more night.

"Then we'll have another chance to talk, I'm sure."

To his surprise, Tricia wasn't already standing in the foyer when he entered the house. Pleased that he hadn't kept her waiting, he stared at the big grandfather clock gracing the space next to the large staircase that led up to the second and then the third floor. Like his bedroom furniture, the clock looked sturdy and was built of oak. But that was where the similarities ended. While his bedroom set looked new and polished, the clock looked as if it had been around for generations.

He hoped that was the case.

"Brandt! You beat me," Tricia called out.

"Just barely." He smiled at her, trying his best not to let her see how much her appearance affected him. She was so pretty. Her hair, though pulled back under her *kapp*, still escaped in a few wisps. He loved the shade of it. Halfway between blond and brown, the exact shade seemed to change depending on her mood.

Her brown eyes were bright and striking. Allowing his gaze to linger longer, Brandt decided that Tricia's hair made her eyes appear a deeper, richer shade of brown and her brown eyes made her hair seem even more fine and angelic.

But, as always, it was her happy spirit that made her special. Well, that and the way she wrote letters. He was starting to believe that she could write about almost anything. He'd looked forward to every one.

Portions of ice and snow, mixed with piles of dry, brittle leaves, crackled under their feet with each step they took. Here, some of the snow had melted or blown away. Instead of a picture-perfect blanket of fluffy white snow, they were greeted with patches of brown earth, brown, bare tree limbs, and shrubs instead of the vibrant grasses surrounding the area in May and June.

"It's a shame that it's so cold, isn't it?" she asked.

"Why do you say that?"

"Because it doesn't look like winter. I wish the snow still covered everything."

"It feels like you read my mind. I was just thinking the same thing." He shrugged. "Then I reminded myself that lots of snow wouldn't make this mo—I mean, this weekend—any better."

She frowned, obviously curious about what he'd almost said. He hoped she wouldn't find out because it felt as if it was asking too much. He already had more than he'd imagined. He had wanted to see Tricia again, but mainly to prove to himself that she wasn't everything he remembered.

But she was. And now, just an hour after they'd seen each other for the first time in a year, here he was, walking alone with her in the woods. God really was so good.

"So, are there any special qualities you look for in your place-card pine cones?"

One eyebrow lifted. "Excuse me?"

"Do you want them all to be the same size? Do they need to be able to rest on top of the table in a certain way?"

She grinned. "Brandt, you've been thinking about this."

"Well, yeah. I don't want to mess you up."

"You'd never do that. They're just pine cones."

He didn't think they were *just* anything. "How about I hold the tote bag and you choose the cones?"

"That's perfect."

"Do you have paint already?"

"Of course I do. I bought some gold spray paint at the hardware store in Wooster."

"I should've known."

"Indeed you should've, since we're going to need these on Christmas Eve."

Instead of reminding her that he had no experience preparing for a monster Christmas Eve supper, he pointed to the ground. "Here's two."

Tricia bent down, inspected the prospects, but only put one of them in his sack.

He pointed to the rejected cone. "What was wrong with that one?"

"It was lopsided."

"Really?"

"Come on, Brandt. You had to have noticed that."

He couldn't decide if she was serious or just determined to give him a hard time. "I really didn't." He held up the sack. "That's why I'm just the muscle."

She bit back a laugh. "*Jah.* At least you are blessed with

strength." Stopping, she pointed to two cones on the ground that looked just like any of the others they'd passed up. "Oh, Brandt. These are perfect, don't you think?"

"I do. They look like perfect pine cones." He struggled to keep a straight face as she picked up another three.

Tricia looked pleased with his assessment. "I think so, too. And . . . now we have six."

"Tiger, are you planning to keep a running tally of all fifty?"

"But of course."

He couldn't help his smile. *But of course.* She really was kind of adorable.

"Stop teasing, Brandt," she said with a soft pout. "I'm being practical. I don't want to come back out if I don't have enough."

"If you run short, I'll go back out and get you more."

Her smile faded. "You mean that, don't you?"

"Of course." Tricia looked so pleased, one would have thought he'd offered to fetch her the pine tree from which the cones came, too.

On they continued, tromping through the snow, searching for half-hidden pine cones, analyzing them for size and ability to hold a place card, and then moving on. Minutes passed. Then a half hour. Then an hour. It was a task he'd never imagined doing with a woman he'd only hoped to have a real conversation with.

"How long have we been out here?" she asked after he tossed two more cones in the canvas bag.

"A little over an hour."

"Oh, dear."

"What's wrong?"

"I just . . . well, once again I feel like I'm overextended. I promised to do a lot of other things. Plus, you probably have a lot more important things to do than to wander through the woods with me."

"I'm good with anything. Don't worry about me."

"Brandt, of course I'll worry. You're our guest."

"No, I'm your friend." Of course, he wanted to be more than that, but he was trying not to push too hard. "There's a difference, right?"

Looking taken aback, she nodded slowly. *"Jah."*

"As far as I'm concerned, friends help each other out. I would've hated the idea of you being out here doing this chore on your own."

"I would've been able to handle it."

"That's not the point." It really wasn't. He was feeling a little protective of her. Not only did he want to spend time with her, but he wanted to make her life easier. He wanted to be important to her and to make her feel like she had an ally, whether it was handling a bunch of houseguests or gathering pine cones or simply having a sounding board for her ideas.

He wished it was possible to do all those things for her.

"Brandt?"

He'd been so lost in thought, he'd kept walking. He hadn't even realized that she'd stopped. "Sorry." He turned on his heel. "Do you have more cones?"

"Jah." She tossed two more in the bag.

"I think that's number forty-nine and fifty. We have them all now."

"Then we can head back." She pointed to a fork in the path. "If we go left, it will loop back to where we started."

"Sounds good. I'll follow you." Looking shy all of a sudden, she led the way to the fork.

The snow had started to fall again. At first it was nothing more than a few stray flakes here and there. But that changed rather quickly. Soon, it was snowing hard enough that the flakes were sticking to her bonnet and his coat.

"It's pretty, isn't it?"

He smiled at her. "It is." And yes, he was looking at her instead of the snow. It was such a corny thing, but what could he do? Mark would call him smitten.

He would be right.

It was also so wrong. He was Englisch. She was not. She had a wonderful, loving family. He did not.

Her aunt and uncle had invited him to their house and included him in all their festivities. The proper way to repay them was not to kiss her in the middle of a snowstorm in the woods.

That would really be a bad idea.

But when she stopped again . . . gazing up at him with such perfect happiness, he couldn't help himself. He lowered his head and brushed his lips across hers. Then kissed her again.

This one lasted longer than was proper, if there was anything about kissing in the woods that was proper at all.

There wasn't.

He knew that. He also knew he should apologize, but he couldn't do it. He wasn't sorry for kissing her. It was too sweet. Too special.

And, well, he was no saint.

Not even close.

Chapter 4

It was happening. After meeting and talking and writing and hoping and wondering . . . there she was. Right there, next to Brandt. Alone in the woods three days before Christmas, and he was kissing her!

Just as she was getting the hang of things, he pulled away. "Wow. Sorry," he mumbled.

He was sorry? Trying to catch her balance again, she stared up into his face. His cheeks were ruddy. Was it from the cold and the snow . . . or was he embarrassed? Or, maybe, regretting everything?

A better woman would smile sheepishly, shrug off the moment and move on.

Unfortunately, she'd never been that woman.

"What are you sorry about?" she asked.

His expression looked even more pained. Kind of like he'd just walked into the ladies' room at school by accident.

"You know, Tricia."

Now she was becoming embarrassed and confused. "Did you not mean to kiss me?"

"What?" Before she could repeat herself, he spoke again. "No. Of course not!"

"Oh." So, that amazing kiss had been an accident. She wasn't sure how that could be, but she wasn't very experienced. Becoming more embarrassed, she turned her head away. Had she somehow inadvertently thrown herself at him?

"Trish, look at me."

She gazed into his eyes again, hoping against hope that she would see a hint of what was going on in his head.

"I'm sorry. I didn't mean no." He shook his head. "I mean, no, that's not what I meant."

He was being as clear as mud. "What did you mean?"

"What I'm trying to say is that I didn't *not* want to kiss you."

Didn't *not* . . . did that mean . . . "So, you did?"

He sighed, acting as if she was the one who couldn't converse clearly. "I meant, I did want to kiss you, but I didn't actually *mean* to kiss you. I kissed you without meaning to. It was on impulse."

"Ah." He'd kissed her on impulse. Was that good? She still had no idea.

"You don't get it, do you?"

"Sorry, but *nee*." She was pretty sure Brandt didn't go around kissing girls whenever he felt like it. At least she hoped he didn't.

"Come on. Let's get on back to the house." Just as she was about to protest, he flung an arm around her shoulders. "The snow is really coming down, isn't it?"

Looking at her black cloak, she couldn't help but nod. It was fairly speckled with white splotches. When it all melted, both her dress and cloak would be soaked.

So she allowed Brandt to guide her back to the house even though she would rather that he told her everything he was thinking—not only about why he'd wanted to kiss her, but what he'd thought about it.

He chuckled. "Tricia, don't," he murmured.

"Don't what?"

His hand squeezed her shoulder. "Don't worry so much. I can practically see your brain spinning in your head. Everything is fine."

Unable to help herself, she leaned into him. Brandt's body radiated heat. Plus, well, she had a feeling that once they were back at the house, they'd be back to behaving perfectly properly. That was how they should be, of course.

But these moments, stolen and a little daring, felt special.

All too soon, she could hear the faint sounds of conversation and spied the glow of the solar-powered lights that came on whenever anyone approached the barn. "Looks like we're almost back."

"Are you going to paint the pinecones now?"

"Not quite yet." She usually liked to spread them out on newspaper and let them sit for a couple of hours. It gave any creepy-crawlies an opportunity to vacate their premises so she didn't have a spider or beetle stuck in or on any of the pinecones.

"So, after supper?"

"Probably."

"I'll be glad to help you, if you need it."

"*Danke*. I'll let you know."

He smiled down at her before leaning closer and giving her a one-armed hug. "Listen, Tricia, I didn't exactly tell you the complete truth earlier."

"You didn't?"

He shook his head. "The truth is that I've been thinking about kissing you for months. Every time we exchanged those letters, I would find myself thinking about you . . . and thinking about holding you in my arms." He blew out a burst of air.

"That's why, when the opportunity presented itself, I took it. Even though I knew I shouldn't. Not because I had changed my mind, but because I respect you and didn't want to scare you."

If he could be honest, then so could she. "I wasn't scared."

"No?"

"I was surprised and flustered because . . ." Did she dare admit the whole truth?

He lowered his voice. "Because . . ."

"Because it was my first kiss and I didn't know what I was doing," she said in a rush. Then she held her breath. Half waiting for him to tell her that her inexperience was completely obvious.

"You did everything right, Tricia," he said.

Her lips parted. "Really?"

"Absolutely. Now hug me back before I kiss you again."

She raised her arms, intending to hug him tightly, when there was a loud snap a few feet away.

She jumped a foot.

"What are you two doing?" Mark called out as he strode forward.

"Nothing," she called out.

"It didn't look like nothing," Mark retorted as he stepped closer.

"How about this then?" Brandt said. "It was nothing you needed to be concerned about."

Her cousin's face darkened with fury. "I think differently. Did you just kiss Tricia, Brandt?"

"Not just now."

Tricia felt like covering Brandt's mouth with her hand. Of all the times to be completely honest, Brandt was picking *this moment*?

Obviously, she was going to need to take things into her own hands. "Please leave us, Mark."

"*Nee.*" Still looking like a fierce rooster at daybreak, he puffed out his chest. "You, cousin, obviously need a chaperone."

"I do not. I'm fine, Mark."

"I'm not so sure."

Fury burned in Brandt's eyes. "Mark, you are overreacting, and all three of us know it," Brandt bit out. "Tricia is safe with me."

A muscle twitched in Mark's cheek. "She'd better be safe. I trusted you, Brandt." Jabbing him with a finger, he added, "Don't let me down."

Tricia had had enough of being treated like a fragile flower. "Mark, stop. Just stop."

"No. This needs to be said."

Turning to Brandt, she reached for his hand. "Come on. Let's go back to the house."

But instead of linking their fingers, Brandt backed up a step. "Tricia, I'm sorry, but I think I need a moment. Will you be okay?"

"Of course."

"Thanks." He turned and walked toward the back of the barn, where his room was located.

When he was out of sight, Tricia picked up the canvas bag nearly overflowing with pinecones. It was a lot heavier than she'd thought. "Come help me carry this into the barn."

Mark didn't budge. "Why do you need to go in there?"

She'd had enough of his silly, suspicious questions. "You caught me, Mark. Brandt and I are conducting a secret romance in your barn. When we're together, we do exciting things like sort pinecones."

"There's no need to be so sarcastic."

"I disagree. I think there's every need to be sarcastic. And angry. Now come help me carry these into the barn, clean them, and lay them out flat. I need to spray-paint them and let them dry before Christmas Eve."

"Why?"

"They're place card holders, you . . . you idiot. Now come help me."

He picked up the bag. "I made a mess of things, didn't I?"

"*Jah.*"

"I'm sorry."

"You have picked the wrong person to apologize to." She lowered her voice. "Brandt is all alone and is here at your invitation. It was so wrong and mean of you to act as if you could take the invitation away at a moment's notice."

"You're right."

Gritting her teeth, she held the barn door open for him. At least there was that.

Chapter 5

Enclosed in the privacy of his barn bedroom, Brandt fumed. Mark's attitude toward his relationship with Tricia hurt. It hurt bad. He was embarrassed about that, too. He was a grown man and had been through a lot in his life—the least of which was being such a disappointment to his parents that they'd distanced themselves from him. After he'd not only started attending the local Episcopal church but had chosen to get baptized, they'd essentially washed themselves of him.

It was as if they couldn't understand that he could love God as much as them. He supposed he shouldn't have been surprised—they had never discussed faith or church or Jesus at all when he was growing up. Christmas had been about Santa Claus and Easter had been about the Easter bunny. Now that he had a fulfilling spiritual life, Brandt had no desire to give that up. He also felt that his life was better with Jesus by his side, but the moment he'd offered to take his parents to church, they'd acted as if he was turning his back on them.

Next thing he knew, his father had accepted a job in Florida.

They'd moved to an over-fifty community in Florida and become immersed in their new, active social life.

Their decision to pull away from him had been hard, but he'd tried to come to terms with it. Most of the time, he didn't let their attitude bother him too much. Everyone made their own way in the world, and they had made their choices. Just as he had.

In addition, he was busy with work at school, his various interests and his wide circle of friends. And, this past year . . . his letters to Tricia.

But at moments like this, when he realized that he might never have a future with Tricia, his spirit sank. He was beginning to feel that he wasn't good enough all over again.

"This isn't the same thing," he told himself in a stern tone. "Don't make it into something it isn't." He reckoned that was good advice. It was just too bad that it felt impossible to follow.

As another wave of anger and hurt hit him, Brandt began to pace. Once he released his anger, he forced himself to examine his actions through Mark's eyes.

Maybe his buddy did have some valid reasons for worrying about his cousin.

He probably could've shown a bit more restraint around her. He probably shouldn't have held her hand for so long. He certainly shouldn't have kissed Tricia. Remembering the feel of her in his arms, he amended his words. "Okay, you might have enjoyed kissing her and she might have enjoyed it, too, but that doesn't mean you couldn't have stopped."

He should have stopped.

The two quick raps on his door forced him to return to the present. He was a guest at the Troyers' home. He needed to settle down and either get his act together or make up an excuse and leave.

"Yes?" he asked as he pulled open the door.

"Hey," Mark said. His buddy looked contrite. "May I come in?"

"Sure." Before he could stop himself, he added, "Did you forget to add a couple of things that I did wrong?"

Mark winced. "I suppose I deserve that."

"I know you did." Reminding himself of the truth, he added, "But I think you had a reason to be concerned, too. I should have behaved more properly around Tricia."

Mark rolled his eyes. "We might be Amish, but we don't live in the eighteen-hundreds. Plus, she's a grown woman, not a young girl. She can handle herself." He groaned. "I'm also not her father. I shouldn't have butted in."

"Is that what you came to say?"

"Pretty much." Studying his face, Mark frowned. "You're still upset with me, aren't you?"

"No."

He exhaled. "I'm glad. *Danke*."

"Hey, Mark, would you like me to leave?"

"Of course not."

"Are you sure?" Meeting his friend's gaze, he added, "I'm going to be honest with you. I wanted to come to this reunion to see you and your family. But . . . I wanted to see Tricia, too. She's come to mean a lot to me. But, if you—or you think your family—are going to be upset if I spend a lot of time in her company, it might be best if I go. I don't want to cause problems." He shrugged. "I'm not unpacked yet. I can be out of here before you know it."

Mark shook his head. "You aren't going to cause any problems. Like I said, the problem was mine, not yours."

"You sure?"

"I'm positive. You can't spend Christmas alone, Brandt."

He wasn't eager to do that, but he was less eager to stay someplace where he wasn't welcome. He especially wasn't in the mood to attempt to avoid the woman he'd come to see. "How do you think my visit is going to work, then?"

A line formed between his buddy's brows. "It's going to work like it did last year. You're going to join in the festivities, eat too much on Christmas Eve, and then open presents with everyone on Christmas morning."

"What about you and me?"

"What about it?"

"Are you going to be wishing I wasn't here or attempting to supervise my every move around Tricia?"

"I just told you that I wouldn't."

"I know." But some promises were hard to keep.

"Brandt, we've been friends for a long time. I'm never going to wish you weren't here," Mark said slowly. "As for the other . . . well, I'm going to try my best to leave you two alone."

"I reckon I can't ask for anything more than that." Feeling that it needed to be said, Brandt added, "I'll treat her with respect."

"I know." Stuffing his hands in his pockets, Mark said, "So, are we good now?"

"Yeah. We're fine."

"*Danke.*"

Eager to move on, he grinned. "So, what's next on the agenda?"

"Let's see. If you want something to eat, there are sandwich fixings in the kitchen and a pot of soup on the stove. Go on in and help yourself. Then, there's nothing planned until this evening."

"What's tonight?"

He grinned. "The scavenger hunt."

His stomach sank. "I didn't think you all were going to do that again. Didn't your father say it should be an every-other-year event?"

"Why wouldn't we have the hunt? It was everyone's favorite part."

Oh, no it wasn't. Already feeling a bit of dread at what was about to happen, he folded his arms across his chest. "Where are we meeting?"

"At the front door of the house. Be there at a quarter to five. Wear boots and don't forget to bring gloves and a hat and such. You're gonna need it, since this year we're going to have the hunt at the old Dennison property."

Brandt actually knew which house that was. It was a large, sprawling place that had essentially been abandoned in the 1980s. "I'll be ready."

"*Gut.* Now, if you'll excuse me, I have to go spray-paint a mess of pinecones."

"You're going to do it?" He'd been kind of looking forward to helping Tricia.

Looking as if he was going to clean a dirty chicken coop, Mark nodded. "I don't have much of a choice. It's my penance for getting in between you and Tricia."

Brandt laughed. "I wish you well with it, then."

"I'll be fine. How hard can spraying pinecones be?" He slapped Brandt on the back before heading into the barn. "See you in a spell," he said as he opened Brandt's bedroom door. "And don't forget, there's always sandwich fixings in the kitchen. Help yourself."

"Thanks, I will."

"Oh, hiya, Carter. May I help ya with anything?" Mark asked.

"Thanks, but I'm good. Brandt and I have gotten to know each other a bit. Whatever I need, I'm sure we'll figure it out between the two of us."

Obviously feeling as if he had enough on his plate, Mark nodded, then opened the thick door that separated the horsey part of the barn from the two guest rooms where Brandt and Carter were staying.

When the barn door shut behind him, Carter said, "Did I hear *scavenger hunt*?"

"You did."

"Great."

"Wait a moment. You look like you've just swallowed a frog. I guess you've participated in one before as well?"

"I did. Two years ago. How did last year's go?"

Courtesy to his hosts warred with honesty. Remembering how taken aback he'd been last year by the chaos of the activity . . . honesty won. After all, guests needed to stick together. "It went well . . . but it was also exhausting."

Carter grunted. "Exhausting sounds about right."

"It's going to be cold, too."

"We're going to be outside?"

"I've heard it will take place both outside and inside the Dennison mansion."

Carter groaned. "I know that place. It's enormous and about two big gusts of wind from falling down. Some of the windows have been broken out. And there are also a bunch of big, overgrown trees scattered on the property."

"Now I understand why Mark told me to be sure to wear boots."

"You don't think Abel and Annie will expect us all to climb trees, do you?"

"I think anything is possible."

"I was afraid of that," Carter said with a moan.

"We work in teams, so get someone younger to climb the tree."

"But what you're saying is that I won't be able to get out of the rest of it."

"I'm afraid not. Participation is expected. I mean, it was last year."

Carter rubbed his back. "Maybe I can pretend to have hurt my back or something."

"Mark's great-uncle is eighty-seven. Last year his team came in second place—and he found the hardest item for them. Age won't get you a pass."

"Great. It's going to be cold."

"Yeah, it is. Don't forget to wear boots and a hat."

"Thanks," he muttered as he walked back to his room.

Finally alone, Brandt closed his own door and sat on the end of his bed. He needed a minute to process all that had happened in the last couple of hours. He had real feelings for Tricia. Mark felt as if he was betraying his trust but was willing to step aside out of respect for their friendship and love for his cousin.

And now he was going to be placing himself smack in the middle of it all—while participating in yet another scavenger hunt.

This Christmas reunion was becoming more and more challenging, and it was only the first day.

Chapter 6

Tricia was wearing a new dark blue dress, thick black stockings, black boots, a red sweatshirt, and red wool mittens. On her head, she wore both her *kapp* and a black bonnet. She also had on a black wool cloak and a thick knitted muffler in a pretty shade of hunter green that her grandmother had knitted for her last year.

She was feeling a bit like a child on the way to school in February. The many bulky layers didn't allow one to move all that easily.

It was also rather warm in the confines of the shuttle bus the family had hired to carry all fifty of them around that evening.

On a positive note, everyone else looked just as uncomfortable. Well, everyone except for Mark's parents. As usual, Uncle Abel and Aunt Annie looked as delighted as ever about the upcoming excursion.

Next to her, Frieda—who she was pretty sure was one of Mark's sisters-in-law who lived out of state—shifted uncomfortably. "I love Abel and Annie, but after last year, I swore that I wouldn't do this again," she whispered.

Tricia looked at her with sympathy. Last year, her Uncle Abel had borrowed a friend's camel, which had carried the grand prize on its back. Unfortunately, the camel wasn't pleased to be out of its pen and disliked having a bunch of strangers attempt to grab a blanket off its back. More than one person had been spit upon.

It had been awful.

That wasn't even the worst thing that had happened in recent history. Flooded floors, a firepit in need of a fire extinguisher—and the broken bridge, which had given someone a broken foot—had instigated a lot of arguing and hurt feelings.

Jah, the annual scavenger hunt was a lot of fun, but it was also maddening and exhausting. All the hunting and running around didn't always agree with each member of the party. "You're not the only one who gets on this bus with a sense of misgiving," Tricia said in what she hoped was an encouraging tone. "But the hunt really does bring everyone together."

Frieda looked skeptical for a moment before she smiled. "You're right. Mixed in with all the memories of being cold and frustrated, I do recall laughing an awful lot with more than one new friend I'd made. Why, once I even met Simon from Kinsinger Lumber in Charm. He was great fun. He even got me a deal on some new French doors."

"There's your silver lining."

Frieda patted Tricia's hand. "Ach. I think you are my silver lining, dear. It's all about one's attitude, ain't so?"

"Indeed." Warmed by the thought, Tricia couldn't resist glancing Brandt's way. He was sitting next to Carter, the other Englischer, who was also housed in the back of the barn. From the way they were talking, they'd become fast friends—which was another wonder of the season. Aunt Annie often liked to say that she had a gift for bringing people together. The occupants of the bus were a testament to that. They were family, friends, colleagues, and friends of friends. Somehow, they all mixed together in such a way that everyone felt as if the Lord's hand was on their shoulders, offering support and guidance and assurance to one and all. If that was the case, then it was certainly all that anyone could ask for.

As the vehicle groaned to a stop fifteen minutes later, Uncle Abel stood up with a microphone in his hand. "*Gut ohvet!*" he called out.

He laughed as nearly every one of the folks sitting down responded "good evening" in kind.

"Since I have a microphone and you all are a captive audience, I wanted to take a moment to say a few words before we begin this year's scavenger hunt."

A couple of lighthearted moans and comments greeted him, but for the most part everyone was quiet. Tricia even found herself leaning forward, eager to hear what her uncle had to say.

"When my Annie and I decided so many years ago to start this gathering, we had no expectations beyond selfish ones. You see, we missed so many of you. Everyone had gotten so busy that writing a letter seemed to take too much time, let alone paying a call on someone in person." Glancing at Aunt Annie, he smiled. "That's when *mei frau* here suggested we ask everyone to join us for a spell. She thought that if we were feeling a bit isolated, then maybe others felt the same way. And since we liked everyone we invited very much, we reckoned the folks who came might enjoy each other's company too."

Looking at all of them, he coughed. "And now, here we are. Five years later with a full bus."

"You're gonna have to have a barn-raising just to house more people!" someone sitting in the back joked.

Annie took the microphone. "Don't give him any ideas, Ted," she said in a stern voice.

Reclaiming the microphone, Abel continued. "In any case, I want to thank each and every one of you for joining us this weekend—and ask you to please bow your heads. I know we usually say silent prayer, but I'd like to say a prayer out loud this evening. I fear my heart is too full to keep my thoughts to myself."

As they collectively bowed their heads, he said, "Dear Heavenly Father. We're so blessed by your presence in our lives every day. Thank you for bringing us all together to celebrate the wonder and miracle of your birth. Please keep us safe during our travels—and give us each a moment or two to reflect on the many blessings you've given us. In your name we pray."

"Amen," Tricia whispered with the others.

"Okay, everyone. Here's what's going to happen next. Each of you has a card printed with your name on the table near the front door of the building. Open the card up. It will not only give you your team's color but will list the other members in it. Around the entryway are signs with each color. Find your color, wait there for everyone else, and then wait for instructions."

Annie stood up. "There are refreshments of coffee, tea, and hot cider in one of the hallways, and the Porta Potties are off to the right."

"Now that the logistics are taken care of, I hope all of you have a good time, and may the winner not be too cheeky!"

As they all stood up and filed out, Frieda reached for her hand. "Forgive me, Tricia. I shouldn't have burdened you with my complaints practically the whole way here."

"You didn't do that at all. You were simply being honest."

"Well, now I honestly wish I had behaved better. I hope you have a good time tonight."

"I wish you the same." She smiled as she got in line, finally spying Brandt. He'd not only been talking with Carter, but also with several Amish and Mennonite men surrounding him. She was proud of him. Though she knew he sometimes felt out of place, he'd quickly ingratiated himself to everyone he met.

The thought warmed her as she made the short walk into the Dennison's dusty, sparsely furnished house.

Just as in years past, a sense of excitement filled the air as everyone crowded into the front door, looked for cards with their names on them, and opened them up.

"Here, Tricia," her mother called. "I found your name."

"*Danke*, Mamm." Eagerly taking her envelope, she took a moment to admire the way her name had been printed on the outside before breaking open the seal.

There were four people on her team. To her amusement, it was Frieda, herself, Brandt, and his barn mate, Carter. They were team gold.

She was the last one to join the group but the recipient of everyone's well-wishes.

"I can't believe that we're on the same team, just moments after I was complaining to you," Frieda said.

"I guess the Lord and Aunt Annie knew the four of us belonged together." Smiling into Brandt's eyes, she added, "I think we're going to do just fine."

"I hope I don't slow you three down," Carter said. "I wasn't too good at solving the clues two years ago."

"There's no pressure from me," Brandt said. "It's all in fun anyway."

They were prevented from further discussion when her uncle spoke. "Here are the basics. You will have seven clues. Each clue leads you to the next one. However, don't forget to follow the directions on the cards. Sometimes you have to find your item and bring it to the table before you are permitted to search for the next one. If, for some reason, you inadvertently discover more than one clue or find someone else's prize, you must not take it, hide it, or tell anyone. We're on the honor system here."

General laughter followed before he said, "In your areas,

each of you has a red metal box. On the bottom of it is your first clue. Don't forget, the scavenger hunt is over when the last team turns in their last clue."

"That's for you, Mary P!" someone called out with a laugh.

"I learned my lesson five years ago!"

"We remember!"

As more gentle ribbing continued, Tricia hurried to the gold area, where Carter had his hands on the box, obviously waiting for all four of them before he flipped it over.

"You ready, everyone?" he asked.

"We're ready," Brandt said.

Carter turned over the box, then read the clue. " 'You'll find this mighty important piece where children are nestled.' "

"Ugh. How am I supposed to figure that out?"

"I do," Carter said. "Don't forget the 'Night Before Christmas' poem."

" 'Children all nestled snug in their beds' . . ."

" 'While visions of sugarplums danced in their heads,' " finished Brandt.

"We need to go upstairs to the scary empty bedrooms."

"And find what? Sugarplums?" Tricia asked.

"Why not? I can think of worse things to look for," Brandt commented. "Let's go."

And with that, the four of them headed toward the stairs while other folks walked outside, and one group descended into the basement.

The scavenger hunt was on, and she had the best team in the whole place.

What could possibly go wrong?

Chapter 7

Brandt thought that the second floor of the old house looked like something out of a scary movie set. It was dark, the lights didn't work, and the narrow beam of their flashlight seemed to only make every nook and cranny more foreboding. It was also really cold, thanks to the fact that about a fourth of the windows had broken panes.

He wasn't a fan of the Dennison mansion. Not at all.

He wasn't afraid, but he didn't like wandering around in the dark. Some of his buddies in high school had loved to visit all the haunted houses in the area every October. He hadn't been one of them.

Worse, Frieda seemed nervous enough to jump out of her skin. Every time they encountered a shadow, she gasped or cringed. Meanwhile, Carter seemed to only be going through the motions—as if the activity was only slightly better than getting a root canal. Though Brandt could relate, he was competitive enough to want to do well. As far as he was concerned, if they had to participate in this crazy hunt, they might as well get the prize.

The only person who seemed to be of any help was Tricia, but it was obvious the other people's moods and actions were taking a toll on her. Some of the brightness that had been in her eyes at the beginning of the night had faded.

Brandt was beginning to think it was up to him to pull their team out of the doldrums.

Standing in the third bedroom the four of them had wandered into, he cast the flashlight into all four corners of the room. "Does anyone see anything promising?" he asked.

Carter didn't wait a second before replying. "Nope."

"I don't either," Frieda whispered.

Noticing that the woman was already edging toward the door, Brandt held up a hand. "Come on, everyone. We need to give this a better try than that. We need to look."

"I'm not sure what to look for," Tricia said. "There are neither beds nor sugarplums in here."

Carter folded his arms across his chest. "There sure isn't any way of discovering if anything has ever been dancing in anyone's heads either."

Brandt couldn't deny that, but he wasn't about to let them all give up so quickly. "We need the Ghost from Christmas Past to pop up and give us a hint," he joked.

Frieda gasped. "This place is scary enough. The last thing we need are visiting spirits."

"He was making a joke, Frieda," Tricia said. "And a reference to *A Christmas Carol*."

When Frieda looked as if she couldn't care less, Brandt said, "I'm sure everything is fine. No need for anyone to be nervous."

"Ack!"

Boy, that Frieda sure didn't want to calm down! "Frieda—"

"*Nee*, Brandt," she interrupted. "I think I found our clue." She pointed above her head. Practically in unison, they all looked

at the ceiling. There, suspended from a few pieces of sturdy looking yarn, was a note in an envelope.

"Oh!" Tricia said. "I can't believe it."

Carter laughed. "Frieda, that's terrific. Good for you." He
lifted one arm. His fingers grazed the bottom edge of the envelope, but it was obvious he was too short. "Brandt, can you
reach it? If not, we'll have to lift Tricia on our backs or something."

He was a little taller than Carter, so he could reach the envelope, but clutching it between his fingers wasn't easy.

He attempted to jump and grab it. The first time he missed,
but on the second try he found success. One tug from his hand
pulled the item from the strings. And then there it was. Resting
in his right hand.

"Oh, *gut* job, Brandt!" Tricia clapped.

"Here you go, Frieda," he said with a smile. "Since you discovered the clue, would you like to read the message out
loud?"

Even in the dim light cast by the flashlight beams, he could
see that she was pleased to have found the first clue. "*Danke*,
but you go ahead."

He tore open the white envelope. Out fell both a red card
and a lollipop.

"I think that's supposed to be a sugarplum," Tricia said.

"I reckon so. Here's what it says. " 'Pa rum pum, pum, pum.' "

"What is that supposed to be?" Tricia asked.

"It's a song," Carter blurted. "You know, 'Come, they told
me, pa rum pum pum pum,' " he sang, every single note off key.
"It's 'The Little Drummer Boy.' "

"But the problem isn't the song . . . it's what are we supposed to do with that information?" Brandt asked.

Tricia frowned. "I don't remember a lot of the words. All I
remember is something about " 'Come, they told me' . . ."

"It goes something like this." Feeling a little foolish—and slightly pleased with himself because he wasn't quite as out-of-tune as Carter—Brandt began to recite the words to the familiar tune. Carter, Frieda, and Tricia listened intently.

"All it keeps talking about is how the little boy doesn't have a good gift like the Wise Men," Frieda complained. "All he can do is bang on the drum."

"Have any of you seen any drums lying around?" Brandt asked, only half joking.

"We've already been in all the bedrooms," Carter said. "There wasn't a drum in sight."

Tricia sighed. "I guess that means we need to head downstairs."

"Or . . . didn't Annie say that there was an attic?" Carter asked.

Tricia answered. "She did. And I even happened to notice how to get up there. There's a ladder in the closet in the first bedroom."

"Let's go check out the attic, then," Carter said with a new note of enthusiasm in his voice. "An attic sounds like a logical place to store old instruments."

Realizing everyone was in agreement, Brandt waved a hand toward the door. "Lead the way, Carter."

So off they went. Back down the hall, past the second bedroom and into the first. Just as Tricia was opening the closet door, Brandt heard his friend Mark call out his name. He stepped back into the hall to acknowledge him.

"You good?" Mark asked.

"We're doing fine," he replied, glad that his group's mood had improved. "What about you? Is your group having a good time?"

"More or less." Mark was scanning the area. "How's it going for you?"

Suddenly realizing that his friend smelled a little like a barn, Brandt shrugged. "Pretty good. We've gotten one clue."

"Oh. We have two."

He realized then that Mark looked irritated instead of pleased. "Why don't you look happier?"

"Because the second was in a pile of straw on the ground." He wrinkled his nose. "It wasn't soiled, but it wasn't exactly clean. Now instead of wanting to find the prize, I just want a shower."

He did smell pretty bad. "I bet."

Mark groaned. "I smell, don't I?"

"Yep."

"Maryanne was just starting to smile at me, too. I told my parents that I shouldn't have to do this. They disagreed."

"Brandt?"

"On my way!" Turning back to Mark, he said, "That's Tricia. I have to go."

Mark craned his neck to peek into the room. "Where is she?"

There was something in Mark's eyes that gave him pause. "Why are you up here?" Brandt asked.

"Uh, doing a scavenger hunt."

"But where's your team?"

He averted his eyes. "They sent me upstairs to look for a clue."

Mark had been feeling him out! "You wouldn't be trying to cheat, would you?"

"Never."

"I hope not. Because if you were, that would be a real shame. Especially since Tricia is your cousin and I'm your best friend."

"Brandt? Brandt, where are you?"

"I'm coming, Tricia!" As he started walking, he peeked back over his shoulder. "Don't you follow me, Mark."

"Fine," he grumbled. "But don't you expect me to help you out when you get in a bind."

"We won't. We're going to sail through this hunt and win."

"You wish."

"I know," he said as he hurried into the room—and closed the door behind him. It probably wouldn't keep Mark from following him, but it might slow him down.

As he climbed the ladder, Brandt couldn't help but think about how nice it would be to gloat for a whole year over winning the hunt. He would, too. He was a lot of things, but he wasn't above participating in a little bit of good-natured ribbing.

When his head popped up into the floor of the attic, he noticed all three of his teammates frowning at something on the floor.

"What's going on? Did you find anything?"

"You could say that," Carter said.

Concerned, Brandt approached the trio. "Is it a drum?"

"It's a drum major's uniform," Carter said. "And, because you were taking your time, I went ahead and read the note."

"It said we only get credit for this clue if one of us wears the jacket."

"So, who's going to do that?"

"I'm an old Amish woman," Frieda said. "I can't do that."

Frieda was forty if she was a day. "Carter?"

"I can't fit into it, son." He patted his belly. "It would never button."

"All right then. Tricia?"

"I think there's a spider or a beetle or something living in it. Wearing this is a man's job."

Frieda smiled sweetly. "That's you, dear."

"Next year, tell your aunt and uncle to plan a different activity. Like charades or something."

Tricia's lips twitched as she watched Carter bend down, pick up the uniform jacket and give it a good shake before handing it to Brandt.

And . . . there popped out a spider. Things were going from bad to worse by the second.

Chapter 8

It turned out that Brandt's drum major uniform was a hint of things to come. Two hours later, when everyone gathered back in the large living area on the main floor, almost everyone was wearing some piece of clothing, tag, ribbon, or carrying a bulky, awkward item. One poor woman was carrying a stuffed bird in a cage.

Once again, Tricia was feeling that she'd gotten off easy. All she'd had to do was carry a wreath.

But God was so good. As if He was pleased with their bedraggled group, the general mood lifted after just a few minutes. Soon, everyone was good-naturedly teasing each other about their adventures, mishaps, and the items they had to carry around.

Even Carter was laughing and showing off the crown he was wearing, in honor of "Good King Wenceslas."

Of course, everyone's good spirits might have had something to do with the snacks, hot cider, and trays of cookies that were laid out for all of them. Tricia was yet again amazed by Annie Troyer's scavenger committee. How they'd been able to arrange everything in such a short amount of time was a minor miracle.

When Annie and Abel appeared, looking far neater and cleaner than any of the scavengers, everyone in the room clapped.

"I'm mighty glad each of you made it," Abel said as soon as everyone quieted down. "I know this year's hunt was especially difficult, but each of you came through with flying colors." As he looked around at the ragtag group, the corners of his eyes crinkled with merriment. "Better yet, I betcha some of you made some new friends."

Thinking about Frieda and Carter, Tricia smiled, then met Brandt's gaze. He was standing next to her. And in spite of the fact that he was wearing a smelly band uniform jacket, she didn't want to be anywhere else.

Honestly, it felt as if their relationship had taken a big step forward that evening. Running around the house and grounds, problem-solving, working together, had brought them closer together as a couple—and that was how she thought of them now. There was something about Brandt that felt right. Even though there were many differences between them, they agreed on a lot of things. Best of all, he seemed to be thinking the same thing.

At least, she hoped he did.

As her uncle continued to talk, her mind drifted. She was already dreading the end of the gathering. She didn't want to wait another year to see Brandt in person.

"And so, without further explanation . . ."

"You mean procrastination!" someone near the back of the room teased.

"The winning team is Team Teal. Team Teal, come up, let us see how you are looking, and claim your prize."

Exchanging glances with Carter, Frieda, and Brandt, Tricia shrugged. She knew they hadn't arrived first, but the winners had not only had to return quickly but with all the correct items, too. That was the tricky part. They'd all believed that they'd had a small chance of being declared the winners.

However, none of them seemed all that surprised or upset about not winning, either. That was a blessing.

"Do you know any of them?" Brandt whispered in her ear.

As the winning team walked to the front of the room, she nodded. "Two of the women are friends of my mother's. Another was in school with my older sister, I think. I don't know the Englischer though."

"Are you disappointed that we didn't win?"

"Not even a little bit. What about you?"

"I feel the same." His expression warmed.

Feeling that they were sharing something more than just words, she cleared her throat. "Ah, the scavenger hunt isn't about the prize, anyway. It's the experience."

"All I know is that I wouldn't have traded these last couple of hours for anything."

Tricia felt butterflies flutter. She meant something to Brandt. Something warm and special. Better yet, she felt the same way about him—although she'd been too afraid to admit her real feelings out loud. She smiled at him, and even went so far as to lean toward him before remembering herself.

What was she doing? Allowing herself to care about Brandt could be a recipe for disaster. He lived in the city, she did not. He was Englisch, she'd always assumed she'd be baptized Amish and live in her community forever.

If she chose him—and, granted, there were a lot of steps between their current relationship and the future she was imagining—Tricia would have to leave everything she held near and dear in her heart.

But how could she ignore the way she was feeling?

If she walked away from the man the Lord might intend for her—the man who could make her happy with just a single glance—would she always regret her choice?

Yes. Yes, she would.

Oh . . . what was she going to do?

"Hey, Trish, are you okay?"

Tricia blinked as she focused on the speaker. It wasn't Brandt; it was Mark. She lifted her chin. "Of course."

"Well, then, come on. Everyone is getting in line."

To her dismay, her cousin was right. The room had thinned out significantly. There was also a pile of props and clothes on tables near the door. So much had happened while she'd been staring into space! "Where's Brandt?"

Mark's frown deepened. "Didn't you hear him? He told us he'd meet us on the bus. He had to visit the Porta Potties."

"Oh."

"Yeah, oh," he teased. "What's going on with you? Are you just tired?"

Though that wasn't the problem, Tricia grabbed hold of the excuse. "Oh, *jah*. Exhausted."

"Take my hand, then. I'm half afraid if I don't keep tabs on you, you're going to wander off and no one's going to be able to find you."

"Don't be ridiculous." But even though she'd made sure to sound offended, she still allowed him to take her hand. The last thing she needed him to realize was that she was falling for one of his best friends.

When they got on the bus, the only available seat left for her was next to Brandt. Mark didn't look as if that had been a coincidence, but he didn't say a word as he moved to his seat in the back.

Moments later, the bus pulled out and the overhead lights turned off. Nestled in the comfortable seat with just the faint glow from the streetlights outside, Tricia was only aware of Brandt. He was warm, and even after running around the dusty house, he still smelled like soap and his aftershave.

"Do you have enough room?" he asked.

He'd moved to the aisle seat when she'd arrived so she could have the seat next to the window. "Of course."

He shifted again. "My mom always complains about sitting next to me on the plane. She says my shoulders get in the way."

Tricia felt like rolling her eyes. As if she was going to complain about Brandt having broad shoulders! "Your shoulders don't bother me none."

"That's a relief."

She could hear the smile in his voice. It made her smile, too. Taking a risk, she said, "I can't think of anything about you that bothers me."

He chuckled under his breath. "I'm relieved, but that's most likely because you don't know me real well yet."

That's what she wanted to do, but admitting such a thing would be more than she was willing to do. "If we get a chance to know each other better, I'll let you know if I find something bothersome."

He chuckled. "I'll look forward to it."

Glad that she hadn't ruined their easy conversation, Tricia allowed herself to rest her head against her seat. Around her, everyone else's conversations seemed to have slowed as well. Perhaps she wasn't the only one ready to go back to the farm. She needed to wash her face, put on a flannel nightgown and take a few moments to rest her mind.

Being in Brandt's company felt at times as if she was playing hopscotch. She was constantly worrying about stepping in the wrong square or fumbling her words during their conversations. Some of the letters she'd written him had taken almost an hour to write. She'd chosen each anecdote with care and made sure never to sound like she was complaining, tired, or stressed out.

You were trying to be perfect for him, a small voice inside her head said.

She kind of was, but not exactly. No, she'd been trying to be a better version of herself. Now that she and Brandt were sharing so many conversations, she didn't have that luxury. And because of that, she seemed to be in a constant state of nervous anticipation.

She didn't know if that was normal or not.

"Hey, Tricia?" he whispered. "You asleep?"

She wasn't. However, for the first time, she didn't think she could handle another conversation with him. So, she kept her eyes closed and gave thanks for the darkness. If he could see her better, Brandt would probably notice her features were too stiff for her to be asleep.

After a second, he exhaled and shifted. His left shoulder edged slightly toward her as he tried to get comfortable. Then, he curved an arm around her shoulders. Holding her securely.

Before Tricia realized what she was doing, she'd shifted as well, and rested her head on his shoulder.

And then, as if her body had finally found the comfort it had been seeking, she relaxed completely.

This is where you belong, she told herself. Even if choosing Brandt meant making a lot of changes and maybe even some growing pains, she realized it would be worth it. She would be happy with Brandt. Happy and secure and loved.

Finally, finally, the internal battle her mind had been waging eased.

At last, oblivion found her.

Chapter 9

Brandt woke up groggy on Christmas Eve morning. After rubbing his eyes and remembering where he was, he reached for his cell phone. When the numbers 9:23 flashed back at him, he was shocked. How could it already be after nine?

More surprising was the fact that he wasn't in any hurry to get out of bed. Nestled in his barn room, he pulled the flannel covers over his shoulders and flipped onto his side. Even though he felt obligated to get up, he couldn't seem to make himself do it. His room, with its sparse furnishings and private location made him feel completely relaxed.

A rarity when it was so close to Christmas Day.

He usually hated this time of year. That wasn't something he was proud of—and he really hoped that neither Mark nor Tricia would ever learn he'd spent a number of Christmases essentially alone until last year. Learning that someone's parents had moved away on Christmas Day just made things awkward.

And for folks like the Troyers, who not only valued their

family members but worked hard to reach out to other people, well, his circumstances didn't make much sense.

His parents had moved when he was a senior in high school. Though they'd offered to take him with them to their new home in south Florida, he knew their offer hadn't been exactly genuine. He'd had college plans and plans for his last semester in high school. He couldn't ignore everything without paying the price in a number of ways.

They hadn't completely left him on his own. They'd made arrangements with the families of his friends, who'd been kind and had developed a kind of rotation system for him until he graduated, but that got old quick. Sometimes he was in a guest room, sometimes on the couch. The entire time, even when the parents tried their best, he felt as if he was an interloper.

The day after he graduated from college, he'd asked his parents for help paying a couple of months' rent on a studio apartment and then went out on his own. That had come with a lot of challenges as well, but at least he'd regained some stability in his life.

It was nothing like the Troyer family, though. Everything about their lives was filled with stability and care. He loved being around them.

No, he loved being with Tricia.

What he wasn't certain of was what to do about that.

When he finally opened his door, he was surprised to find a small basket with two muffins, a cup, and a carafe of coffee. Pleased by the thoughtfulness, he carried the basket into the main barn. When two horses popped their heads out and nickered, he sat down on a stool next to them.

"Happy Christmas Eve, horses," he said as he poured his first cup of coffee.

When one of the goats bleated, he grinned.

Sure, he was surrounded by farm animals, but he would take

this crew over a lot of people he knew. At least they let him drink his coffee in peace.

He was almost done when Mervin Troyer, Tricia's father, wandered in. He chuckled when he caught sight of Brandt. "Look at you!"

"Good morning." When he moved to stand up, Mervin waved away his effort. "No need for that. I'll join you . . . unless you've decided that horses are better company?"

"I'll be glad of the company, though I must admit that they listen well and don't say much."

"I can't argue that point." Pulling up a stool, he grinned. "Ah. Now I understand. You got one of the breakfast baskets."

"Are they a thing?"

"Kind of."

"Hmm. I didn't receive one last year."

Mervin kicked out his legs. "Annie has five or six of these sets. If she has time, she sets them out at a few people's rooms every morning." He gave Brandt a sideways look. "Usually, she delivers the basket to a person or couple she feels might need a little bit of a helping hand."

"Hmm."

"Is that you?"

"I'm not sure." The idea didn't make him feel too good. He didn't want to be an object of pity.

Mervin's good-humored expression turned more serious. "I spoke in jest, but I'm ready to listen, if you've got something on your mind. I've always found that burdens grow lighter when shared."

Brandt's instinct was to say he was fine, but he knew if he didn't say what was on his mind today, he was going to have to do it one day in the future. Putting off this important conversation didn't seem like a good idea.

But he figured he should give the man some warning. "I . . . well, I've been thinking about Tricia."

Mervin froze for a second before he regained his composure. "My Tricia?"

"Yes." He poured himself another cup of coffee so he didn't have to look the man directly in the eye.

"I see."

It was obvious that Mervin didn't. A thousand questions were embedded in those two words.

But maybe it was time that Mervin learned how he felt? "I don't know if you realize it, but last year, when I came to your reunion, Tricia and I became friends."

Mervin's posture relaxed a bit. "I realized that. Her mother says that you two have been writing each other. Is that true?"

"Yes. I, um, never considered myself to be much of a letter writer. I guess I always thought it was too much work. But with Tricia, I began to look forward to pulling out a sheet of paper and a pen. Her letters were always fun to read and full of little details about her life that I wanted to know more about." Not wanting to drone on and on about their personal notes to each other, Brandt cleared his throat. "Our every-so-often letters became weekly. Sometimes more than that." He glanced at Mervin. "Needless to say, I had hoped to receive another invitation from Abel because I wanted to see Tricia again."

Mervin seemed to think about that for a moment. "You could have simply come to the house, you know," he said after a moment.

The man was not wrong. "I guess I could have done that."

"You wouldn't have even had to wear a band uniform for two hours last night."

He laughed. "Good point. I didn't think about doing that, though. It seemed too forward. And . . . like I was crossing a line."

"What line would that have been?"

"The line that divides friends and"—he paused, attempting to think of a suitable descriptor—"sweethearts."

Mervin's eyebrows rose so high, Brandt could barely see them beneath the brim of his hat. "Is this roundabout story your way of telling me that you have made my daughter into your sweetheart?"

Ouch. Despite the cold temperature, Brandt felt a trickle of sweat roll down his back. "Not officially."

"I'm sorry, but that don't make me feel any better."

"I reckon it doesn't."

"My Tricia is a good girl."

"I think she is, too."

Mervin narrowed his eyes. "*Nee*, pup." His voice lowered. "I mean that she is a good and decent woman. She is not deserving of your shenanigans."

"I'm not partaking in any shenanigans," he blurted. Feeling his cheeks pinken, he added, "Or anything else."

Mervin's frown turned into a deep scowl. "I should hope not."

What had he been thinking? Why had he thought he could share his feelings for Tricia with her father and it would all go well? Had he really thought he'd be able to gain acceptance from Mervin? He must have lost his senses.

Taking a last sip of coffee, he carefully set the empty cup in the basket and stood up. "I think I'll go take this into the kitchen and thank Annie properly."

Mervin stood up, too, though he looked a bit like a rooster ready to pick a fight. "Brandt Holden, look at me, if you please."

Though the words were phrased kindly, they certainly weren't a suggestion. They were a demand. Brandt turned to face Tricia's father. "Yes?"

"This conversation is not over."

"Oh?" His back was up. He might have shocked Mervin, but Brandt wasn't a kid and didn't want to be talked to like one. "What else do we need to say?"

To his surprise, Mervin's eyes lit up, as if he was amused by

Brandt's feistiness. "I reckon it's not what else, but who else you need to be talking to."

"Pardon me?"

"Son, here's the way I see things. See, while I appreciate the fact that you are pouring your heart out to me, I think you are speaking to the wrong person."

"You want me to speak to Tricia, even without your blessing?"

"If you love my daughter and aim to spend the rest of your life making her happy, then you already have my blessing."

Oh, man. Now he was about to tear up. "Thank you."

"Hold on. You're still going to have to work on saying the right words to Tricia. She canna read your mind, you know."

Mervin was right. He needed to tell Tricia how he felt. "I'll speak to her soon."

"I'm glad that we got that settled."

"Me, too," Brandt replied, though he wasn't completely sure what actually had been settled.

"Get on your way now, Brandt. Go visit with Tricia and tell her how you feel. Then, if the two of you could let me and her mother know what your plans are, we'd be mighty grateful. We're thinking of taking a vacation in the summer, you see. If you two start planning a wedding and such, we're going to have to rethink our trip to Florida."

This was truly one of the strangest, most unexpected conversations he'd ever had in his life. "I'll do my best to keep you informed."

"*Gut.*"

And with that, Mervin walked back into the house, leaving Brandt alone with his thoughts. And a new nervous energy running through his veins.

It was time to find Tricia, take her someplace private, and pour out his heart.

Chapter 10

It was a long-standing tradition in the Troyer family for everyone to eat together on Christmas Eve. Whether it was eight people, or fifty, Annie Troyer wouldn't have it any other way. Fold-out tables were lugged inside from the storage areas in the barn and basement, fifty metal chairs were unstacked and carefully wiped down, and most of the living room furniture was pushed against the walls.

And then the women got to work. Crisp, white tablecloths were spread out over each table. Next, plates, silverware, and glasses were distributed, and pine boughs were carefully cut down and spread along the center of each rectangular table. Finally, gold place card pinecones were put out so each person knew where they were supposed to sit.

That was the easy part.

The hard part was preparing all the food for the big event. Some folks hosting fifty people might have gone the casserole route. Chicken and rice casserole was easy enough to prepare for ten, twenty, or fifty folks. Some might go with lasagna.

Annie refused to serve something so mundane to her best friends and family.

It was a blessing that the Troyers had so many hardworking and experienced cooks. Most of the women had grown up cooking for large numbers, and feeding fifty people Christmas Eve supper didn't faze them in the slightest.

It was also a blessing—though few were brave enough to say it out loud—that Annie Troyer was bossy. She had no problem giving everyone around her something to do. Both Tricia and Mark had learned at a young age that the jobs they were assigned were absolutely not suggestions.

In years past, Tricia had sometimes resented her extended family's traditional Christmas family reunion. More than once she'd asked her mother why they couldn't have their family reunion in the summer like other people. Having time to relax and enjoy the miracle of Jesus's birth sounded like a good thing.

All her mother had done was smile, give her a hug, and go help her Aunt Annie.

Now, however, as she was seated next to Brandt at the end of a long table and the supper was finally underway, Tricia felt that all the blood, sweat, and tears had been worth it. She was glad she had a family that went to such great lengths to gather together—and to include so many other people in the gathering. It was a blessing.

In fact, everything would be wonderful if she wasn't getting the feeling that Brandt was bothered by something.

"Are you all right?" she whispered. "Are you too cramped?" They truly were sitting as close to each other as sardines in a can.

"I'm fine, Tiger."

He wasn't looking at her though. No, something was absolutely not quite right. "When we're done, we can go sit down somewhere," she added. "We won't have to wash dishes all night."

"I'm not worried about dishes."

But did that mean he was worried about something else? She drew a breath. "Oh, if you—"

He reached out under the table and squeezed her knee. "Stop worrying and relax. Okay?"

"Okay."

Looking pleased, he removed his hand just as Uncle Abel stood up.

Mark, who was sitting across from them and therefore blissfully unaware of their exchange, leaned back in his chair.

So did several other people who had been guests at the meal.

Tricia didn't blame any of them for attempting to get a little more comfortable. Her uncle's traditional Christmas Eve speech was historically long-winded.

"It's that time again," Abel said as soon as all conversation stopped. "As I look around this room, my heart feels full to bursting. We make a right nice group, ain't so?"

"Here, here!" Carter said.

Everyone laughed.

Her uncle continued. "I'm also filled with gratitude for my *frau*, Annie. She and many helping hands worked tirelessly to once again create a weekend to remember. *Danke*, Annie!"

Aunt Annie beamed as the room erupted into a round of clapping.

"I'd also like to take the opportunity to acknowledge the group of eight newlyweds who both organized and cleaned up yesterday's scavenger hunt. I think it was our best yet." After another round of applause, he looked around the room. "I cannot wait to see what next year's team comes up with!"

"Don't start making plans yet!" someone from the back called out.

"Oh, I'll wait until New Year's Day to do that," he joked.

Looking more serious, Abel cleared his throat. "You know, every so often someone will reach out to me about September and hint that maybe we don't need to gather together yet again. Or perhaps suggest that going to every other year might be better. Sometimes I even believe they have a point. Many of you go to great lengths to be here."

Though she didn't feel her uncle's gaze settle on her, Tricia felt as if it might have been.

He stretched his arms out wide. "But then, just as I start asking God what His opinion is about the matter, I'll meet someone at an auction or the market or even Walmart."

"You do enjoy a trip to the supercenter like no other, Abel!" her father called out.

He grinned. "I canna help it. I'm only a man . . . with a fondness for wandering around aisles." He took a deep breath. "Seriously, though, what always seems to happen is I'll run into a friend or one of our own and we'll get to talking." He lowered his voice. "And I'll learn that maybe the year hasn't been all that easy for him. People get sick. Animals do, too. Work gets hard or there are layoffs. Or the crops don't bring in what was expected." He swallowed. "Or, even, perhaps, there's something else that's going on that's only between him or her and the Lord."

When he paused, Tricia was fairly sure one could hear a pin drop. Every eye was trained on Uncle Abel. "And then that person admits this gathering means the world to them. Because it's a happy time." He chuckled. "Sure, it's also chaotic and crowded. We do silly things, like go scavenger hunting in old houses. But I have to say that I feel the Lord is always with us. Everyone is surrounded by love, and sometimes we even find love here. And no matter what happens, I know that the miracle of Jesus's birth is always close to our hearts."

He stuffed his hands into his pockets. "And so, even though I've already prattled on too long, I want to tell you that I'm real glad each of you is here. This reunion is worth all the trouble and headaches and work because in the midst of it, there are moments like this, when I am reminded of how blessed I am to know each of you. And because I have a sneaking suspicion I'm not the only one who feels that way. Merry Christmas and thank you for being here." He held up his glass of water.

Feeling tears in her eyes, Tricia held up her glass. Everyone else in the room did as well.

Just as Abel sat down, George, one of their neighbors, stood up. "I just wanted to share that I was a person who told Abel I was real glad we were gathering this weekend. I'm not your kin and I'm also as English as they come. But the acceptance and friendship I've found here means the world. My December would be a lot harder to get through if I didn't have this to look forward to. So, I propose a toast," he said as he raised his glass. "To Abel and Annie Troyer."

"To Abel and Annie!"

Annie stood up. "I love my husband and am fond of his speeches, but it's time to eat. Let's bow our heads in silent prayer, then start passing dishes. It's time to dig in."

Dutifully, Tricia bowed her head, gave praise to the Lord for bringing them together and for the food and the hands that prepared it. *Also, Lord, if you could be with me and Brandt tonight, I would be grateful for that, too*, she added silently.

Two hours later, she and Brandt were sitting alone in the barn. He'd pulled out an old steel trough, flipped it over, and tossed a horse blanket on top. There was just enough room for the two of them to sit side by side.

"I can't believe this is the only place we could find to be alone," she said.

"I don't mind—I've been kind of enjoying the animals' company this weekend."

Noticing that two horses had poked their heads over the

stalls and were watching them with interest, she chuckled. "I think they might be enjoying our company, too."

Brandt grinned. "We'll have to see if they start speaking tonight."

"What in the world are you talking about?"

"There's an old myth that the Lord gave the animals the power to speak after midnight when Christ was born. They helped spread the word that Jesus had come."

"I've never heard of that myth."

"Well, it is a little fanciful. I've always liked it, though. I like the idea of God's son coming for everyone, even animals in the stable."

"All creatures great and small," she murmured.

"Exactly." He smiled at her in the dim light, but then his expression turned worried yet again.

She couldn't take the suspense any longer. "Brandt, whatever is on your mind, just tell me." Reaching out for his hand, she added, "I promise, I'll be happy to listen to whatever you have to say."

"I hope you mean that."

"I do. Just say it."

"All right." He inhaled, blew out a deep breath. Then at long last, spoke again. "Tricia, I've fallen in love with you. I know that there are lots of reasons why we shouldn't be together, but none of those matter to me. Not like you do. The only thing I know for certain is that one day I want to go to this reunion with you by my side." He swallowed. "One day I'm going to want you to be here not just as a Troyer, but as a Holden, too."

As a Holden. He was talking marriage. Love and marriage. Tricia stared at him in shock.

Looking upset with himself, Brandt wrapped his other hand around hers. "I'm sorry. In my head, I practiced what I would say a hundred times."

"A hundred times," she whispered. This wasn't a sudden thing. He'd planned it.

"Okay, not a *hundred* times, but a lot." He ran his fingers through his hair, making it stand up this way and that. "I mean, I tried to think of the perfect words. I'm no poet or anything, but I thought I could handle that." Still looking as if he was talking to himself instead of her, Brandt muttered, "I never thought I'd blurt everything out like that."

Her heart went out to him. He was tearing himself up for not being perfect when she didn't need that. "Brandt—"

He cut her off. "No, Trish. It's okay." In a rush, he added, "You don't have to say a thing."

He was going to let her off the hook. She could smile, act relieved, and Brandt would understand.

Tomorrow morning, he'd probably act as if this moment had never happened so she wouldn't feel awkward. That was the man he was. No, that was the way he treated her.

But she wouldn't be okay with that. All she had to do was figure out how to respond. It was too bad the horses and goats in the stalls weren't eager to start talking right about now. She would welcome their help.

After a long silence, she realized that she needed time to think. Her reply would not only affect her future, but her family's, too. A decision this big probably warranted hours to respond.

"Brandt, I want to answer you, but I want to think of the right words, too. Can I come back in the morning and give you my answer?"

"You don't have to say anything."

Everything in his posture and expression told her that he'd given up on them. She felt guilty for making him wait, but she didn't want to say a single word that she would regret. Not for something this important.

"I'll be back here at six," she said.

"Six in the morning? That's early."

"I know, but I'll be up. It will be Christmas morning, after all."

"All right. I'll be waiting here for you at six." He glanced at his watch. "In six hours."

"It's midnight?"

Looking dazed, he nodded. "It's Christmas. Merry Christmas."

"Merry Christmas, Brandt." She backed away before she gave in and flung herself into his arms. "I'll see you soon."

When she walked out of the barn, she shivered in the cold air, gazed up at the sky and noticed that hardly any stars were out. Clouds had come. Snow was on the way.

They were going to have a white Christmas. It was going to be a great day.

Thinking of Brandt, she shook her head. No, it was going to be glorious.

Chapter 11

December 25

There was no coffee basket outside Brandt's door when he opened it. Though he was glad that no one in the Troyer family had gone to the trouble, he was still a little disappointed. He'd barely slept last night. A cup or two of scalding hot coffee would have helped him prepare for whatever Tricia was about to say to him.

What was he going to do when she gently let him down? Not only would he feel the need to escape the Troyers' farm as soon as possible, but Brandt knew that he would probably never return to their Christmas reunion. Oh, he knew he'd get an invitation. Even if Mark didn't deliver it, Abel or Annie would send him a note. They were good and decent people. Kind. They'd offer him a place to celebrate Christmas so he wouldn't have to be alone.

But there was no way he'd be able to take them up on next year's invitation. Christmas was a time of joy and hope. Not a time to dwell on the mistakes he'd made.

Certainly not the time to make lovely Tricia Troyer feel awkward and uneasy.

"Hey, what are you doing up so early?"

Turning on his heel, he spied Carter approaching with a coffee basket in his hand. "I, uh, was just up. What about you?" He noticed then that Carter had on a crisp-looking pair of slacks, a sweater, boots, and a coat. His suitcase was outside his door.

"I'm on my way out." He grinned. "My niece called to tell me that she had her baby two days ago. She invited me over for lunch."

"Hey, that's wonderful. Congratulations."

"Thanks." Looking sheepish, he added, "To tell you the truth, I'd forgotten the baby was due so soon. I'm not going to ignore her invitation, though."

"Of course not." He held out his hand. "It was good to meet you, Carter."

He shook his hand. "Same. I hope to see you again one day."

"That would be great."

"In the meantime, here." He pulled out a business card from a pocket and tossed it in the basket. "Feel free to call, email me, text . . . whenever you have a moment or two to spare. I'd love to keep in touch."

"Thank you. I'll do that."

"And enjoy the coffee."

"You don't want it?"

"Not this morning. Like I said, I'm anxious to get on my way. Plus . . . I think you might be needing it more than me."

Taking the basket from Carter's hand, Brandt grinned. "I'm not going to refuse it. Thanks. And merry Christmas."

"To you, too." Walking over to his suitcase, he called out, "I was serious about staying in touch, Brandt. I want to know what happens between you and your girl."

The lump that had eased in his throat returned in full force.

"I'll be sure to let you know." He wasn't sure when he'd be able to do that, though. Receiving Tricia's rejection was going to be hard enough without sharing the news with a man he barely knew.

As Carter waved a hand, then started rolling his suitcase out a side door, Brandt opened the door to the main barn and walked inside.

Right away, two horses popped their heads out of their stalls and a goat bleated.

"Good morning, everyone," he said. "Merry Christmas."

"Merry Christmas."

He was so startled he practically dropped the basket. "Tricia!"

Standing next to a stall near the back, she giggled. "Sorry, I didn't mean to scare you. But come look!"

After depositing his coffee basket on the ground, he strode to her side and looked in the stall. There, nestled against a silky-looking white goat was a tiny one. It was curled in an awkward-looking ball. The little thing—was a newborn goat called a kid? He wasn't sure. Whatever it was called, all he knew was that it was as cute as could be. He smiled at her. "One of the goats had a baby."

"She sure did. I think it took my cousin by surprise. Mark is usually the one who tends to the goats."

Standing next to her, he copied her stance, resting his forearms and elbows on the top of the stall door. "It's a nice surprise though, yes?"

"Oh, *jah*." Sounding a bit dreamy, she said, "Even though no one in the family can remember a goat being born in December, it's a blessing for sure and for certain. Added to the fact that it was born in a barn on Christmas Eve, well, it feels right, you know?"

He nodded. His mouth had gone dry. Yet again, he seemed to be mentally unprepared when he was beside her.

"Brandt, would you like to sit down in the same place we were last night?"

"Sure." Noticing that the bench was still in the same spot, he gestured for her to lead the way.

"You got *kaffi*, too?"

"No, Carter did. He had to leave early so he passed it on to me. I haven't opened the thermos yet," he muttered.

"I'll fix that." Tricia retrieved the basket, deftly opened the thermos, and poured him a cup. "Here you go."

"Thanks, but you didn't have to do that."

"I've found that I kind of like looking after you, Brandt."

That sounded positive.

After taking a fortifying sip, he sat down next to her. "I think it's supposed to be the opposite, Tricia. I think I'm supposed to be taking care of you." If she allowed him the honor, of course. "I mean, if we were a couple."

Her expression softened. "You sound worried."

"Of course, I am. I put you on the spot last night with my clumsy speech."

"I think I'm the one who did that by making you wait until early this morning to respond."

"That was your prerogative," he said as he took another sip.

"I suppose." She flashed him a smile before staring straight ahead. "Last night, after we parted, I walked into the house. There must have been a dozen people in the living room chatting with my parents."

"Did you join them?"

"*Nee*. My mother called out my name, but I told everyone good night. Like you, I wasn't eager to be around a lot of people." She sighed. "Anyway, as I walked into my room and saw my bed waiting for me, right in between my sister's bed and a fold-out cot that one of her friends was using, it occurred to me that I was making everything too hard. I started thinking that maybe I should be a little bit like Mary and Joseph."

She'd lost him. "What do you mean?"

"Even in that crowded room, there was a place for me," she whispered. "It wasn't exactly what I was used to, but it was fine. I had my pillow and quilt and I didn't have to worry about anyone taking it or pushing me out of the room."

"Of course not, it's your room."

"*Nee*, it's more than that. You see, I started thinking about Mary and Joseph walking into Bethlehem and needing a safe place to stay for the night. Sure, there was no room in the inn, but they made do in the stable. I could be wrong, but I don't think they were worrying about much beyond having that baby and being safe and warm."

"They knew the Lord was going to look out for them."

Turning to face him, she smiled. "He did. Angels came and shepherds and Wise Men, too. And then later, they raised Jesus even though they hadn't been parents before, and he was special. Their best was good enough." She paused. "Don't you think?"

"Well, yeah."

She chuckled. "I guess all that is my roundabout way of telling you that becoming Tricia Holden is going to involve a lot of changes for me, but I know it will be okay. Because I'll have you."

She was saying yes. He was shocked and thrilled and honored. And his heart was so filled with love for this woman. Reaching for her, he said, "You're right. You'll have me and you'll have my heart because I love you."

"And I love you, too."

"So . . ."

"So I'm saying yes to you, Brandt Holden."

He didn't have a ring in his pocket. He wasn't on one knee. There weren't flowers lying beside her or soft music or any of the things that he reckoned a girl wanted when her future husband proposed to her.

But obviously he'd had it all wrong anyway. They didn't need any of that to find a happy life together. Just each other and the willingness to have faith in their future.

They certainly had that.

Some of the light shining in her eyes faded. "Brandt?"

"Sorry, I was just . . ." Oh, what did it matter? Pulling her into his arms, he tasted her lips again. Held her close as he realized that this was just one special moment in many, many of them in their future.

Just as he wrapped one hand around her jaw, pulling her toward him again, the barn door opened.

"Just wait until you see how cute she—" Mark stopped. "Brandt Holden, what are you doing?"

"Looks pretty obvious to me," Abel Troyer said.

Brandt had no idea how many people were standing there, maybe eight? After settling Tricia back on the bench—she'd been practically on his lap—he stood up. "I was . . . well, I was kissing my fiancée."

"Tricia, you agreed to marry this Englischer?" Mervin asked as Tricia got to her feet as well.

"I did, Daed. Just, um, about five minutes ago."

Before Mervin could speak, Abel grinned. "While I reckon there's lots to say, I think all of us should probably give these young'ens a minute or two of privacy, ain't so?"

"Ack," Tricia muttered as everyone started walking back out, except for Mark and his father.

"Are you happy, Tricia?" Mark asked.

"Very happy. As happy as I've ever been."

"That's all that matters then. Right, Daed?" he asked.

"Oh, *jah*," Abel said as he threw an arm over Mark's shoulder. "Especially since next year we're only gonna have to worry about having one room to house the two of them. That's a blessing, right? We'll be able to invite another guest."

"I was afraid you'd say that."

When the barn door closed again, Brandt started laughing as he pulled Tricia back into his arms. "If that is a taste of how everyone is going to react, I think we're going to be just fine."

Resting her head on his chest, Tricia nodded. "Very fine indeed. Just about perfect."

"What an amazing, incredible Christmas," Brandt said, though whether it was to Tricia, the animals, or to the Lord above, he didn't know.

He supposed it didn't matter anyway. Everyone already knew it was.

Or maybe what they knew was that every Christmas was amazing and incredible. It was Jesus's birthday, after all.

We Gather Together

LENORA WORTH

To Alicia Condon,
thank you for allowing me to write my Amish books
with Kensington.
You are a great editor. Enjoy your retirement!
I will miss you!

Chapter 1

Lucas Myer tugged at his barn jacket and stared out over the choppy waters of Lake Erie. He should be up at the big inn where he and most of his family would be staying for the whole week, but he'd always shied away from big gatherings. And an Amish reunion of more than twenty family members was what he considered a big gathering. Thankfully, they wouldn't all be staying here at the Shadow Lake Inn. His grandparents and his parents were all settled in nice rooms here, but the others would show up and stay in various places nearby for the big feast on Saturday, two days before Christmas.

He'd see some cousins and other relatives near his age, but he'd be expected to hang out with them a lot when he only wanted to go somewhere peaceful to contemplate life.

He wished he could find a quiet place to just think. His *mamm* said he was an overthinker, but Lucas liked to find his way through his thoughts before he made any decisions. Now that he was past Rumspringa, he wanted to get on with his life. Only he couldn't decide how to make that happen.

The lakeshore seemed like the perfect spot to think things through and come to a decision his folks might support. He was alone out here in the cold at this early hour of the morning.

Then he heard a feminine voice humming a familiar hymn. An *Englisch* hymn? "We Gather Together"! Of Dutch origin, if memory served him. But he'd heard German versions, too.

The sweet humming made him see the lyrics in his head, both in *Englisch* and in Pennsylvania Dutch, which was actually High German. So beautiful and soothing, the tune lifted his spirits and made him want to sit and listen more.

Lucas glanced around and spotted the source of the soft music. Then his heart did its own little hum.

A young Amish woman stood staring out over the choppy lake, her head tilted to the morning sun, her gloved hands held together against her heart. She had golden-brown hair, a few strands sparkling underneath her dark winter bonnet, which had slipped away from her pretty, heart-shaped face.

"Uh, *gute mariye*," he said so he wouldn't startle her.

She gasped and whirled around, her cheeks red from the cold. "Oh, I didn't see you there. *Gut* morning to you."

Lucas noticed her bright green eyes and wide smile. "I liked your tune."

She blushed and tugged her dark cape closer as the wind picked up. "I like to hum to myself when I'm trying to figure something out."

He moved closer. "What are you trying to figure out?"

She gave him a solemn stare. "Why my younger sister is getting married before me," she said, her tone firm and unabashed.

Lucas chuckled. "It wonders me how you have not married," he said. "You are for certain sure pretty and you seem rather nice."

She grinned at him, then frowned. "And you are rather bold. So who are you, anyway?"

Direct. He liked that. "I'm Lucas. Who are you?"

"I'm Kayla. And I came out here to be alone."

"So did I."

"Then we have a problem."

"We could be alone together," he replied. "I don't find that a problem at all." He shrugged. "I'm not much of a talker."

She moved closer. "I won't hum if it bothers you."

"It was actually quite nice," he admitted.

They stood quiet for a moment, and then he asked, "Would you like to sit on that bench over there?"

She turned to see him pointing at a curved wooden bench near a tree. "*Ja*, since it's in the sun and I am freezing."

Lucas guided her over to the bench. "It's warm to the touch."

Kayla bobbed her head. "I know it's silly, coming down here when the weather is so chilly, but I needed some fresh air."

They had that in common. "Same with me."

She gave him a direct stare, which made him want to talk.

"So your sister is getting married soon?"

"*Ja*, here at the inn, on Saturday."

Lucas perked up. "So you'll be here all week, just like me?"

She turned to stare at him again. "I suppose so. Why are you here?"

"A family reunion, also on Saturday. I don't like crowds, however. Not even people I'm related to."

"I don't either," she said. "I love weddings and such, but sometimes I have to sneak away so I can think straight. And try not to think about being the last unmarried woman in my family."

Lucas thought she'd be married one day. She just had to find the right man. She was pretty and apparently opinionated but also a loner like him. That gave him an idea.

"We can be alone together all week."

Kayla's brown eyebrows did a high lift. "That sounds a bit naughty, and I'm well past my Rumspringa."

"We are adults, right?"

"We are," she replied. "My sister is eighteen and I'm twenty. I suppose I can have a friend while I'm fretting about her beating me to the altar."

"I can be that friend if you'd like. I'm not married and my *mamm* is forever regretting that."

Kayla gave him an appraising stare. "We are certainly in a pickle here."

"I don't like pickles, but I think we'll be just fine," Lucas said. "Meeting you has been the highlight of my day."

Kayla's smile outdid the sun shining on their faces. "Mine, too. Although the day is young yet."

Lucas grinned. "Wanna get some hot chocolate? The innkeepers have a big pot of it under the pavilion. And there's a firepit going there."

"You've checked the place out already?"

"I read the history of Shadow Lake Inn. It's owned by an Amish family that inherited it from an Englisch couple who had no children."

"Yes, the King sisters run it now." Her eyes brightened. "They are famous around here. They make quilts about their lives—their love lives—from what I've heard. The quilts are on display in the library."

"I haven't seen the library yet, but that's probably where I'll be hiding most days."

"I had thought the same," she said, her tone a bit hesitant. "I don't think you'll be a problem."

"Oh, you mean you won't get tired of me shadowing you at the Shadow Lake Inn?"

She laughed and then shook her head. "You have a streak of humor underneath that stern persona."

Lucas grinned. "I have to admit, you seem to make me smile."

She smiled back. "I think we're going to be *gut* friends, Lucas."

Then she looked at the sun. "Oh, I have to get back. Wedding stuff."

"I'll walk with you. I have to find my family for breakfast in the inn's café."

They hurried back up the pebbled path and approached the long front porch lined with rocking chairs and decorated with fresh greenery and red ribbons.

"We're eating there, too," she said when they paused near the steps to catch their breath. "Who is your family?"

"The Myers," he replied, glad they would see each other again.

Kayla stopped in her tracks before they made it up the steps. "Myer?"

He nodded. "What's your last name?"

"Hollinger," she said, her tone weak, her gaze darting around him.

"It can't be." He looked at her and then he stared up at the inn.

Kayla lowered her voice and held her head high. "If you're the Myers from Spartansburg, we have a big problem."

"Because you're with the Hollingers from there?" he asked, his heart sinking like a wrecked ship.

"The very same. My *grossdaddi* is Claude Hollinger."

"And my grandparents are Tobias and Berneta Myer," he said, seeing her through disappointed eyes now.

"Sworn enemies despite the tenets of the Ordnung."

"Despite everything," she replied. "What are we to do?"

Chapter 2

"We don't need to do anything," Lucas finally said after he'd guided her up onto the porch, his tone firm. "This is not our feud."

Kayla took his words in, thinking she'd finally met a man who seemed so well matched to her—shy—introverted, the Englisch called it—studious and serious, when everyone else seemed shallow and silly. And now, she'd discovered he was part of a family her elders did not like at all.

"I've never understood why they dislike each other," she admitted. "I didn't grow up in the Spartansburg community. We live in Shipshewana, Indiana."

Lucas's worried expression looked a little calmer. He sure was handsome with his curly brown hair and those big dark eyes. Probably the most handsome man she'd ever seen. Telling herself to forget that notion, she watched him absorb this new information, his expression serious but also hopeful.

"As I said, this is not our feud, it's theirs and it's time someone convinced them to put a stop to it."

"Where did you grow up?" she finally asked, hoping it wasn't Spartansburg.

"Lancaster County," he said. "We rarely visit this area, so while I'm aware of the feud, I don't know all the details about the disagreement that occurred between our grandfathers."

"I've heard about it all my life," she admitted. "They were young—about our age—and they both fell for the same girl, but my *grossdaddi* married my *grossmammi* Ethel, the woman he eventually grew to love. She died five years ago, and we can all see that he still mourns her." Kayla's eyes misted over. "Yet I know she always wondered if she was second in my *grossdaddi*'s heart."

"I'm sorry," Lucas said, his dark eyes full of sympathy now. "My *daed* rarely talks about that. He was hesitant to attend this reunion for other reasons, however. My grandfather Tobias can be a hard man at times, and my *grossmammi*, Berneta, fusses at him for still holding a grudge. He won the girl—her."

"*Ja*, my grandfather's parents sold the land next to the Myers and moved to the other side of the community. It was that bad between them. But that's where he met the woman he truly loved—my grandmother."

Kayla wondered how much tension they could stand, all being here together. She loved her *grossdaddi* and he was, for the most part, a kind man. She couldn't see him causing a scene, especially now, when one of his granddaughters was about to be married. "Berneta, *ja*. That's the woman. You'd think they could forgive each other now. It's been over fifty years, after all."

Lucas lifted his chin toward the house. "As I said, we don't need to be part of this feud." Then he pivoted to face her. "Or we could do something. If they find out we're friends, maybe we can help them heal this rift and be done with it." He shrugged. "I do know their animosity grew beyond their competition over a woman. They feuded about everything from goats to wheat fields."

"That's why my elders moved," she replied. "I don't want us to fight like that. I just met you."

"We won't, no matter how they act."

She glanced toward the big windows, hoping none of her family had come down to breakfast yet. "But if we are seen together, it could cause all sorts of trouble. My *grossdaddi* would forbid me to even speak to you."

"We will part ways right here," he said, checking their surroundings. "It's early yet and no one is about. I'll go around the building and enter through the back way."

"*Denke*," she said, checking again. "This is silly, but also exciting."

Lucas stared into her eyes, a hint of anticipation in his own. "A forbidden friendship."

"*Ja*, forbidden. But I'm not afraid."

Lucas gave her a curious once-over. "I do believe that. You seem fearless to me. But will you think about what I said? We're friends, right?"

"*Ja.*"

"Then this should be between you and me, not for them to decide."

Kayla stood quaking in her winter boots, but she wouldn't give in to her fears and doubts. Her grandfather could be stern, but he was also kind and loving to his family. And he'd seemed so sad since Grossmammi Ethel had passed. She'd always believed that he had truly loved her *grossmammi*.

But now she wondered.

"I'm not fearless," she admitted, pushing her doubts away. "You seem nice, Lucas. What harm can there be in just having a friend for a week?"

"No harm," he said, hands up. "We can go our separate ways once this week is over and done."

"*Ja.* A perfect plan. Whether we keep it a secret or not."

"The only plan," he replied. His dark eyes made her think of rich tree bark. "I really like you, and we do have a lot in common."

"Starting with two stubborn, grudge-holding grandfathers, ain't so?"

Lucas leaned close, his hair falling down over his eyes. "What if we could be the bridge that brings them together? Wouldn't that make it the best Christmas ever?"

Kayla could only hope. "They do need to let this feud go and forgive each other, for certain sure. They aren't following the Ordnung at all."

"We'll come up with a plan," he said. "Meet me near the pavilion after the noon dinner and we'll find a place to plan and see what we can do."

Kayla liked that idea, not because she wanted to plan, but because she wanted to be with Lucas again. And that prospect was dangerous enough to make her wonder if she should just stay away from him.

"You look doubtful," he said, as both of them jumped apart when one of the inn workers walked around the corner. The big, muscular man smiled and waved. He had helped them with their buggy yesterday. Jonah.

"I'll be there," she said after smiling at Jonah. She was not one to miss out on a good time.

"I'll see you then," he replied. "I'd better get inside. Maybe I'll see you at breakfast."

"That should be interesting," she reminded him. "We will all be gathered in one room."

"Together," he said. "Just like your hymn."

Kayla watched him go, then took a deep breath. She'd never been good at keeping secrets, and this one would be a whopper.

What would Mamm and Daed think about her new friend?

*   *   *

Kayla walked inside and felt the warmth from the lobby's massive fireplace. Putting her gloves in her cape pocket, she glanced around and spotted Colette King Mueller, the youngest of the King sisters.

"Hi," Colette said as she placed a tray of crisp bacon on the buffet table, next to a bowl of biscuits and a tray of pastries. "Did you have a *gut* walk?"

Kayla nodded as she placed her cape on one of the many hooks lining the entryway. "I did. The lake is so lovely, but the cold is brutal."

"I can see that by your red cheeks," Colette replied, her blue-green eyes shining bright. "My sister Abigail loves to walk down there. It's how she found Jonah. He used to have another name, Kane Dawson. But he changed his name to Jonah King."

Confused, Kayla laughed. "And he married Abigail King."

"It's complicated," Colette said with a shrug. "Finding a man near death in the lake brings all kind of trouble, but it all worked out."

Kayla almost blurted out that she'd found a man by the lake, too, but she caught herself. "I saw a few people out bracing the cold."

"Matthew and I prefer a warm fire and some hot tea and cookies," Colette replied.

When they'd checked in yesterday, Colette had told Kayla and her sister Becky about her own wedding here a year ago. Apparently, the King sisters had all found true love and their husbands now lived and worked on the property. A total family affair, without feuds or arguments.

"I suppose I did stay out a bit too long, but it was a lovely morning with bright sunshine."

Colette nodded. "And this weather should hold for the wedding. Your *mamm* is in the kitchen talking to my *mamm*.

They are going over the wedding feast." She whirled to glance over the menu. "Breakfast will be ready in about five minutes."

"I'll go freshen up," Kayla said. Then she asked, "Are we the only ones having breakfast? I mean, do you have another big group eating now?"

"*Ja*," Colette replied. "The Myer family. They have a reunion coming up the same day as your sister's wedding."

Kayla didn't tell Colette she already knew that. "So it will be my family and theirs, here for breakfast together?"

Colette gave her a curious stare. "*Ja*. All of our guests eat breakfast at the same time, unless we have latecomers. Is something wrong?"

"*Neh*, just me being nosy," Kayla said. "I don't like large crowds."

"Oh, now I understand," Colette said, her smile full of compassion. "The Myers are nice people. They have that big table by the front window. And your family has the one next to the library. Not the best view of the lake, but you get the cozy corner closest to the food."

"That's a plus," Kayla said to offset any concern on Colette's part. "I'm starving."

Colette laughed. "Then get freshened up and I'll let your *mamm* know you're back. Your sister was looking for you earlier, too."

"Becky is always looking for me," Kayla replied. "You know, the bride who demands everything."

"I think I was that kind of bride," Colette said. "Weddings can be stressful, for certain sure."

"And don't I know it," Kayla replied as she waved Colette away. The pretty young woman headed back to the kitchen, calling out orders as she moved.

Kayla envied Colette's station in life. She ran this kitchen with her older sisters, and they took care of this beautiful old inn. Their husbands helped with the stables and the gardens and maintenance. They had chickens providing fresh eggs, and goats to make milk and provide all sorts of nice lotions and soaps. They even made their own candles. The place was so self-sufficient, she marveled at how they all kept up. Like a farm, but so much bigger and so well run. Like a castle, but still plain and Amish, with fresh greenery and handmade cards and pretty original Christmas paintings here and there.

And now she had found a friend in this beautiful place. It was almost like some of the fairy tales she'd read without her *mamm*'s knowledge. But she reminded herself that fairy tales were not like real life. Look what had happened with her grandparents. But would it hurt to enjoy having a secret friend for a few days?

Laughing at herself, Kayla thought she usually didn't like big, busy places like this one. But everyone here had been so kind and considerate to her family. Would the atmosphere remain so congenial once both families came down to breakfast?

She soon found out. Her sister's voice carried from the kitchen as Becky and Mamm came walking through the side door that led to the gardens and pavilion behind the huge inn.

"I can't find her anywhere," Becky was saying. "Why does she always run off when she's needed the most?"

"Becky, she got up early to see the lake. I gave her permission. Neither of us expected you to need help at six in the morning. You were still asleep after our long trip to get here last night."

Becky kept at it. "She shouldn't be out alone at that time of day."

"I'm a grown woman," Kayla said as she met them near their table. "I had a nice walk and then I stopped to chat with Colette."

Becky sighed. "Never mind. Abigail helped me stitch my dress. I found a spot that was unraveling and needed you to mend it."

"You know how to mend," Kayla replied. "I'm not at your beck and call, you know."

"Let's stop this," Mamm said, motioning them to the table. "Your *daed* is coming down and your *grossdaddi* with him. We don't want to upset either of them with this childish bickering, now do we?"

"*Neh*," Kayla said, thinking that statement was a bit ironic. "I'm glad you got your dress fixed, Becky. Now you can adjust your attitude."

Becky's dark eyebrows lifted as she stared at Kayla.

Kayla waited for her sister's insults, but Jason, Becky's groom, came up beside them and took Becky's hand. "There you are. You look as pretty as always."

Becky's angry frown turned into a dazzling smile. Kayla turned away just in time to see the other family coming down the stairs. She counted six people. An older couple—grandparents, she guessed—another couple that had to be Lucas's *mamm* and *daed*, and two younger teenaged boys who must be his brothers. They favored him.

She studied the grandmother, a pretty woman who seemed shy. Was this the woman her own grandfather had held a grudge about for all these years? If he'd loved Mammi Ethel, why would he pine for a woman he'd lost?

Her mother guided her toward their table. "Here's your father and grandfather. They've been taking in the property with Abe King."

Kayla's nerves trembled and twitched. She should have warned her parents, and now it was too late. Where was Lucas?

Just then she spotted him walking up the back hallway at the same moment her grandfather and her *daed* stopped to find their table. Lucas cast her an almost apologetic glance before heading toward the other group.

Kayla's younger brother, Billy, whizzed by, always looking for food. But her *grossdaddi* stopped in his tracks and stared at the group gathering around the other table. He gasped, his gaze landing on the older woman walking with the man.

"This cannot be," he said, his hand lifting as he pointed toward the other group. "What are they doing here? Surely Becky didn't invite them to the wedding?"

The other group grew quiet as the older man turned toward her *grossdaddi* and glared at him. "What are *you* doing here?"

Grandfather Claude stepped forward. "I'm here for my granddaughter's wedding, and you are not invited."

Lucas rushed toward his family. "I'm sorry I'm late. I went for a walk."

The older man ignored Lucas as he moved around the table, his gaze on Claude Hollinger. "I'm here for a reunion, but not one in which you would be included."

At about that time, Eliza King Lapp hurried out of the kitchen, her whole staff behind her. "Breakfast is served," she called. "Please take your plates to the buffet and enjoy your meal. We will bring out the *kaffe*, and there is more in the urn on the buffet table."

The staff fluttered into action, trying to bring smiles to tense faces.

"I'm leaving," Claude said, trying to turn.

"I'll leave first," the other man shouted, also turning to walk away.

"Daed!" Her father stopped Claude. "Remember why we're here. Becky is getting married."

Becky burst into tears. "What is going on?"

The room went quiet. Her *grossdaddi* realized he'd made a mistake.

"Nothing is going on," he said, moving with shaking hands toward the table. "Let's eat our meal in peace."

The other man reluctantly sat down, but he glared at her grandfather until his wife put her hand on his arm and forced him to look away.

Lucas shot Kayla a glance that held so many emotions, she wanted to cry right along with her sister.

"Will someone please explain?" Becky said, still sniffling.

"I'll tell you later," Mamm replied. "Let's say our prayers and eat."

Kayla sat and lowered her head, but she gave Lucas a quick glance while everyone else was still praying.

He saw her and shrugged. Then he lowered his head and shut his eyes.

They'd need a lot of prayers to get through this long weekend. Now everything she'd believed had been challenged. Had her grandparents loved each other? Or had they married on the rebound and made it work with a mere show of love?

And where would this feud leave her and Lucas? How could they be friends now?

Chapter 3

Lucas searched for Kayla after the awkward breakfast. At least their *grossdaddis* had each stayed on their own side of the room—for now. But they had a whole week here and while the inn was big and rambling with a huge yard both front and back, it would be difficult for the two families to avoid each other. It would also be hard for Kayla and him to hang out together.

He couldn't find her, so now he sat in the library, staring at the pretty quilts displayed there. Women loved their quilts, but none of these patterns made sense to Lucas.

Jonah walked in and smiled at him. "Looking for a book or thinking about joining the quilting lessons this afternoon?"

Lucas swallowed. Jonah was an intimidating man, but a kind one. "Neither. I'm worried about my family reunion."

"Ah, family." Jonah slapped his leg and sank down on a side chair. "What was that all about this morning?"

Lucas explained the situation to Jonah. "They've held this grudge for many years. Since they were my age, I think. It started with a woman—"

Jonah chuckled at that. "No surprise there."

"But it didn't end there. The grudge built and built, from what I've heard. We moved away but I reckon what happened this morning proves they will never forgive each other."

"That was some kind of drama," Jonah replied, glancing back toward the now empty café. "But they are both *gut* men. I've talked to them each in passing. Both have a love for family."

"But not a love for forgiveness?"

Jonah had washed up on these shores and made a home here. Maybe he could share some insight.

"You've been through a lot," Lucas said. "I've heard about you. How would you deal with this situation?"

Jonah chuckled again. "In the past—I'd have used violence to solve a problem. But those days are over. I suggest you find a way to help them make peace."

"That's a tall order," Lucas replied. "Any suggestions?"

"Show them, Lucas. Show them with your love how they can forgive a long-ago fight. Make them see they should be ashamed of themselves and that they need to remember we are to forgive and then forget. That's why I'm here and part of this family. I confessed all of my past and I studied the Ordnung word for word—translated to Englisch, but still word for word. I live by those principles now, no matter what I had to leave behind."

"They sure need to leave their anger behind, and this meeting is the perfect opportunity for them to do that," Lucas said. "Christmas and this big historical place—how can they stay angry?"

"This place has a way of changing things," Jonah replied as he stood. "It brings people together."

A small figure at the door caught Lucas's attention. Kayla.

Jonah glanced from her back to Lucas, his catch-all eyes missing nothing. "Oh, I see. You two together—is that the plan?"

Kayla blushed and swirled to leave.

"Wait," Jonah said. "Just ignore my teasing. You two make a cute couple."

She turned back around, her head up and her nose in the air. "We are not a couple. I only came to look for a book."

Jonah did an eyeroll. "Of course, but if you two were to become friends, that could help this situation."

"Or make it worse." Kayla's whispered words were low and solemn, but her face held a trace of guilt. "Don't tell anyone we're friends."

"It's not my place," Jonah replied. "I see and hear a lot around here, but most of it stays with me. You have my word I won't rat you out."

Kayla looked down. "Rat?"

He shook his head. "Sorry, old habits. It means I won't tell anyone about you two."

Lucas looked over at Kayla. "I believe Jonah, so don't worry. We've done nothing wrong. They probably won't even notice us anyway."

"I don't plan to do wrong," she said, lifting her head up, her spine going straight. "But I won't let their ridiculous feud ruin my chance to make a new friend either."

Jonah tried to hide his smile, but when Kayla glared at him, he only shrugged. "As you said earlier, Lucas. It starts with a woman, but this time and this woman could be the perfect beginning of a new friendship. Or maybe even more."

He nodded at Kayla and left them standing there, staring at each other.

Lucas pulled her over by the window, out of sight of the lobby. "What are you really doing in here?"

"I truly came in for a book. My sister is napping—from exhaustion she said. But she's like an infant. I try to take advantage of her naps by making time for myself, and reading seemed like a *gut* idea."

He put on a mock frown. "So you weren't even trying to find me?"

She blushed again, her cheeks pretty and pink. "I did think about you and I had hoped I'd . . . run into you."

Smiling, Lucas sat her down on the small sofa. "I hoped the same. That's why I came in here. That and the warm fire."

She laughed at that. "So should I find a book or can we just talk?"

"Let's talk. Then you can take a book upstairs with you as proof that you did visit the library."

"I like the way you think," she said after a giggle.

Lucas leaned close. "I like the way you look. You're pretty, Kayla."

She stared back into his eyes. "*Denke*. No one has ever told me that."

"Hard to believe, but maybe they don't see you the way I see you."

She looked down at her hands. "My sister is the pretty one, Lucas."

"Does your sister know how to sing the way you do?"

Kayla snorted another giggle. "She can't hold a tune at all."

"So that means she can't hold a candle to you. You should remember that."

Kayla's expression filled with a sweet joy that pierced his heart. "I will, but only because you told me to do so."

"How about we go for a walk later and decide how we're going to get our families together so we can enjoy our time during this Christmas season."

"I'd like that. I pray Becky sleeps all afternoon."

They laughed, then sat back and discussed books, beginning with the Bible and moving on to other interesting stories they'd been allowed to read. Then he told her about his talk with Jonah.

"He thinks we need to find ways to bring them together and show them how wrong they are to continue this feud."

"But how?" she asked, her hands on her lap. "Our *gross-daddis* were both upset this morning."

"We create events where they can't show their anger, where they can only show the *gut* in their hearts."

"So we embarrass them into behaving?"

He laughed. "*Ja*, don't you think that would work?"

"I can ask the King sisters," she said, her tone perky now. "They seem to understand this kind of stuff."

"That is an excellent idea. We should be able to find one of them around here. They're usually in the kitchen, right?"

"Let's go," she said. "We might find some pie and hot chocolate while we're at it."

"I like this plan." He held out his arm as she stood, and together they checked the lobby, then started toward the kitchen.

Lucas felt better about things, but then, Kayla had a way of making him feel happy about everything. But they were only halfway to the kitchen, when they found Becky standing on the stairs, her searching gaze landing on them.

"Kayla, what are you doing?" her sister asked, her nose up as if she were sniffing something unpleasant in the air. "I thought you'd be in that stuffy library."

Kayla's heart shook but she quickly recovered. She had to learn to stand up to her demanding sister. "I was," she replied, realizing that Lucas's presence beside her was giving her courage. "Lucas and I are going to the kitchen for a snack."

"Oh, Lucas and you? I see. Does Mamm know this?"

"Mamm told me to take some time for myself."

"But not by yourself?"

"What do you need, Becky?" she asked, tired of standing there while her sister hovered above them.

"I'm worried about the wedding menu," Becky said. "We should go over it again."

"Can that wait?" Lucas asked. "I really wanted to show Kayla the big pavilion and get some hot chocolate."

"I need her with me," Becky said, her voice rising. "And you need to mind your own business."

Abigail King came walking up, a serene smile on her face. "I couldn't help but overhear. Becky, I'd be glad to go over the menu with you. Again. We're planning to serve the traditional wedding menu and a few side dishes celebrating the season, so if you want to make changes, we need to pin that down now. The menu requires cooking for days and storing food to be warmed up, so we can't make changes after today. Shall we go and make some hot tea and finalize everything?"

"I . . . uh. I don't know," Becky said. "Kayla shouldn't be alone with *him*."

"My *daed* and some of the others are out by the firepit," Abigail replied. "They will keep an eye on these two."

Having no argument left, Becky nodded. "That's so kind of you, Abigail." She came down the stairs, her smile pasted on as she passed Kayla. "Do not be late for supper."

"I won't. I love the food around here," Kayla replied before she shot Abigail a grateful glance. "We won't linger. It's getting so cold."

Becky grunted. "You'd better stay well for the wedding."

"*Denke* for your concern," Kayla retorted. Then she and Lucas grabbed their winter coats from the hall rack and hurried along the hallway to the side door.

Once they were outside, Kayla started laughing. "I've never before stood up to her like that. We fight and she tries to bully me and usually wins. But now, knowing what our families have been doing to each other, I'm not going to feud with my own sister. I'll be firm with her."

"And I will do the same with my family," he replied. "We can end this thing, Kayla. It's gone on far too long."

"But what's our next move?" she asked, excited to have a mission.

"How about we start with finding a project that will involve all of us?"

"And what would that be?"

Snow started falling in thick white flakes.

Lucas held out his hand. "We could have a snowman competition and encourage everyone to get involved. And I mean everyone staying here, not just our families."

"That might work, but what if they fight anyway?"

"We won't let them. We'll tell them all the *kinner* staying at the inn are going to help build the snowmen and decide whose is best."

"They won't show anger in front of the *kinner*, right?"

"I hope not."

They headed for the hot chocolate stand and soon had two cups to warm their hands.

Kayla had never had so much fun, and having a snowman contest would be another opportunity to get to know Lucas better. And avoid her sister as much as possible.

Unless their families messed up the whole plan.

Chapter 4

"A snowman contest!" Eliza King Lapp danced around like a five-year-old after they found her in the kitchen the following day and told her their plan. "I love that idea. We have at least a half-dozen *kinner* here and they need something to do. I'll make a flyer and announce it at supper."

Kayla grinned and glanced at Lucas. They'd put the finishing touches on their plans yesterday, hoping their second day with their families might be better than the first. "This will be so much fun."

Eliza motioned toward the window. "That snow is coming down and it will be perfect for making handsome snowmen or pretty snow women. Amish, with hats and bonnets. We can put old straw hats on them and wrap garland around them like scarves."

Lucas let out a sigh of relief. "Okay, so that's settled. This afternoon?"

"*Ja*," Eliza replied. "Now you two can go out to the stables and feed Samson these carrots." She lowered her voice. "And have some time alone. There is a very special old rock beyond the stables. It's a favorite spot for privacy."

"Really?" Lucas smiled widely, making both Eliza and Kayla laugh.

"Someone seems to want to be alone with you, Kayla."

Heat flushed Kayla's cheeks and her warm clothes became too warm. "*Ja*, we should go on another walk before anyone finds us and tells us we can't be friends."

"*Neh*, you will not go on any walks with him."

Kayla turned to find her *grossdaddi* staring across the room at them.

"It's only a walk," she said, wishing she could slip through the floor.

"I said you will not go and that is final," Claude Hollinger replied, his voice rising. "Your sister is upset with you. She told me you were down here with the Myer boy."

"We're just hanging out together," Kayla tried to explain.

"Which you shouldn't be doing," her grandfather said, his tone firm while his glare sent a razor-sharp zap toward Lucas.

"How about I have Levi escort them?" Eliza asked, clearly trying to defuse the situation. "It's so lovely out there right now."

Kayla walked to her grandfather. "Please, Daddi. Lucas is kind and just a friend. Becky and Mamm are so busy with the wedding, and I'm bored and all alone. Can't I have a friend? I'm old enough to take care of myself and mind my manners."

Her *grossdaddi* looked surprised, and then his expression filled with embarrassment as he glanced around. "I'm sorry but he's a Myer, Kayla."

"That's his name, not his attitude," Kayla replied. "He's not part of your feud."

"You will not speak to me in that manner," Grossdaddi said. Then he gave Lucas a shrewd stare. "You look like your *grossdaddi*."

"Does that mean you don't like me?" Lucas asked, his tone clear and firm.

"I don't know you."

"Exactly," Kayla replied. "We mean no disrespect, but we think the ruckus between you and Lucas's family is being disrespectful to God's word."

"Do not talk to me of theology, young lady."

Kayla tried again. "Grossdaddi, you know how much I love you. I won't do anything to dishonor that love. It's just that Becky is getting married and I'll be all alone at home, and I'm older than she and still . . . single. Lucas is kind and interesting, and we are only keeping each other company. Don't ask me to give up a new friend while Becky is happy and has a big wedding about to happen. Can't I have my own kind of happiness for a brief while?"

Her grandfather looked ashamed, his stern expression changing to a cloud of regret and a hint of understanding. He glanced from her to Lucas but stayed silent.

Eliza stepped close to Kayla. "I will chaperone them, Claude. I had asked them to feed Samson for me, but I can go with them. He loves carrots and I thought they might enjoy meeting Samson. He enjoys taking guests on sleigh rides."

Kayla stared up at the grandfather she loved, hoping he'd concede. "Please?"

He finally nodded. "If Eliza goes with you—and do not stay out with this boy all day." Then he nodded at Lucas and turned toward the front parlor, his gait slower than Kayla remembered. He was getting on, so why keep up this silly grudge?

Eliza took them both by the arm. "Let's go before he changes his mind."

She hustled them out into the snow. Kayla's sturdy boots sank into the soft snow and its depth almost toppled her. Lucas reached to help her but she shook her head.

"*Denke*," Kayla said, "but someone might report that you touched me."

He dropped his hand, a frown on his handsome face. "It's *baremlich*."

"It is indeed terrible," Eliza said, sympathy in her eyes. "But your idea will help in so many ways. What other plans to do you two have cooked up to keep your families busy and hopefully happy?"

"Buggy or sleigh rides would be nice, as you mentioned," Lucas said. "If we could go on one in peace."

"And we thought sledding down one of the hills would be fun for the *youngie*," Kayla said. "If the adults can behave long enough."

Eliza's snort indicated she understood. "Why didn't you stick to the plan most young people usually employ—sneaking around?"

"We had that plan," Lucas said, "but the scene at breakfast yesterday ended that. I won't hide my friendship with Kayla. If it forces our families to change, then so be it. I saw a flicker of regret in Claude's eyes just now."

Kayla was thankful her grandfather had conceded a bit. "He's really so sweet when he isn't judging people."

That made them all laugh.

Yet she couldn't let go of the fears and doubts that had always kept her from committing to anyone. Could someone love her completely? Hearing about this ugliness between the elders of their families had really thrown her for a loop. How could she ever know if someone truly loved her?

"Yes, Claude reined in his feelings, but you might see a flicker of anger next time," Eliza warned, bringing Kayla out of her musings. "You two handled yourselves well back there though. We must be respectful to our elders, no matter what."

They made it to the stables and went inside. Eliza turned to them. "You have fifteen minutes to go visit the rock I told you about. I'll feed Samson and wait for you to come back and help me finish up. Levi and Jonah went into town for supplies. This weather is only going to get worse."

"I hope it doesn't mess with Becky's wedding," Kayla said, worry in her tone. "She'll make life hard for all of us if that happens."

"We'll have the wedding inside if the snow gets worse," Eliza said. "Plan B. But for now, get out there and enjoy the weather."

"We'll hurry," Lucas said, reaching for Kayla's hand.

She took it without drawing back. Putting her concerns away, Kayla glanced over at him. She didn't like sneaking but honestly, couldn't her family understand she'd met a man who checked all her boxes, and she wasn't about to let him slip away without getting to know him better?

They had so much to learn and so little time to really get to know each other. She ran with him, their boots digging into the snow, until they found the huge rock jutting out like a big bench behind a copse of shrubs and trees.

Kayla stopped and took a breath. "Look at that view, Lucas. I can see the big lake from here."

Lucas studied the constantly changing water and held her hand tight. "It's always amazing seeing the big lake, but this is the best view. No wonder people come up here to be alone. It's breathtaking."

"And romantic," Kayla said. Then she clamped her hand over her mouth. "Not that I expect romance. Not at all."

Lucas settled with her on the rock and shivered. "This is not a warm rock."

"*Neh.*" She straightened her skirts and her cape. "Brrr. That morning sun is beautiful but the temperature isn't cooperating."

"Now about that romance," he said, his hand still over hers. "I know we've only just met, but I've never really walked out with a girl before. I mean, I've liked girls and flirted and all that, but I've never felt this close to anyone this soon. Maybe too soon, but we are on a tight schedule."

Kayla smiled at him, relieved that he had some doubts, too. "In a hurry?"

"Kinda." His eyes darkened. "On the other hand, I want to savor this time together because we found each other here in such a unique way and it all seems perfect. As if it were meant to be."

"I understand," she said, her heart pumping warmth throughout her body. "We can't rush anything, but I do know we will be friends when we leave here. We can write to each other."

"I'd like that," he said. "And there are ways to visit each other. Buses, trains, vans. Or I'll just saddle up my horse, Donut."

"You have a horse named Donut?"

"I do. He looks like a donut because he has a spot of white hair, almost a perfect circle on his nose. It stands out against his tan skin."

"And you'd ride Donut all the way from Spartansburg to Shipshewana?"

"In a heartbeat," he replied. "I like you."

"I like you, too," she said. "I wish this week could last longer and that our families could make peace. Then we could truly be the best of friends."

Lucas leaned close. "Regardless of that, one day I'm gonna kiss you. But not yet. I want you to be sure."

"Do friends get to kiss each other?"

"I think at that point we will be beyond friends, ain't so?"

The heat of a blush warmed Kayla's cold cheeks. "I would think so, *ja.*"

They sat still, smiling at each other, shivering in the cold, snow covering their clothes until Eliza called out, her voice soft in the snowfall.

"We must get back," Lucas said. "The kitchen staff is doing their part to avoid tension by letting our families take turns in the café for noon dinner, but I hope to see you at supper if all goes well with today's plan."

"I will look for you."

"And let's hope we won't have any more outbursts," he replied as they trudged back to the stables. "We only want peace such as this snowfall."

"A peace beyond understanding," she replied. "Today, we build snowmen and hope that joint activity brings out the joy in our families."

"I do not want to make a snowman."

Lucas looked at his *grossdaddi*'s frowning face and let out a grunt. "So you won't help the boys? They specifically asked for you to be on their team. Besides, it's Christmastime. Have some fun."

Tobias put his hands on his hips. "I do not care for fun, not out in the cold. My old hip can't take that."

"I'll help," Mitch called out as he ran toward his grand-father. The eleven-year-old adored Tobias Myer, as did Lucas and his middle brother, David. "Please, please. We need you to help us, Grossdaddi."

Lucas gave Tobias a hopeful stare. "C'mon. Just try."

Finally his grandfather grabbed a handful of snow. "Well, let's get started. I can't stand here freezing all day." Then he threw the snowball he'd shaped at Mitch, hitting his grandson on the arm.

That started a round of back-and-forth snowballs until Grossdaddi finally held up his hand in defeat. "If I am to build the biggest, best snowman, I need to catch my breath."

Lucas laughed and glanced over to where Kayla and her younger brother Billy were already dragging her parents and grandfather toward the area of the yard where Colette and Eliza had organized the snowman competition.

"I'm not so sure about this," Cella Hollinger shouted. "It's a bit chilly."

"Perfect snowman building weather, Mamm," Kayla said. "And the winner gets a pecan pie."

"Pie?" Billy grinned, his shaggy golden bangs hanging over his eyes. The teenager was way more outgoing and energetic than his pretty older sister Kayla. "I want pie."

Claude laughed until he saw the Myer family gathering across the way. "I might need to sit this one out."

"You can't do that," Billy said, ignoring his grandfather's grumpy face. "Mamm, make him stay and help."

"I'll try." Kayla's *mamm* looked worried as she acknowledged the other people gathering. "But I won't stay long. I have things to do."

Billy tugged his mother toward the heavy snow. "You haven't played with us since we got here. Why do you hang out with Becky and no one else?"

"Your sister is preparing to get married," their mother said, glancing at Kayla. Then she amended. "I do have a few minutes, now that I think about it."

Lucas saw the sadness in Kayla's smile. Her sister took all the air out of a room with her demands for attention while Kayla stood back and watched and waited. He wanted her to have a great time this week. She was a special person, and it was time her family noticed that.

Eliza stepped to the center of the area where the two families had somehow gathered on each side, along with a few other daring people with their own *kinner*, some Amish and some Englisch. Lucas hoped the extra families would cushion the growing competition.

"Here's how this will work," Eliza explained. "You all have baskets full of scarves, aprons and hats, along with carrots and buttons to make noses and eyes. You have thirty minutes to create your snow people. The winning family will get a pecan pie and some other goodies to enjoy in your suite later with a warm beverage."

Everyone clapped. Lucas watched as the Hollinger family got their basket and waited for Eliza to announce the start. Claude stared across at the Myers who'd gathered—Mamm and Daed with Grandfather Tobias and Lucas's brothers. Mitch motioned for him to join them. Where was Mammi?

Lucas took a quick glance at Kayla with her mother and brother. Her father had walked out to the stables with Levi Lapp, Eliza's husband. They might need some help, but he was committed to the Myers' snowman for now.

Eliza lifted a red handkerchief and counted. "One, two, three. Go."

Tobias Myer immediately called out, "We need to win this and show those Hollingers a thing or two."

"Just try," Claude called back. "My family knows how to have fun and create beautiful things. Snowmen included."

"We shall see about that," Tobias shouted back. "And don't try to steal ours."

Then they both started working on their snow people, each of them grabbing buckets and instructing their teams on how to make the perfect snowman. The shouting got louder and fiercer with each minute that ticked by.

Kayla glanced at Lucas with fear in her pretty eyes. "Bad idea," she mouthed, her eyes wide and her cheeks red with cold and embarrassment.

He shook his head. "It's okay," he mouthed back.

Then his grandfather called out, "Lucas, whose side are you on?"

Lucas gave Kayla another pleading glance and then turned to face his *grossdaddi*. "Yours," he called. "Always yours."

"*Gut*," Tobias replied, the smug grin on his aged face a clear stab at the Hollinger gang working on the other side of the open area. "We aim to keep it that way, don't we?"

As Kayla heard the conversation, the brightness left her eyes.

Lucas didn't answer his grandfather's question, and he couldn't face Kayla right now. Instead, he went to work on making a nice snowman. While he prayed he could salvage this competition and their friendship.

Would their idea turn out okay, or make things worse between the two patriarchs of their families?

Their whole plan might have just gone up in a snow fight to end all snow fights.

Chapter 5

"This has turned into a disaster," Kayla said as she dragged Lucas away when no one was looking. "The other families are making *wunderbar* snow people." She pointed to an Englisch couple with two little girls. "They've made a snow family based on their own family."

Lucas glanced at the corner spot where the family had indeed made a *daed* and *mamm*, and two dainty little snow children. "Give 'em time. Their family might fall apart one day."

Kayla slapped at his snow-covered barn jacket. "Don't say that. We can't let our *grossdaddis* make us feel the same way they do."

"Well, look around," he said, lifting his hands in the air. "They're making snowballs to hit each other, rather than creating something cute that would merit pie."

"You go and help my family, and I'll go help yours," she said, shoving him toward her laughing, arguing siblings. "Go," she ordered, giving him a challenging stare.

Lucas didn't stop to think. He hurried over to where her grandfather was struggling to make another snowball to throw.

Grabbing the bucket they'd abandoned, he filled it with snow and went to the half-finished, sad-looking figure that leaned to the left.

"What are you doing?" Billy asked, shocked. "You're supposed to be over there." He pointed to the Myer bunch. "They don't know a thing about making a snowman."

"Says who?" Lucas replied. "I came to help you with this one since your *grossdaddi* is too busy trying to hit my *grossdaddi* with a snowball."

"They didn't listen to the rules," Billy said, sighing. "You'll help me?"

"Sure. Let's get busy," Lucas said, glancing to where Claude was giving him the stink eye. "We'll show all of 'em."

Billy laughed and started back on the poor fellow in front of them. That brought Billy's *mamm*, Cella, to help. She glanced at Lucas with a smile.

Becky came running out, her hands on her hips. "What is going on? I need help and I can't find anyone."

One of Lucas's younger brothers hit her in the face with a snowball. Becky let out a scream that stopped everything, and her fiancé ran to check on her.

Claude spotted the shenanigans and glared at Lucas. "I'm done. I won't have someone harming my granddaughter."

"You have two," Billy pointed out. "Kayla looks fine, and Becky just wants attention."

Claude let out grunt, then glanced to where Kayla was finishing up a nice snow lady. Lucas's *mamm* was helping her and they were laughing. Mamm had a kind heart and she was probably secretly happy that he'd found a pretty girl to flirt with. Mamm wanted grandbabies.

Becky kept fussing but soon turned with her fiancé and went back inside. Claude stomped away and Tobias did the same, but both in different directions.

After that, everyone finished up with little fussing or fighting. Eliza announced the thirty minutes were up, but the two patriarchs were nowhere to be found.

Lucas glanced around. The other families had made nice snow people, while the Myers and the Hollingers had made a big mess. The one snowman he and Billy had finished toppled over before it could even be judged.

The pecan pie and goody basket went to the family of four who'd made a family of snow people. At least they'd had the right idea and followed the directions. Their snow family had smiling faces and big red and green scarves and cute carrot noses. They wore colorful bonnets and hats. They stood confident and sure amid the half-finished attempts and melting snowballs all around them.

Eliza gave Kayla and Lucas an apologetic glance, then shouted, "Hot chocolate and pie for everyone."

Lucas didn't hesitate. He hurried to Kayla and motioned. "Let's get some pie. We deserve it, ain't so?"

"*Ja*," she said, giving her remaining family members a defiant cheeky grin. "I'm starving."

Kayla returned to their suite soon after the midday meal had been served. Her family ate early to avoid the Myers, so she didn't get to see Lucas again after they'd shared pie and hot chocolate out by the firepit.

The pavilion was being set up for her sister's wedding this weekend, so they'd watched as the husbands of the sisters—Jonah, Levi, and Matthew—worked to string fresh evergreen branches together to make the open platform more festive. Lucas got up and offered to help and they'd readily agreed.

At least the King family didn't have a feud with anyone. They worked together in an almost choreographed way, going through their daily duties with laughter and playful teasing.

She and her sister needed to be like that, but they'd fought from day one, according to their *mamm*. Kayla had loved her baby sister until Becky took over the limelight and began getting more attention. As the years passed, they'd had some precious memories and some horrible quarrels.

Was she jealous? *Neh*, she was a little envious but she wanted her sister to be happy. Kayla had accepted that she might not ever fall in love and marry, that she would be a wallflower rather than a beautiful rose. Becky told her she needed confidence, but Kayla wasn't sure if Becky had confidence or just too much pride.

But now, when she thought about Lucas and his beautiful smile and sparkling eyes, she longed for her own wedding day, her own family, her own life. Only, he was part of a family her relatives disliked because of a childish feud that should have ended years ago.

Maybe some people never completely grew up.

These thoughts had danced through her head as she and other visitors watched while the men hung handmade wooden Christmas renderings that looked like Christmas cards all along the swirls of black iron trim that followed the roofline. She'd helped make some of the wooden cards while sitting in their suite at night. She and Becky and Mamm had been painting them for weeks, and the sisters had helped finish them up once they'd arrived here.

After Lucas got busy, she'd waved to him and then headed inside for a quick bite of more nutritious food, and now she was here in the room she had to share with her sister. Becky's bed was covered with clothes and decorations, while Kayla's was neat and clear. She sank down on the soft starburst quilt trimmed in red, green, and gold. It was festive but still plain. She loved the coziness of the little room and the comfort of the bigger room where her parents were staying. They had a small sitting room between them with a fireplace and a snack table.

She had a view of the back garden from the window in the

smaller bedroom, so she found the book she'd been reading and settled into a nice chair to enjoy the scene.

After a few peaceful moments of reading an Amish romance, Kayla stood and stretched, then glanced out the window.

Lucas walked by, stalking, his hands fisted at his sides. Then she spotted his *daed* and *grossdaddi* following him, calling out to him. Lucas kept walking.

Had he gotten into trouble because of the snowman fiasco?

Watching in fascination, she saw his *daed*, John, following him. John caught up with him and reached out to Lucas in a gentle way, his hand touching his son's shoulder. Lucas turned to face his father and John said something, a smile rather than a frown on his face. Lucas listened, his stance softening. He lowered his head and said something to his *daed*, and then he smiled, too. The tender moment between father and son held her heart with its sweetness. The way they'd looked at each other, their frowns changing to smiles, showed a deep, abiding love.

But Tobias Myer watched their exchange, then lifted his hands in the air and stomped away.

Could they be discussing her?

As if they knew someone was watching, both father and son glanced up, and Lucas spotted her standing there. He gazed at her for only a moment, his expression telling her so many unspoken things. He gave his *daed* one last pleading glance, then looked away, the frustration in his expression telling her despite the tight smiles, he was not happy.

Putting her book down, Kayla was headed for her cloak when Becky came into the suite and blocked her way.

"Excuse me," she said, trying to pass her sister. "I need some fresh air."

"*Neh*," Becky said, shaking her head. "You do not need to go out and find that boy."

"What makes you think I'd do that?" she asked, her own

anger boiling like a kettle with a flame under it. She'd have to show restraint or the situation would only get worse.

"Are you serious?" Becky asked, her hands on her hips, her eyes bright with smug triumph. "Tobias Myer made it clear to Daed that you are to stay away from his grandson."

"He did what?" Kayla whirled and went back to the window. Lucas was nowhere to be found.

"If you're thinking to meet him, he's probably gone back to his room, per his grandfather's orders," Becky said. "So you can get over the notion that you two can be friends. You need to steer clear of him, Kayla. He's a Myer. We all know what that means. Or at least most of the family does."

"What exactly does being a Myer mean?" Kayla shot back. "Lucas didn't start this feud and he doesn't even live in Lancaster County. We met here and we enjoy doing things together. Why is everyone so against that? And why are you, of all people, against it? You're getting married and yet you can't allow me a bit of happiness with a man I happen to like a lot."

Becky started to say something and then stopped, her eyes going wide. "Oh, my. You really do have feelings for this boy?"

"He's not a boy," Kayla replied as she sank down on a slipper chair covered with a lush floral pattern. "He's a grown man and I'm a grown woman, the older sister in fact. But everyone seems to have forgotten that."

"Are you jealous of me?" Becky asked, but for once her question held a different tone. An almost apologetic tone.

"I'm not jealous," Kayla replied. "I'm happy for you and Jason, but I'm sad for me. You're the outgoing, pretty Hollinger sister, Bec, and I'm the plain unmarried older sister who keeps getting offers to take home stray cats. We have enough cats around our house."

Becky started giggling, her hand going to her mouth, her eyes misty.

"You think this is funny?" Kayla began to pace, the well of

emotions she'd held inside for so long bubbling to the surface in a heated rush. "All I've heard for the last few months is wedding, wedding, wedding. And you are one of the worst brides ever, with your demands and your assumptions and your thinking I should be at your beck and call. I only want to get to know a man who seems to accept me—me—Becky. Just the way I am. Plain and simple."

Becky reached for her arm to stop Kayla's pacing. "I'm not laughing at you. I'm laughing at the idea of you surrounded by cats. You are pretty, Kayla, but you hide your light under a bushel as the verse goes. You sing like a beautiful little bird but you're too shy to let the world know that. You quilt better than I ever will and when it comes to cooking, Mamm always turns to you."

"Because you are never there," Kayla retorted, stinging at her sister's depiction of *her* life. "You're mostly out doing things."

"I enjoy being with people, that is true," Becky said. "And I'm probably overdoing things with the wedding, but I'm nervous and marriage is a big step and what if I mess up? You never mess up, Kayla, because you never take risks or step outside what is safe and easy."

"I'm trying to do that very thing right now," she said, wishing her sister wasn't so daft at times. "I like Lucas and I'm going to keep getting to know him. How is that for stepping out?"

"I think it's about time," her sister said. Then Becky hugged her in a tight grip. "And now that I can see the truth through your eyes, I'll back off, just to see it happen."

Shocked, Kayla glanced at her sister to make sure Becky wasn't teasing. "So why come in here and jump all over me about Lucas?"

"I was trying to warn you about Tobias," Becky replied. "I'm sorry if I sounded self-righteous and overbearing." Becky grimaced, her cheeks turning pink. "I reckon I did, at that."

"You?" Then Kayla started giggling. "You'd never do that to me, ever."

They both started laughing then. Mamm came in and gave them a once-over. "Well, this is different."

"We just made a pact," Becky said. "I'm not going to be the mean bride anymore and Kayla is going to step out with Lucas a lot more."

"Becky," Kayla said, embarrassed.

"You did say that," her sister reminded her. "And I *am* making a pact with you. I need my sister to be happy, and not just for my wedding, but in her own life, too."

Kayla glanced at Mamm and saw no animosity. More like shock and awe. So she was equally honest: "I'm going to step out and I'm going to be happy. I really want to spend time with my new friend."

Mamm absorbed, accepted, and then nodded. "Okay then. I'm going to take a nap."

Chapter 6

On the Wednesday before the upcoming weekend wedding and the Myer family reunion, Kayla and Lucas met down by the lake. The snow had softened and stopped, but the whole countryside was covered in a brilliant white coating that looked like quilt batting, all fluffy and heavy. The fresh sunshine beamed against the stark white, highlighting each gentle snowflake with a shimmer, as if someone had scattered tiny crystals all over the earth.

"Beautiful," she said, taking the cup of strong *kaffe* with cream he'd brought for her.

"Very beautiful," he replied, his own paper cup cradled in his hands.

But he wasn't looking at the choppy lake or the blanket of snow.

Lucas watched Kayla with bright hope in his eyes. For a moment they stood silent, letting the earth talk for them. Birds flew by, cawing and chirping. A beautiful red cardinal perched on a snow-covered limb, its keen gaze taking in its surroundings. The lake waves hit the shore and then fell back in the same age-old pattern, breaking icy water as they shifted.

Kayla tried to read his face, tried to find a hint of regret or remorse. "Are we really here, alone, without anyone shouting at us?"

"*Ja,* here we are together and alone," Lucas said, his voice husky and low. "Day three of the Lucas and Kayla adventure, and this is one special moment. But we have much to do still. The sisters have scheduled cookie decorating next."

"I know," she replied, sighing as reality burst their little snow globe bubble. "We have a few minutes before chaos breaks out again." Then she smiled and shrugged. "They seem to have backed off a bit."

She told him about her conversation with Becky. "She's being nice to me, and she likes you, Lucas. That's a win right there."

"She should be nice to her sister," he replied. "I'm glad you were honest with her."

"I'm learning to speak my mind," she admitted. "I couldn't have done that without your encouragement, without meeting you."

"Gott's will, I hope," he replied before sipping his black *kaffe.*

"Or maybe two people being willful for the first time?"

"That too, but he led us here, ain't so?"

"*Gut* point."

She shivered and took a sip of her creamy brew. "Mamm seems okay with us, and Daed is staying out of things. He's longed for some sort of reconciliation with your family, and it's been a bone of contention between him and my *grossdaddi* for years."

"So many emotions between us, like a river that runs deep with ebbs and currents we can't contain. But we can control what happens in our own lives, with Gott watching over us."

"So we follow his path, not the one everyone else thinks we should follow?"

"I believe so," he replied. Then he finished his *kaffe*. "Meeting you has been the highlight of this week, maybe the highlight of my life. Would Gott lead us here to each other only to force us to give up these feelings we have in our hearts?"

"I sure hope and pray not," she replied, amazed at how well he understood her and the attraction between them. "If we keep forcing our families together, they will have to find a way to forgive, *ja*?"

"It's worth a try." He glanced up at the inn looming off in the distance. "We should get back since we're the ones who asked for these competitions."

"And we are to blame if our *grossdaddis* keep competing in a bad way."

"I hope today will be better. At least my *mamm* got to know you a bit more. She really enjoyed visiting with you even if the snowman competition didn't work out the way we'd planned."

"Your *mamm* is very nice, Lucas." They started walking back up the stone path. "And my brother Billy couldn't stop talking about you last night at supper. Daed frowned and Mamm smiled, but she will win Daed over because she knows you and I are friends. I was firm on that."

"You, firm." He laughed. "Show me your firm expression."

She pursed her lips together and made an exaggerated frown.

Then they both burst out laughing.

Kayla laughed so hard she almost slipped on one of the stones, but Lucas caught her and tugged her into his arms.

They stopped laughing and stared at each other for a brief second. Then he drew close and kissed her gently on the lips. Gently, but a spark was lit, and soft warmth glowed in her heart, then took off in a sizzling dance down her spine.

The kiss was sweet and simple and quick, but it told her

what her heart knew already. She was beginning to care deeply for this man she'd only just met.

He drew back, his gaze moving over her face. "Should I be sorry?"

"For what?" she asked, breathless and still stunned.

"I kissed you, or did you miss that entirely?"

"I didn't miss a thing. I was fully aware of that kiss."

"In a *gut* way?"

"In the best way, Lucas. I like you and I liked that kiss."

"But?"

"But we just met and I'm so afraid this fragile longing will break apart like that ice out on the water, and we'll go our separate ways, and our families will never approve, and—"

He kissed her again, putting a definite stop to all her worries.

Then he leaned back, held her chin with his gloved fingers and grinned at her. "We are going to get through this. We might have to go our separate ways for a while, but, Kayla, I'm not letting you go. I want you in my life, so we will tolerate our families and they will have to accept that you and I are not part of their feud. We are two adults who have decided to be friends and . . . maybe more, understand?"

"I do understand, but you know it's not that simple."

"Our kiss was simple and easy and *gut*, right?"

"Oh, *ja*," she said with a sigh. "So easy. So *gut*."

"Then we take things step-by-step, slowly and surely. We both have level heads, and we are rule-followers. We don't rebel and make a fuss. We won't do anything to dishonor our families or our faith."

"*Neh*," she replied, wishing they could get back to the kisses.

"But we will be the ones to decide what happens next," he told her. "We have to stand firm or we'll be swept up in this awful feud and it will never end. Or worse, I'll be fighting with my own family."

She shook her head. "I won't let that happen."

"What do you mean?" he asked, his brow furrowed.

"I mean, if staying apart means keeping the peace, then we'll have to walk away. I won't *kumm* between you and your family, Lucas."

"Nor would I do that to you. But we shouldn't let them keep us apart either. If we stand firm, they should see that we care for each other and be happy about that. Their grudges shouldn't stop us from being together."

"But you and I being together could make things even worse," she pointed out. "I will not let that happen."

They realized the complications and the impact of their declarations.

Kayla looked out at the water and then back at him. "So either they allow us to be friends, or we end it here and now."

He shook his head. "I don't like that idea, but we could use that premise to our advantage. In fact, our ending it in a big ol' fight might just get their attention and bring about the peace we all want."

Kayla thought about that, then frowned. "You mean, fake it?"

He glanced up at the house. "If it comes to that, it would be our last resort."

Kayla had to agree. "Seems we have a new plan. A sneaky, conniving plan, but sometimes you have to fight fire with fire."

He pulled her close for one more quick kiss. "And sometimes you have to play dirty to get what you really want, what Gott has planned for you. And I know now that I want you in my life for a long, long time."

She grinned and touched his long bangs. "I want the same. As my deceased *grossmammi* used to say, 'You can mess up now and ask for forgiveness later.' We might need to do that, for certain sure."

"I just wonder if either of our *grossdaddis* have ever thought to ask for forgiveness," he replied. "That would be the best solution for all of us."

By the time they made it to the café where the cookie decorating would be held, they had a solid plan in mind.

But when they entered the doors and saw all the people gathered and ready for this next competition, they could only look at each other and shake their heads.

Everyone was shouting at everyone else as the two families confronted each other. Tobias and Claude were pointing fingers and talking over each other, while Grossmammi Berneta was almost in tears. And both their *mamms* were standing there glaring at their elders while the *kinner* and teens looked on in embarrassment.

"Maybe we should sneak out," Lucas whispered to Kayla.

Before she could answer, Tobias spotted them. "Well, here are the two lovebirds now. Don't try to deny it, Lucas Myer. We all saw you kissing this girl out there in the light of day." Moving his pointed finger from Kayla's grandfather to Lucas, he shouted, "And after I told you this must stop, you defied me."

Lucas tried to speak, but Claude jumped right in. "Kayla, you can find better friends when you get home. Why are you latching on to a Myer? What is it about him?"

Kayla was about to speak when a loud whistle shrilled through the air, stopping the fuss and causing everyone to turn toward the kitchen.

A well-rounded older woman stood with a large kitchen spoon, her dark eyes filled with a fire of her own. "I am Aenti Miriam—Sarah's sister—and along with my friend Edith, we are working extra hours here, helping the King sisters keep things in order. You are all adults but look at you, fussing like *kinner* while the *kinner* are watching. You will reap what you sow. So I suggest you stop fussing and get on with decorating these cookies. With smiles on your faces."

Kayla glanced at Lucas. Lucas glanced back at Miriam. Then they both nodded toward their families.

"We agree with that," Kayla shouted before she could change her mind. Then she took a bold breath and said, "*Ja*, we kissed each other and look—we're okay. We're all okay here because we are all blessed. Can we have peace for one hour, please?"

"Just one hour," Lucas echoed, glaring at all of them. "Then you can fuss at me privately for kissing Kayla. But I do not regret kissing her, not at all. Just to make that clear."

The room quieted and Miriam stood still, her spoon at the ready, a twinkle in her assertive eyes. Then two more older women came bustling out of the kitchen, their aprons crisp and tied tight.

"I'm Gayle, and this is my sister Gloria," the elder one with gray hair explained. "We moved here last Christmas and joined the kitchen staff. We oversee the desserts."

She stopped smiling and held up a large rolling pin. "We can't do our work amidst fussing and fighting. If we wanted that, we'd go home to our sons and their families."

Gloria looked troubled, but she held up her hand for quiet. "So for one hour we want you to work peaceably together."

Miriam stood with the two other women. "Any questions?"

No one said a word. Wives glared at husbands and husbands glared across the room at each other. But they all finally nodded their approval and acceptance on this matter.

"That's more like it." Miriam approved the quiet. "Let the cookie decorating begin." She whipped around to the kitchen, the two employees following, thus leaving the families stunned and afraid to say anything.

"Peace," Kayla whispered to Lucas. "Let's make the best of it."

Lucas whispered in her ear. "We can't cause a scene now with our own fight. It has to look real to convince all of them."

"I understand," she said. "I don't feel like fighting anyway."

They parted and each took their place with their families, the tension between them fizzling down like a dying ember in a fireplace.

For now, all was quiet. And then everyone starting laughing and grabbing at cookie dough.

Chapter 7

Three dozen sugar cookies and a lot of messy icing later, the café grew quiet again. Colette and her husband Matthew had taken the *kinner* for a quick buggy ride along the path that had been cleared in the apple orchard, each child munching on a messy cookie. Eliza and her older sister Abigail were in the kitchen supervising the lobster bisque and freshly baked cornbread.

Kayla sat in a chair by the fireplace, staring at the book she was pretending to read. Becky was upstairs with her friends, who'd arrived after being delayed by the heavy snow, and Mamm was talking to Miriam and the other taskmaster of the kitchen, Edith. Miriam had explained they were both retired, and she helped out with Levi's *mamm*, who needed assistance at times.

"But we both *kumm* back to help during the holidays. We love being in on the action."

Happy there wasn't any action right now, Kayla sat warm and sleepy, hoping Lucas would walk back in and talk to her. He'd left to help Eliza's husband, Levi, in the stables since the weather was getting worse. Lucas liked to stay busy, and he knew a lot about horses and farming. She'd seen him talking to Abe King, the patriarch of the inn's working family. Even though he was quiet and studious, Lucas could talk to anyone. She wished she could be more outgoing like her sister, but Kayla just didn't have it in her to show off or act out. Lucas accepted that, rather than teasing her or trying to get her to change. Right now, she had to wonder if she could learn to stand up for herself more and be firm, but kind, when dealing with controversy.

She watched as Sarah King, the mother of the three sisters, came strolling through the big lobby, where leather chairs sat near floral sofas and the fire and *kaffe* were always going strong. Sarah had a serene aura about her. Surprised to see her own *mamm* following Sarah, she waved to them.

"Hi, Kayla," Sarah said. "I was just about to show your *mamm* the quilts in the library and explain how each of my daughters made them with help from all of us. Would you like to join us?"

Kayla put her book on the table and nodded as she hurried across the big room. As she crossed the lobby, the desk clerk, Henry Cooper, waved to her. Although he was Englisch and had recently remarried, he loved his job; his new wife helped out at the front desk and the café on a part-time basis.

Sarah smiled as Kayla entered the cozy little room. "I see you're enjoying some of our books."

"I am," she said. "Although that fire was trying to lull me to sleep."

"We all need a nap after that cookie contest," Mamm said. "I hear you and Lucas had the idea to hold these competitions."

Heat burned across Kayla's cheeks. "We're trying to end the Myer-Hollinger feud. But I'm afraid it is bigger than the both of us."

"Don't give up," Sarah said as they stood looking over the

WE GATHER TOGETHER / 137

quilts that told the stories of her daughters and their true loves. "These quilts are a testament to staying the course and waiting for the Lord. Each panel and pattern was stitched with grit, determination, forgiveness, and love."

As Sarah explained how Abigail had found Jonah, and Levi had returned for Eliza, and Matthew and Colette had almost lost each other, other women came slipping into the room. Berneta Myer stood off to the side with Lucas's *mamm*, Dina, and even Becky and her friends rushed in to stand beside Kayla.

Then Abigail, Eliza, and Colette each came in. The room was soon full of laughing, sighing women. When Sarah had finished, with comments from all of her daughters, Miriam stuck her head in the door.

"I suggest the Myer women and the Hollinger women make a quilt together, to show what they remember about the *gut* in their families."

At first, Berneta Myer looked pale. Then she cleared her throat and sighed. "They say this started with me, but I know for a fact that Ethel had a crush on Claude, and he did walk out with her a few times. He could never make up his mind, so I made the decision to help him. I loved Claude and I loved Tobias. I prayed and told the Lord I would take whichever one came to me first and told me he loved me. They were both *gut* men but I knew my friend Ethel had an eye for Claude and they'd make a good match. Tobias came to me first, but that made Claude mad. Ethel and I talked it out. She loved Claude, and now she had an opening to tell him her true feelings. She didn't pursue him. She waited until he came to her. And they fell in love. We both found *gut* matches. End of story."

"Did you ever try to explain that to the men?" Sarah asked.

"We did. We tried several times, but they'd only wind up in an argument every time we sat them down together. Ethel and I decided this fight wasn't about us. It was about the two of them wanting to be the first to get to anything. New wives, new equipment, a new barn, a new milk cow. They had an ongoing competition."

"And they still do, obviously," Kayla said. "Maybe our idea was a bad one."

"*Neh*," Berneta said. "It's a perfect time for them to see that even though they are elders now, they are still acting like teenagers during their Rumspringa." She sighed. "It's complicated."

"Why *is* love so complicated?" Becky asked, her blue eyes on the quilts. "It's plain as day on these quilts. The patterns are like photographs and they explain things." She smiled at the King sisters. "You three figured it out."

"It took a lot of prayers and listening to advice we didn't want to hear," Abigail said. "But Mamm always told us to remember Gott's will, and so we abide by that."

Miriam snorted. "Men sometimes don't see things in the same way as women. Don't get me wrong. We love our men, but . . . we have to show them the way at times."

Dina huffed. "And sometimes, people can't see the forest for the trees." She glanced at Kayla. "You are a sweet woman and Lucas is smitten with you. And that makes me happy. I am proud of you two for trying to mend this situation, but I don't want either of you to get hurt in doing so."

Kayla's *mamm*, Cella, lifted her chin. "Dina and I have been talking and we have a lot in common. It's a shame we can't all be friends. We only have three days left here together." Then she glanced at the quilts. "But we've wasted so much time all these years. I've prayed Tobias and Claude would make peace with each other before it's too late. I know my mother-in-law wanted that, too."

Berneta stepped forward. "I agree, Cella. I think we're all here for a reason, and I believe Kayla and Lucas have the right idea. We are gathered here together, for two very important events—a wedding and a reunion. What better time than

Christmas to merge the two and find some peace? Ethel died wondering if Claude loved her as much as he loved me, but she and I wrote letters back and forth for years and I assured her that Claude loved her with a deep abiding love."

"If you had it to do over again, would you do it any differently?" Kayla asked Berneta.

The older woman stood, petite but with a ramrod-straight backbone. "*Neh,* child. I'd not change a thing. I love Tobias, even when he's acting daft in the head. And I'd like to have this feud forgiven and over with before I go to meet my maker."

Miriam clapped her hands together. "Then we just make another quilt, ladies. Not faceless Amish couples falling in love, but a quilt that shows two families gathering together in peace and joy, with *gut* tidings for all. Or something like that."

"I like that idea," Berneta said, tears in her eyes. "But we don't have much time."

"Many hands," Sarah said. "If we start today, we have two days before the big events. We can take turns making small panels, and if we don't get the rest done before you all leave on Sunday, my daughters and I will finish it later, but we will display the panels and let everyone see what it can become. Kayla, if you don't mind, instead of racing on the sleds, let this be our next competition. We won't fight like the men have been doing. We'll take turns and get as much done as possible and if we aren't finished—"

"We'll explain the rest," Berneta said. "Something I should have done a long time ago. We will tell our men they need to make the future better." She glanced at Kayla. "For those who take over our family legacies and carry them to the next generation. For those who will add their own panels."

Kayla's eyes misted with tears. "*Ja,* I like that idea. And while we are all quilting, Lucas can find a way to bring the men together to talk this out, I hope. He can go ahead with the sled races, I reckon."

"I'm sure our husbands can help with that," Abigail replied.

Becky made a face. "I'd hate to be in charge of that group."

Sarah's soft smile beamed. "I'll put my husband, Abe, in charge of the menfolk. He has a way of getting his point across."

"True, that," Abigail said, giggling. "Just ask Jonah."

"Or Levi," Eliza added.

"And especially Mattie," Colette said.

Those comments made everyone laugh.

"So we have a plan," Sarah said. "Now, I'll see you all at supper. That lobster bisque is going to hit the spot."

"I hope that will be the only thing hitting the spot. No food fights," Berneta replied, her sharp gaze moving over the room.

"I hope that, too," Kayla said. "For Lucas's sake if nothing else."

After Abigail put up a pretty flyer in the lobby, inviting lunch and supper guests to join those staying at the lodge to make quilt patterns for a very special project, and then announced it again at supper that night, they had a dozen or so women wanting to help out. Some were locals who could walk home through the snow; others were staying in nearby hotels but loved coming to the inn for meals.

Miriam announced she was in charge, and everyone followed her to the quilting room after dessert at the noonday dinner. Gayle and Gloria would help, too. They were expert quilters, and after witnessing their stance at the cookie decorating task, no one would tell them they couldn't help.

Even Becky fell into step with Kayla. "I've got a lot to think about, but all the wedding arrangements are finished. I had so much help, and you did your part, Sister. So I shall return the favor to you."

"Very kind," Kayla replied. Then she stopped and took her sister's hands in hers. "I'm glad we're friends again."

"Me, too," Becky said. "I've been a real pill and I'm sorry."

"All is forgiven," Kayla told her. "I don't want us to be like our *grossdaddi* and never forgive each other."

"I agree, and I'm so happy about you and Lucas. No matter what, he seems like a nice fellow and you two make the cutest couple." She nudged Kayla in the ribs. "Maybe we'll be back here next year for your wedding."

"Don't get carried away," Kayla replied even as that image floated across her mind. "Lucas and I want to let our relationship ripen and grow over the next few months. Long distance until we can meet again."

"Then let's make a quilt that might change your life." Becky dragged her toward the big room near the kitchen and soon they'd both picked out floral patterns that represented the four seasons. Spring, summer, fall, and winter.

Sarah and her sister Miriam (the one who seemed to think she was in charge) explained what they wanted to create.

Sarah spoke to the women. "We want the patterns of life to be on this quilt. It will represent families and *kinner* and life—the kind of life that brings us to this season and our plain, quiet—well, mostly quiet—Christmas celebrations."

The women in the room laughed and chatted at that comment, nodding their heads.

Sarah allowed them a chuckle and then continued. "We want to paint a picture from a woman's perspective, a gentle, soft, kind picture of how we rejoice even when we are suffering. *Gott* doesn't want us to rejoice because of suffering; he wants us to rejoice despite suffering. To remember even with bad things happening, there is still something to celebrate in life as long as we have family and faith."

Kayla heard a few "Amens" from the Englisch women and saw some of the Amish women lowering their heads in silence.

Then Miriam said, "Let the quilting begin. Pick your pattern."

After that, laughter and teasing and chattering filled the room all day, even after the last of the sun's feeble rays pushed through the snow clouds and fell across the treetops, causing the snow to sparkle in a golden-pink hue that became a quilt pattern covering the earth much in the same way that their hasty quilt making was completing a story of its own.

Chapter 8

Their first quilting day had gone well. Most of the women who'd volunteered were seasoned quilters, so they went to work cutting the square panels and laying them out. The staff went back and forth, checking on the café and kitchen staff, but since all meals had been served, the kitchen was now quiet and shut down for the night, and they vowed to work until dawn if need be.

Abigail had prepared the batting and found material for the quilt back, while the other women began to sew either on machines or with their hands, each panel matching up to another one as the four-square pattern began to take shape. This easy pattern only required panels of plain fabric with no appliqué work, and the women had fun picking out the colors they liked best.

At around ten, Sarah suggested everyone but Gayle and Gloria should stop and get some rest. They had one more day to work before the happenings of the weekend.

"If you're available tomorrow between breakfast and noon-dinner, we'd love to have you back. Each of you will be given a gift basket courtesy of the inn—*denke* for helping us."

The women liked that idea. "Bribery will get you what you want," Cella said with a chuckle. "But this is good work, and it's *gut* to get to know others who are traveling the same path."

"It is, indeed," Dina replied. "Like you and me. Why did we wait so long?"

"We were forbidden," Cella replied. "But there is no sin in making a new friend. I hope we can keep in touch."

"So do I," Dina said, smiling at Kayla. "Perhaps you and Kayla can visit my home once I'm back in Spartansburg."

Kayla sent her a grateful smile. "I know I'd like that."

"I'm sure Lucas would like that, too," Dina replied.

Everyone went their separate ways, but as Kayla turned the corner by the kitchen to head up to her room, a strong arm reached out and pulled her back.

Lucas.

"Hi," he said with a soft smile. "I wanted to tell you *gut* night."

"That's sweet." She gave him a grin, her heart filling with a deep longing. She quelched it and went on. "With our families eating dinner at different times, we don't have a chance to dine together."

"*Ja*, but it does keep the peace."

"It's hard to eat a meal when your stomach is in jitters," she admitted. "How did the sled races go?"

"Not bad." He chuckled. "Jonah made it clear in his Jonah way that the adults who wanted to participate had better behave in front of the *kinner*. So they did."

"Even our *grossdaddis*?"

"Even they, but instead of racing down the hill on sleds, Abe stayed close to our *grossdaddis* by the fire, explaining he needed their help carrying firewood."

"And they stayed there with Abe?"

"They did. It was awkward at first, but then Abe began to tell them the history of the inn, and though they didn't speak to each other directly, they did listen to Abe. I like the people around here. The King family brings calm to any kind of chaos."

She laid her hand on his shoulder. "That's because they've been through such chaos, Lucas. They know how families can be torn apart, they've known heartache and loss, and now they're happy and they love what they do here. They make staying here comfortable and easy and . . . they bring people together. Which is what we're trying to do."

She explained about the women gathering to make a quilt, to show their two families what forgiveness and peace could be like.

"We hope our *grossdaddis* will see this quilt and realize how much time and energy they've wasted being mad at each other."

"That is a solid plan and doesn't involve screaming or name-calling." He tugged her close. "I like bringing people together. Especially you and me. I don't think I can fake-fight with you."

"Really?" Relief washed over her. "I dreaded even pretending. So we can toss out that plan, ain't so?"

He gave her a quick kiss on her cheek. "It's forgotten already. Sleep well, Kayla."

She touched her hand to his jaw. "The same to you, Lucas."

He watched her all the way up the stairs before turning back toward the fire in the big lobby. Kayla glanced down at him one more time, then sighed and went to her room.

Today had been a *gut* day, after all.

Friday involved last-minute wedding plans and preparing for the Myer family reunion. The patriarchs of the family were trying to avoid each other but not always succeeding. Abe went back and forth between the two like a diplomat, and several members of both families had stood by the always burning firepit earlier. That was an improvement at least.

Kayla had deliberately walked by once just to see if they were behaving.

She'd heard Abe talking to Claude and Tobias. "You both have well-adjusted families, it seems. Clearly, you both know Gott's will."

Grossdaddi Claude had nodded while he silently looked at the fire. Tobias Myer had stared off into the distance as if he longed to be somewhere else.

Remembering what Berneta had told all the women yesterday, she had to wonder if Tobias might feel the same as her late *grossmammi*. Did he wonder if Berneta had chosen the wrong man?

"I appreciate the truce," Abe said, his tone firm and calm. "We don't condone fighting around here, especially with Christmas just around the corner and the *kinner* running around all excited. Understand?"

They'd both murmured something, and Kayla thought with Abe working on them, these two men might finally see the error of their ways. She'd waited off to the side, hoping for a sign.

Claude had said he wanted to go check on something, and Tobias had headed to the stables. Abe had turned and headed up the hill to his own *grossdaddi haus*, behind the cottage where Eliza and Levi now lived with their young son. All three King sisters had homes on this property near Abe and Sarah, who now lived in the *grossdaddi haus*.

Wouldn't it be lovely to have a cottage by the lake with Lucas?

Whoa. She reeled in those thoughts as she sat in the lobby by the fire, staying close in case Becky needed her. But her sister had calmed down and was focusing on her joy at marrying the man she loved.

The snow had stopped falling, and the roads had been cleared for safe travel, but the temperatures kept the countryside beautifully white and pristine—a perfect setting for the upcoming events.

While the reunion would take place inside the café and the wedding would be mostly outside in the pavilion and a heated tent the Hollinger family had rented, Kayla's nerves were still on edge. So much could go wrong between the two families.

Abigail came walking by with her to-do-list clipboard. After glancing at Kayla, she stopped and sat down. "Hi. I need a break and you look like you need a friend."

Kayla smiled at Abigail. She was years older than Kayla with two young *kinner*, but she had shining golden hair and pretty blue eyes and she always looked so calm and in charge of things.

"I'm hoping the wedding goes well," she said. "And I'm also hoping the family reunion goes well."

"So am I, on both accounts," Abigail said with a laugh. "But I will warn you, sometimes the best planned events still hit snags. We do our best to keep that from happening, however."

"I plan on staying in that warm tent," Kayla admitted. "You know weddings can take so much time, and my sister wants hers to be perfect, so she will make sure the bishop and the ministers preach as long as they like."

"Well, once the service is over, then the meal will be served," Abigail said. "We've hired many extra people to help with that, and they should all make it here because the roads are open today and traffic is moving. Even buggy traffic."

"You've all been so kind to us," Kayla said. "I love it here."

"You are *welkom* anytime," Abigail replied. "Now I'd better get back to work. Are you sure you're okay?"

Kayla glanced around the empty room. "Can I ask you something?"

"Certainly." Abigail sank back against her chair and put down her clipboard. "Go ahead."

Kayla swallowed her fears and blurted out her question. "How do you know if you're falling in love with someone?"

Abigail's smile was gentle but her eyes held resolve and a bit of concern.

"How do you feel right now?" she asked Kayla.

Surprised, Kayla placed her hands together and let out a sigh. "Like I'm walking on air. Like the wind has lifted my heart and the rain smells so sweet and the snow is the prettiest ever. The whole world is beautiful to me right now, despite all the things we're dealing with."

"You mean, the things you and Lucas are dealing with?"

"*Ja*. I like him, Abigail. Is this too soon? It's only been a few days and yet, it's as if I've known him forever."

Abigail placed her hand over Kayla's. "That for certain sure sounds like love, Kayla. But you don't have to rush anything. Is this your first serious walking out?"

"*Ja*." She glanced at the beautiful white poinsettias on the check-in counter. "I keep telling myself this can't last. We don't know each other, and we don't even live in the same state, but I want to see if this feeling can last for a long time, maybe."

"You are wise to consider all the obstacles in your way," Abigail said, nodding. "You know my story. Jonah and I had to overcome his amnesia, and his being Englisch and then, his being in law enforcement. He had a violent, horrible past, but I will tell you, Kayla, the day I found him wounded and half-drowned on the shore, I knew he was the man for me. I don't know how I knew that—I just did."

"And he returned to you," Kayla said, her romantic heart beating at the thought of it. "He truly loves you that much."

"He does," Abigail replied with her own dreamy smile. "He

has worked hard to prove it, and he has held fast to our ways and our faith. Jonah is not the same man I found that day. He has been made new again by Gott's will and Gott's grace."

"I'm happy for you," Kayla said. "But I like Lucas the way he is."

"As you should," Abigail agreed. "He's a *gut* person and you and he make the cutest couple. Sometimes, people *kumm* into our lives for a reason and the timing of this week—the way your two families have been forced together here—it shows that Gott is in control. Faith can change hearts and show your families—and you and Lucas—the right way."

"We both believe that," Kayla replied, "but even though they are being tolerant right now, our families aren't so keen on us being together."

"And yet, here you are." Abigail grabbed her clipboard and stood, so Kayla did the same. "Things are changing because of how you and Lucas have tried to handle this situation. I'm guessing by the end of this week, all of your hopes and prayers will be answered."

"In one way or another," Kayla said. "*Denke* for talking to me. Is there anything I can help with to ease your tasks?"

Abigail's brow furrowed. "Would you like to join Colette in folding napkins? She hates that work, but she'd like it better if she had some company."

"I'd be happy to help," Kayla said. "She can probably give me some advice, too."

"*Ja*, but hers might be a lot different from mine," Abigail said with a chuckle. "In the end, you'll find your own answers. You're a smart woman."

They walked toward the kitchen. "I'll show you where Colette is in the employee lounge." Abigail took her down a short hallway. "My *mamm* and several of the women are working on the quilt, so you can drop by and help there later if you'd like. Plus, we have fresh gingerbread cookies cooling on the counter.

One of those and a cup of Christmas tea will help with folding napkins."

"You have Christmas tea?"

"Our very own recipe with mint and cinnamon," Abigail explained. "It makes everything better."

Kayla giggled. "This place is better than the North Pole."

Abigail gave her a girlish wink. "Don't tell Santa that."

Chapter 9

Kayla had been busy helping Colette, and listening to all the gossip, when they heard footsteps outside the open lounge door. People moved through the big kitchen section in the back of the house all day long, but they both glanced up, curious to see if anyone would stop and chat with them.

Lucas stood at the door, his smile wide, his dimples showing, a dusting of snow on his brown barn jacket. "*Gut daag.*"

"*Gut daag* to you," Kayla replied with glee. "I was wondering if I'd see you today."

He stepped into the room, the scents of woodsmoke and evergreen surrounding him. "I was wondering the same about you until a little birdie named Eliza told me where you were," he said. "I've been helping Levi set up the trees around the pavilion. For the wedding."

"My sister's wedding?" Kayla asked, thinking she was being redundant.

"*Ja,* unless you know of another wedding taking place here," he replied, a teasing note in his tone and in his eyes.

Kayla frowned and then she laughed. "Of course, Becky is the one getting married. The only one so far."

Colette's amused gaze moved back and forth between them. "That was kind of you to help, Lucas." Then she pushed back her chair. "I'm going to find us something warm to drink. Lucas, will you help Kayla finish folding these napkins? And what would you two like to drink?"

Lucas grinned and sat down. "I'll have *kaffe*, black."

Kayla gave Colette an appreciative nod. "I'd love some of that Christmas tea."

"I'll be back after I check on a few things," Colette replied. Then she hurried away, leaving the door open for propriety.

"Could she tell I wanted to have you all to myself?" Lucas asked, his cheeks rosy from the cold. "And how do I fold a napkin?"

Kayla laughed and showed him. "It's not that hard." She took the long cotton napkin and pressed it against the table. "This one is rectangular so you want all the edges to meet." She folded it once and then twice. "Then you just roll it up and put a white ribbon on it to hold it."

"Just so people can unroll it and wipe their hands and mouths?"

"*Ja*, because that is what napkins are for, ain't so?"

"You are brilliant," he said. "And kind to help, since I'm sure some of these will be used at our reunion supper."

"Just as you are kind to help put trees around the pavilion where my sister is to be married—out in the cold at that."

"So we are the best, aren't we?"

"We are," she said with a giggle, basking in his compliments and his kind nature.

Then he asked, "And why does your sister want to be married out in the cold?"

Kayla could explain that easily enough. "*Ach vell*, she read a book once about a Christmas wedding with snow and holly berries and real snow-dusted trees, so that became her goal. She'll be all bundled in a mint-green wool dress, with heavy tights underneath and a dark green cape and matching bonnet. An Amish wedding but with a Christmas theme and colors. Becky has always known what she wants."

"And you haven't?"

"*Neh*. Well, not until recently."

He looked up and into her eyes. "Am I on that list now?"

"Top line," she blurted before she could think about it. "I mean, you are my new best friend."

"But you're not sure about anything else yet?"

She had to be honest. "We live so far away from each other, and we only have two days left here before we have to leave on Monday morning."

"A lot can happen in two days, Kayla. Trust me, please. And trust Gott, remember."

"I'm trying," she replied. She was about to say more, but Colette returned with a tray. "Edith sent finger sandwiches along with the cookies. Chicken salad and ham and cheese."

"We have a feast," Lucas said, getting up to help with the big tray. "Will you join us, Colette?"

Colette shook her head. "Mattie and I are sharing a meal at our home. He's on his way up the front drive to walk with me up there. He's been clearing the entryway for the arrival of our guests during the weekend."

"Mostly our combined families," Lucas said as Kayla served their snacks. "They have filled most of the other available hotels and inns around here."

"*Ja*, because we have no more room for anyone else here," Colette replied. Then she held up a finger, "And yet, each year we take in anyone who needs shelter."

Just then, Matthew Mueller came in and smiled at his wife. "How are you feeling?" he asked, his eyes full of concern.

Colette blushed and glanced at Kayla. "Our family knows but keep this quiet for now. I'm . . . we're . . . going to have a *bobbeli* come late spring."

"Oh, how exciting," Kayla said, her eyes misting. "That's so special."

"Very special," Matthew said. "We can't wait."

Lucas nodded and nibbled his food. "A *bobbeli*. I can't even imagine."

But when he glanced at Kayla, his eyes held that longing again. The same one she'd felt ever since she'd met him. The same one that always caused her to blush.

"We should go," Colette said. "I still have a lot to do today."

"Don't overdo," Kayla said, smiling at her.

"I won't. No one around here will let me," Colette assured her.

After the happy couple left, Lucas glanced at Kayla again. "Do you want *kinner*?"

She almost spit out her tea. "I haven't thought about it, but *ja*. Doesn't that happen with marriage?"

He started laughing. "I believe it does, but I'm not rushing things, I promise."

She relaxed. "*Denke*, Lucas, for understanding."

"I understand a lot more than you realize," he replied. Then he grabbed a sandwich and smiled at her. "This is nice."

"It is," she had to agree. "I like having a friend to share a meal with me."

"That's the best part."

She could certainly agree with him on that, but now she had thoughts of marriage and a family in her head. And she liked them a lot.

Lucas went back out to help with marking places for buggies to park near the stables. Most of their relatives would take the local bus or hire a cab to get to the celebration tomorrow, but those who had buggies would need help with the horses. So he worked with Jonah and Levi to make sure all the stalls were clean and the small corral near the back was ready. Unhitching a wagon took time, but he was willing to help as needed tomorrow, too. Staying busy would take his mind off the way he felt each time he was with Kayla.

Or he could remember those times with her while he worked. He liked that idea better. If he kept his mind on Kayla and how amazing she was, he wouldn't have to deal with the feud that could end things between them before they even had time to figure out their feelings.

"*Denke* for helping, Lucas," Levi said after they'd finished up. "I think we've got it all as ready as it can get. The pavilion is set up with firepits on each side and blankets on every bench. We have a nursery for the younger *kinner* in one of the first-floor rooms and we have enough food cooked, and more arriving, to feed the whole town, I believe."

"How do you get it all done?" Lucas asked. "I help my *daed* on the farm and that's hard work, but here you are always surrounded by strangers coming and going."

"We have lots of part-time help when we host big events like this weekend," Levi explained. "We close for Christmas, but we open up again for Second Christmas so friends can come visiting. Then we take several days off, and things settle back down with a few guests here and there. It's a routine I've become accustomed to." After putting away the shovels and rakes they used in the stalls, he turned back to Lucas. "And a lot of our guests are return customers. So we do know them. You should consider yourself one of those now, Lucas. You're welcome here anytime."

Lucas listened quietly and absorbed the majesty of Shadow Lake Inn. Right now, the snow made it look like a postcard, but he had seen what went on behind the façade. Snow was a problem with big crowds trying to get here, and yet the King family stayed on task and planned ahead. This was a true working business.

"Was it hard for you to fit in at first?" he asked Levi.

Levi let out a chuckle. "Oh, *ja*. Eliza hated me."

"Your wife once hated you? No one would ever believe that now."

"She did, indeed. I'd done her wrong when we were young and she did not want me anywhere near her stables."

"Her stables?" Lucas glanced around at the huge alleyway. "I heard she loves horses."

"That she does," Levi said, moving toward their prized Percheron, Samson. "She considers these stables and the barn as her territory. Woe be it to anyone who messes with it." He pointed a finger toward Samson. "This one is her big baby."

Samson gave Levi a side glance and lifted his head to toss his mane while he waited for his afternoon carrot.

Lucas rubbed Samson's nose. "He is a beautiful animal with this grayish coat."

"And loyal to Eliza. Mainly because she spoils him."

"So you obviously won her over."

"It took time and a lot of prayers. We had to let go of the past and get beyond the secrets between us."

Lucas studied Levi, watching the expressions on his face. Levi obviously loved his family. It showed in the way he smiled and each time his eyes lit up. "I'm glad it worked out for you."

"Me, too," Levi said as they closed up his farrier shop at the back of the stables. "Trust, Lucas. We had to learn trust."

"I'm working on that," Lucas admitted. "I like Kayla a lot but she's afraid of all the things that could tear us apart."

"You mean things like feuding families?"

"So you noticed," he replied in a teasing tone. "That's a big hurdle, and the distance between our homes, of course. But I'm willing to work around all of those things."

"So she should be able to do that, too, you think?"

"I want her to do what is right and comfortable for her."

Levi's eyebrows lifted high. "Sometimes we have to do the uncomfortable things to find the truth, Lucas."

Lucas nodded as they walked toward the front of the big barn; the landscape before them was like a painted Christmas card. "I can do that. Now I just have to make sure Kayla can, too."

Levi adjusted the collar of his jacket and looked toward his house on the hill. "Eliza and I overcame some big hurdles to find our way back to each other. I pray the same happens for you and Kayla as you try to find each other. Gott will guide you."

"That's what I believe. We both believe."

After he and Levi parted ways, Lucas wondered if Kayla's doubts would keep holding her back. Could she trust him enough to follow through on their feelings for each other, or was she using these obstacles to hide her fear of falling in love? Could they find their way to each other? Or maybe she was just being kind to him until she could be on her way.

That had certainly happened before with other girls. But Kayla wasn't like other girls. She'd told him she liked him and wanted to get to know him better, and he had to believe she was being sincere. He'd keep hoping, for now.

Chapter 10

The quilting room was busy all day long. Women came in and out, some learning, some teaching, as they went about making the nine-patch quilt. The panels were made with small squares sewed together to make one big square, row after row, when the whole thing was finished. It was a simple and age-old pattern, but with all the many floral patterns and colors, and several people working, it was coming together nicely.

"A people quilt," Sarah said with glee. "Made by many hands."

"Connected hands," Kayla's mother said as they finished their parts. "We've done more in two days than most do in a month. It's not perfect, but it's a gift, a peace offering that we hope will make a *gut* impression on those who can't seem to see the light."

The few women left nodded their heads. It seemed to Kayla that with quilting came talk of marriage, family, children, and husbands. Some serious and some teasing. Every woman who'd participated in making these patterns and patches loved her life even with the ups and downs.

She thought of Mamm and Daed, and again thanked Gott

for their loving, gentle ways. And she thought of Lucas, and what a *gut daed* he'd be one day.

Then she went back to work on the quilt.

Kayla had cut, trimmed, and measured with rulers, and she'd learned more about quilting than she'd ever thought possible. Miriam and the G-Sisters, Gayle and Gloria, ran a tight quilting schedule. They could pin and sew panels faster than a cowboy could lasso a horse.

Tomorrow, the wedding and the family reunion would happen, but the weather had changed and the snow was coming down again in thick flakes.

Becky came hurrying in. "I don't think people will be able to make it here. I keep hearing the roads are closing, people are getting stuck, and well—"

"It will all be as it should be," Mamm said. "The plows are out night and day."

"Cella is right," Sarah said, her hand moving over the colorful patterns that seemed to ripple like a lake wave. "Marriage is about two lives becoming one. I know brides expect pretty weddings, even in winter. But the most important part of the ceremony is when you and your husband agree to follow your faith and to live in a way Gott will approve."

Becky glanced out the window where snow had gathered on the sill like puffy cotton. "I'm worried about the safety of people out there in the storm, but *ja*, I want a nice wedding, too."

"We will move your wedding inside if this keeps up," Sarah replied.

Mamm nodded and touched Becky's sleeve. "You knew that a Christmas wedding could be iffy because of the weather, *liebling*. We also have an inside plan if all else fails, and we made that plan for this very reason."

Kayla couldn't speak, but they had warned Becky over and over she'd be taking a risk by planning a winter wedding. She'd been too stubborn to consider all that could go wrong, and now it was too late to have regrets. Because things were definitely going wrong.

Especially because the Myer family reunion still had to take place in part of the big lobby. An inside wedding would mean they'd be near Lucas and his family at the same time as the reunion dinner. No way to keep their *grossdaddis* apart. Her *daed* had rented that big tent, but with the weather, it would be hard to enjoy being inside a tent, heaters or no heaters.

"Where will you put everyone?" Becky asked, clearly struggling not to have a bridal meltdown.

"We will make room in the lobby and the café," Sarah said. "Just as we explained. You'll have plenty of room for your guests, Becky. You were wise to invite mostly family. At least you know they've arrived in town."

"But getting them here might be a problem," Mamm said. "It's about a mile walk and hard on some in the snow."

"I should have paid more attention to the possibility of complications," Becky admitted, her tone low. "But you are correct. I just want to be married to Jason, so I'll keep thinking about that. We are safe and we have food. And this place is beautiful, no matter what." Then she lifted her chin. "And the café has doors we can close off from the rest of the lobby."

"That's the best attitude," Mamm said, making a face at the door comment. Then she nudged Becky. "And think of the romantic walks you and Jason can take after the wedding is over and the food has been served."

"That would be nice," Becky said. "I don't want my pretty cape to go to waste."

"Nothing will go to waste as long as you and Jason love each other," Mamm said.

Kayla's heart skipped a beat with that advice. She and Lucas kept worrying about what could go wrong. Maybe they should focus on what might go right instead. She said a swift silent prayer, turning her worries over to the Lord.

Becky nodded to them and went back upstairs with her friends. Kayla had wanted to comfort her sister earlier, but she'd been too worried about their *grossdaddi* and Lucas's family. Now, after praying, she reminded herself that things had settled a bit after Abe had taken charge of the two old men, and Sarah had taken on the task of keeping Cella and Dina together in the quilt room as much as possible. Her mother and Lucas's *mamm* had become tentative friends. But the families had also avoided being in the café or lobby together. She could only imagine what might go wrong if they had to share the space for hours during a snowstorm.

Trust.

She heard that word as clearly as if it had been spoken to her.

Trust.

Perhaps the only way to convince their families to forgive and forget would be to get them into the same space and make them stay there and enjoy not only their own festivities, but each other's, too. What better way to replace guests who couldn't make it to either event?

Put them together and share one big meal with both families.

It would have to work. One way or another.

She hurried to find Lucas. They would need to be prepared for this.

She was fast learning to be prepared for everything in life.

A lesson her elders should know but had been ignoring out of pride and anger. And another reminder that Gott was in the details of everything.

She rushed out of the quilt room so quickly, she almost ran into Henry Cooper. "Oh, excuse me," he said, holding his hands out to protect himself. "Where's the fire?"

Kayla stopped and took a deep breath. Henry always dressed

in a suit and tie and looked like someone from the old movies she'd watched at an Englisch friend's house once.

Taking a breath in, she blurted out her fears. "Because of the snow, we might all wind up in this lobby and the café across the hallway, Henry. And you know what that means."

"Fewer leftovers," he quipped. Then he stood back and nodded. "I do know what that means, but the staff here is used to things changing rather quickly, Kayla. You should have been here last year. We had a newborn, a dad lost in the snow, and a bus full of strangers spending Christmas here wherever they could find a place to lay their heads. But we got a Christmas birth out of it, and two marriages, and two new cooks, not to mention we found the dad and he got here just in time to see his son being born, a son that was named after a variation of the three husbands of the King sisters—Liam John Kauffman. Levi, Matthew, and Jonah. His young parents were so appreciative, they moved close by, and now Simon works for the inn as a maintenance man and carpenter as needed. And it doesn't end there. The mama's parents didn't like him as her husband, so they weren't speaking to their daughter. But we found a way to get them here and they all made up, for the child's sake. Leah was so happy to see her family. Now they come and visit often."

He stopped and took a breath. "Whew. That was a lot to tell you, right there."

Kayla stared over at the dapper man who'd been so kind to her family. "Henry, you should write a book one day about this place."

"I just might do that," he said with a chuckle. "The things I've heard and seen here could fill two or three books." Then he leaned close. "I found my true love here during that time, too. Our first anniversary is coming up in February."

"You make a *gut* point," Kayla said, her head spinning. "What a Christmas that must have been, with so much happening and so much love and grace. I hope this one can top it."

"Only if we do our best to prepare and trust," he said. "Trust in the Lord." He nodded. "I'm off to check on the piano. I play at my church, and I need to practice a bit before I'm standing in front of a huge Christmas crowd. If I can even get back home, that is. Marcy might have to hire a sleigh and horses to get me home."

Kayla smiled. "You said you got married last February."

"Valentine's Day. Yep, I met Marcy right here," he said, his dark eyes wrinkling with a big smile. "She came off the bus and walked through those very doors and I was as smitten as a kitten."

Kayla shook her head. "I can see why all the guests love you, Henry. And you play the piano, too. Can I listen in? I love to sing. I go to singings all the time and sometimes sing solo in church."

"You can most certainly sit in," Henry replied. "The piano is in the corner of the café and we rarely use it."

Kayla couldn't believe there was a real piano here. "How did I miss that?"

"We keep it hidden. You know, you Amish don't go for such."

"I'd still like to see one," she whispered. "I won't tell if you don't."

Henry made a sign to show his lips were sealed. "Shall we?"

They hurried to the far side of the big rectangular café. The whole place was empty right now, but the fireplace on this side of the inn glowed brightly and felt warm.

Henry kept an eye on the front desk as he tested the keys and fiddled with his song sheet. "Do you know 'O Little Town of Bethlehem'?"

Kayla nodded. "In Englisch and Deutsch."

"Let's start with English," Henry said, laughing.

He went over the keys, playing the song, then nodded and started playing for her to sing along.

Kayla's heart lifted with each word. She hadn't had time to think about singing at all this week, but now the words telling the story of the Savior's birth filled her soul with peace and contentment. What did she have to worry about? Her family loved her and she came from a *wunderbar* home. She must stop fretting about everything here, especially the things that she couldn't control and had no part of. Thankful for her life, she sang from her heart, her eyes closed in reverent happiness.

At some point, Henry stopped playing the piano, but Kayla kept singing. She realized this was her gift, her release from stress, her way of communicating with and honoring the Lord.

When she opened her eyes to smile at Henry, she noticed a crowd had gathered just inside the double doors of the café.

And Lucas was amongst that crowd with a proud smile on his face and a deep understanding in his dark eyes. At that exact moment Kayla knew she'd fallen for him. Did it matter how or if it was too soon? Did it matter that they had many issues blocking their way?

Neh. She'd find a way. With Gott's help, she'd find a way.

Suddenly, she understood the word *trust.* As her voice lifted to finish the old hymn, her confidence grew, and she concluded with a flourish of joy mixed with humility.

She turned to Henry. "*Denke.*"

"My pleasure," he said, clapping along with the others. "You have a gift, Kayla."

Everyone, from the kitchen staff to her *mamm* to Lucas's *mamm*, clapped their hands and smiled.

It was a moment she'd never forget. And she hoped that if their *grossdaddis* had heard her song, they'd stop and think about what they needed to do to make this a special Christmas.

They needed to trust and obey.

She needed to do the same.

* * *

Lucas rushed to her and took her hand. "That was so beautiful."

Kayla lowered her head, embarrassed now. "I rarely do that."

"What? Sing like a sweet bird?"

"Sing in front of people," she admitted. "Each time I sing at a gathering, I get so nervous I almost make myself ill. But today, it was different."

"Today, you sang for Gott," Lucas replied. "And I had the honor of hearing you." He checked behind them. "We all did. The staff stopped everything and came out here to see and hear you."

"I had no idea anyone would notice," she admitted. "But I did shut my eyes in case." Her stomach still had a few butterflies, but her heart flowed with joy and acceptance. And that trust everyone kept mentioning.

"You should keep your eyes open when you sing," Lucas said. "You have pretty eyes. They tell me so many things."

"*Denke*," she replied, waving to the others as they went back to work while she wondered what he saw in her eyes. Her love for him? Or her fear for their future?

Mamm and Dina walked up to them. Daed stood off by the fire and didn't speak, but his eyes were moist. Had she moved her stoic, quiet father?

"Kayla, that was lovely," Dina said, her eyes on her son. "Lucas told me you have a beautiful singing voice."

Mamm touched Kayla's cheek with her hand. "My precious songbird. You have to quit hiding your gift, Kayla."

"I feel too jittery," Kayla admitted. "But I'll try to get over that now."

Mamm nodded. "Your *daed* and Claude were outside, but they came in and caught the last of your song. Surely you can sing some other hymns for us."

"Maybe when we get home," she said, not liking all the attention she was getting. But she had enjoyed singing and right now, she for certain sure enjoyed the way Lucas looked at her. He didn't know her true feelings, however. Looking was one thing. Loving was quite another.

She could imagine singing while washing dishes, with him holding her close, her back against his chest, as they finished the day together.

Would that dream come true one day?

Chapter 11

"So the quilt is done then?"

Kayla nodded in answer to Lucas's question. "It is done. I've never seen so many women working all at once. Most quilts take days, weeks, even months, but this one was put together with an assembly line, and it's finished. Just a little trim here and there and then it will be displayed in the library along with the famous King sister quilts. Hopefully in time for our big events."

They were sitting in the library now, so Lucas pulled her close, the sweet scent of vanilla and lavender wafting up from her hair. "Do you think our stubborn elders will see the point?"

She started giggling and he looked over at her. "Points," she explained. "I learned all about connecting the points on this quilt. I'm guessing the ladies in charge used that word over and over and made points on this quilt to make a point to both of our *grossdaddis*."

"So will they see the point," he repeated, "or is this whole thing pointless?"

"We will find out tomorrow," she said, smiling up at him. Then they looked out at the white satin snow gleaming in the night. "Snow everywhere. A real blizzard."

"But this forced togetherness will bring the feud to an end, either way."

"I'm praying for the best possible outcome," she said. "If your grandfather could just see that he won, and let this go—"

"And if your grandfather could remember the woman he was married to, and not that he lost my grandmother."

Kayla pulled back. "He does remember Grossmammi Ethel, Lucas. You haven't been around him a lot. He's still mourning her death, but he can't let go of this grudge because of pride."

Lucas could see the aggravation in her frown but he couldn't stop defending his family. "And my *grossdaddi* can't help it if he won the woman he loves. The woman who loved him more than she loved your *grossdaddi*."

"How can you be sure of that?" Kayla asked, her expression filled with doubt, her eyes bright with questions. "Maybe Berneta still has feelings for Claude. They've never really discussed that because of the constant fighting."

Lucas didn't like the tone of that suggestion. "*Neh*, she loves Tobias, *my grossdaddi*."

Kayla remembered what Berneta had said earlier in this very room. It wasn't her story to explain to Lucas, however. "Have you asked her about it? I believe she loves Tobias, but what if he thinks she doesn't? That might be the reason he is still angry at Daddi Claude."

"It's not my place to question my grandmother, Kayla."

"But you are questioning my grandfather, assuming he didn't love Ethel. You're wrong, Lucas."

She stood, her chin jutting out, her usually sweet face twisted in a disapproving frown. "You see, it's happening. This long-standing feud feeds itself and keeps growing. Now we are fighting about this situation. This is what I've feared, Lucas." She pivoted and started pacing. "This is why I've held back. We tried not to get involved, but we are involved because we tried to fix things that can't be fixed."

"Is one of the things that can't be fixed *us*?"

She looked at him, her eyes full of dread and defeat. "Maybe there never was an *us*."

He followed her to the double doors. "We don't have to fight, Kayla. We decided not to fight, remember? If you could trust me, and trust that our elders married the ones Gott picked for them, we would be able to work through anything. I never wanted to hurt you."

"But this is hurtful, Lucas. You're accusing my *grossdaddi* of not loving my *grossmammi*. That is hurtful."

"I wasn't accusing. I was speculating in the same way you were just speculating." Frustration overcame him. "We've never asked either of them, any of them, how they really feel. And now, we're fighting over something I said."

"Something you implied," she corrected. She couldn't tell him she'd heard some of the truth from Berneta.

"I never figured you for stubborn, Kayla," he blurted, then instantly regretted his words.

"And I never thought you'd say something so mean about my *grossdaddi*. I'm going upstairs. Tomorrow will *kumm* soon enough."

"It can't come soon enough for me," he said to her back. "I want this over with so I can go back home."

"I feel the same." With that, she was gone, practically running up the stairs to get away from him.

Lucas stood watching her, wishing he hadn't said those things, wishing she didn't fear their future. But at least now, he knew she did have doubts. Big doubts. And he wasn't sure how to overcome her feelings and still remain loyal to his family.

"What a mess I've made," he said to no one.

"Sure looks that way."

Lucas glanced up to see Tobias standing a few feet away in the kitchen hallway.

"How much did you hear, Grossdaddi?" he asked, wishing he could fall through the floor.

Tobias motioned to the sofa in the library. "Enough to know you and I need to have a long talk," he said.

Lucas followed his grandfather into the library. Tobias sank onto a side chair while Lucas took the small sofa by the window. "Talk to me, please," he said.

Tobias studied the new quilt on display and then glanced out at the snow. "I am sorry," he said, his words trembling. "We've made a big mess of this whole week, a mess that needs to be cleared up before we all go our separate ways again."

"I couldn't agree more," Lucas replied, "but you're too late. Kayla is angry at me and I'm not too happy about all of this myself."

"Kayla is upset and irritated, and I can't blame her," Tobias replied. "Your *grossmammi* has been upset with me most of this week."

"Why?" Lucas asked. "Why has this gone on for so long?"

"Because we are human and we let pride and past misunderstandings get the best of us," Tobias replied. "But I want you to know, Abe has helped me see how wrong I am. He brought me here earlier and showed me this quilt and made me see the meaning of this work."

"I'm glad to hear that," Lucas told him. "But I've lost Kayla, so where does that leave me?"

"You don't let her go," Tobias replied. "You fight for her, but not in the way I fought for your *grossmammi*. You fight with a reckless love that will show her you care. Don't give up and don't let the mistakes we've made slow you down. You both proved your worth this week, trying with all your might to make us see the error of our ways. And look, it worked.

Maybe you and she had to clear the air a bit, too, before you could truly commit to each other."

"So you're telling me you'll reach out to Claude and his family?" Lucas asked, a glimmer of hope giving him strength.

"I will, tomorrow," Tobias said as he pushed himself off the chair and struggled to stand. "I'm tired. So tired of this long-held grudge."

Lucas helped Tobias to the stairs. "Will you be all right?"

Tobias turned and put his hands on Lucas's shoulders. "I will now. I know you will carry on and keep our family strong and on the right path, even after I'm gone."

Lucas felt the weight of that statement. "You'll be around for a long time, Grossdaddi."

Tobias sent him a lingering smile. "I'll be around until Gott calls me home. And I need to mend these fences before that time *kumms*."

Lucas stood there in the dark, watching the last embers of the fire.

He'd won the battle, but he'd lost someone he had come to love and cherish. He said a silent prayer, hoping Kayla would forgive him. Tomorrow would be their last day together.

He'd find her and make her see how much he loved her.

Kayla didn't sleep. She tossed and turned while Becky snored softly without a care in the world. After going back over her fight with Lucas, Kayla knew in her heart why she'd been so hesitant all week.

If their grandparents couldn't straighten things out, how could they ever be free to love each other? Her fears and doubts came from a deep place that she'd tried so hard to hide—that spot in her heart where she would always be second, would always be the plain sister, would always wonder if the man she'd fall for could truly love her back.

She'd been afraid to let go and enjoy her feelings for Lucas, such new and fresh feelings that they had overwhelmed her and left her confused and unsure. But now she could see—Berneta had told the quilters she loved Tobias, and that Ethel and Claude had loved each other. Thinking back, Kayla could now see how her *grossdaddi* had showered Ethel with love by working hard, by bringing her freshly cut wildflowers, by making sure she had a nice home and good food, and by laughing with her every day.

Why hadn't she remembered the *gut* between them, rather than assuming her sweet grandmother had been slighted. Yes, Ethel held doubts, but she and Claude had made a *gut* life together. The best life. Because of the one thing Berneta had said the other day.

Ethel had waited for Claude to come to her. She hadn't forced him. He'd come to her and he'd fallen in love with her. The plain one.

Had Lucas fallen for Kayla in the same way? Had her own doubts brought about their fight?

Pondering how she'd handle seeing him today, she got up and dressed in the small washroom between her room and the one where her parents were sleeping. When she returned, Becky was sitting up in bed waiting for her.

"Are you all right?" Becky asked. "I thought I heard you crying last night."

"You did," Kayla said. "Lucas and I had a fight."

Becky gave her a sympathetic stare. "Will this feud continue then?"

"Not if I can help it," Kayla replied. "I'm going after the man I want to marry, same as our *grossmammi* did. She did it the right way, and so will I. But I don't have to wait to find out if Lucas loves me. I'm going to show him that I love him, then let him decide."

Becky yawned and then she grinned. "The snow has stopped

and it's my wedding day, so whatever plan you have, please don't let it involve a food fight."

Kayla shook her head. "There will be no fighting today, Sister. Not if I can help it."

Now she just had to find Lucas and make him see how much she loved him. Then a thought popped into her head. She knew the perfect way to calm everyone in both families. She just prayed it would work.

Chapter 12

The roads were clear. The sky was a wintry blue. The sun shined across the snow-covered hills, where the glittering trees looked like a Christmas garden waiting for a celebration.

"We will not need to bring the wedding inside," Sarah announced to the staff and to Kayla's anxious parents with a sigh of relief. "However, the inn will be open to anyone who needs to come inside, and the gardens are open to anyone who needs some fresh air outside. I hope everyone can agree and honor this compromise."

"We will," Becky said, nodding to her parents and Jason's family members who'd finally made it through the snow last night.

Kayla hoped everyone could get along. She had yet to see Lucas.

She had just turned to set her plan in motion when Berneta walked up and pulled her to the side. "We need to talk."

Worried, Kayla followed Berneta to the far side of the inn's big lobby, out of earshot. "Is everything all right? Is Lucas okay?"

Berneta calmed her with a hand on her arm. "Everything is fine, child. Lucas went for a walk along the shore."

Kayla let out a breath. "What do you need to tell me?"

Berneta smiled. "It worked, Kayla. Tobias came to me last night and told me he aims to make amends with your family, with Claude."

Kayla put a hand to her heart, the warmth of her light green wool dress bringing her comfort. "That's amazing."

"It is, indeed," Berneta replied. "And the quilt helped with that. He was returning to see it again when he heard you and Lucas quarreling."

"He heard?" Kayla's skin grew warm with a flush of shame. "I'm sorry that happened."

"*Neh*, he needed to hear and see what this discord has caused. He couldn't take seeing his grandson so unhappy." Then she added, "And you couldn't take wondering if your grandparents truly loved each other. Believe me, they did. Don't let the past taint your feelings for my grandson. I'd be honored to have you as a granddaughter in my family one day."

Touched, Kayla wiped her eyes. "But Lucas is so angry. I want to make it up to him. To find him and let him know how I feel."

"Then go and find him," Berneta replied. "Dress warmly and be careful, but go down to the shore and find my grandson. He needs you in his life."

Kayla went to find her cape and then hurried back downstairs to go in search of Lucas, but her grandfather called to her before she got out the door.

"I'll be right back," she said, needing to find the man she loved.

"*Neh*," Claude replied. "You need to hear this."

Thinking he'd talked to Tobias, she stopped and turned back. "Of course, Daddi Claude."

He ushered her into the library, where she spotted the quilt the women had worked so hard to finish. "I saw this quilt and came in to study it after one of the staff members told me how it had come about. I was so touched, I went to Tobias and we walked up to Abe's place to talk."

"You did?"

Claude nodded. "We aired all our grievances, face-to-face, and realized finally we both married the women we needed to marry. We have fine families who love and care about each other, especially our two oldest grandchildren, who have shown more maturity all week than we have in fifty years. I'm so sorry, Kayla." He held out his arms. "Can you forgive me?"

Kayla fell into her grandfather's arms and hugged him. "Already done, Grossdaddi."

Claude chuckled and placed his hands on her shoulders. "Then go and find Lucas. That is where you're headed, correct?"

"*Ja,*" she said, laughing. "Can this day get any better?"

"It will, I promise," Claude replied. "Oh, and one more thing. I loved Mammi Ethel with all my heart. I tried to prove that to her and in the end, she knew how much I loved her. Never doubt that, and Kayla, never doubt yourself."

Kayla flew down the porch steps and hurried to the shore. She saw Lucas standing by the bench where they'd sat almost a week ago. He was dressed in his best Sunday clothing and a dark hat.

Lucas turned and spotted her, then hurried toward her. "Kayla."

They ran into each other's arms.

"I'm so sorry," she said, breathless but happy.

"I'm sorry, too."

Then they both began to talk at once and soon learned from each other how their grandfathers had talked and agreed to let go of their rivalry.

"We did it," he said as he snuggled close to her on the bench. "Our fight was the final catalyst, and the quilt helped them see the truth, too."

"And we didn't even fake it," she replied.

"Gott knew," he whispered. "Gott knew."

She bobbed her head. "I had one last plan if things went wrong today."

"Oh, and what was that plan?"

Kayla whispered in his ear. Lucas looked over at her. "I think you should go for it anyway. As a celebration and a new beginning."

"I like that idea," Kayla said. "Let's go up."

They reached the inn, where all of Lucas's family had gathered for the reunion. "Wait here," she said, as she hurried to spread the word so her family could meet her in the big lobby.

Soon Becky was coming down the stairs with her cloak over her wedding dress. "What's going on? My wedding starts in an hour."

"This won't take long," Kayla said, her nerves shimmering with joy.

By the time they'd found everyone and got them into the lobby, the chatter level was high. But no one was fighting. In fact, Kayla and Lucas watched as their grandfathers shook hands and then hugged each other.

"Are you ready?" Lucas asked, pride in his eyes.

"I'm about to cry," she admitted. Then she glanced to where Henry stood behind the check-in desk. He gave her a thumbs-up.

Lucas held her hand and then stepped back.

Kayla began to sing, her voice rising over the noise. " 'We gather together . . .' "

The chatter and the discussions ended. The room grew silent as she sang with all her heart. Kayla took it all in—her eyes misty but her voice strong. Seeing the crowd of both families smiling and grabbing hands showed her that love had been here all along. She only had to trust that Gott would reveal the love and forgiveness offered to all of them.

When she finished, everyone clapped and many wiped their eyes, including her grandfather. He walked up to her and hugged her, then whispered, "You remind me of your *grossmammi*."

Kayla had never had a better compliment.

Edith and Miriam came out of the kitchen, followed by Gayle and Gloria. "We have an announcement," Edith said. "Tobias Myer and Claude Hollinger have asked that we merge the two dinners together as a celebration of this day. All of the food will be served here in the inn after the wedding ceremony is over. But you are free to go back and forth for desserts and warm drinks."

The King sisters and their husbands got to work serving cinnamon rolls, *kaffe*, hot tea, and hot chocolate.

Lucas grabbed Kayla by the hand and they hurried to the big rock behind the stables. He had two cinnamon rolls and two containers of hot chocolate in a basket. Spreading out a blanket over the rock, he reached for her and held her in his arms.

Then he kissed her and whispered, "This time next year we will return here for our wedding. But we will make sure we have it inside."

Kayla nodded and kissed him. "And our families will be in attendance as we gather together once again."

Lucas kissed her temple. "I can't believe it but, *ja*, the feud is over at last, and we are free to marry. Would you like that?"

"I would like that. Gott will show us the way," Kayla said, smiling as the warm sunshine fell across her face. "This is the best Christmas ever."

"*Ach vell*, just wait until next year." Lucas touched a finger to her chin. "I love you."

"I love you, too," she replied. Then they kissed as the snow began to fall softly around them. "I love you, Lucas," she said once more, her words echoing out over the countryside. "And we have a celebration to attend."

They ate their breakfast, then ran down to join in the festivities, their hands held tightly together as they hurried toward their families.

Hitting All the Right Notes

RACHEL J. GOOD

Prologue

Boom! Clang! Rat-a-tat!

Nine-year-old Mark Troyer jerked upright, the horse feed tumbling from his hands. The neighbors were at it again. On Christmas Eve.

He bent and picked up the fallen bale of hay. If he hurried, he could sneak over and listen. Haphazardly, he plopped hay in the horses' feeders as his feet danced along to the loud, insistent bass. His heart swelled to the rhythm and matched the staccato beat. Between horses, his fingers tapped out the tempo on the wooden stall doors.

The second he finished, he slipped out of the barn and checked to be sure nobody in his family was peeking out the windows. Daed would be upset if Mark didn't go straight into the house, but their Englisch neighbors had two teens who played in a rock band. They practiced in their garage, filling the air with the enticing thump of drums, the twang of electric guitars. Because the Amish didn't play music, the band fascinated

Mark. He sneaked over to their house as often as he could to listen to practice sessions.

Something about music, any music, touched his soul. He loved singing hymns from the *Ausbund*, and once his older sister whispered he had a great voice. If Daed had overheard, he'd have scolded her for encouraging *hochmut*, but Mark treasured her compliment, even if it made him feel a little prideful.

Humming along to the tune drifting from the garage, he sneaked across the stubble of his family's small cornfield to crouch in the bushes beside the Musslemans' house. Concealed from view of his parents, he closed his eyes and lost himself in the music.

He wished he'd been born into this family. All of them were musical. Mrs. Musselman taught piano and voice lessons, Mr. Musselman played the saxophone and trumpet, and when their two boys were younger, they took violin lessons. Now, as teens, the boys and their friends gathered to practice with different instruments. Instruments that enchanted Mark. The bangs, plinks, and high-pitched wails vibrated through his body.

Whenever he could slip away from his chores, he hid outside their house to listen to the tinkling of piano keys or the smooth alto tones of the sax. Even the screeches of beginner violins fascinated him. But of all the notes flowing from this house, Mark's favorite came from the garage. The syncopated beat of the drum, the strumming of the guitar, and the throaty voice of the lead singer merged in an exciting blend that took Mark's breath away.

He smiled as he recognized the song. He'd heard it many times before. Tipping his head back, Mark belted out the lyrics. If Mamm heard them, she'd wash his mouth out with lye soap. The crashing and banging from inside the building drowned out his voice, so he sang to his heart's content.

A hand descended on his shoulder, and Mark gurgled to a stop. Fearing his parents' wrath, he slowly opened his eyes.

"I'm sorry," he said, although he wasn't really sorry. The only thing he regretted was getting caught.

But when he glanced back, Mrs. Musselman smiled down at him.

"You like music?" Her eyes appeared friendly and appreciative. She must like music as much as he did, but—

He hung his head. He shouldn't have been listening or singing Englisch rock lyrics. "*Jah*," he whispered.

"You have a wonderful voice." Her soft words flowed over him with a comforting warmth. "Would you like to come in and watch the boys play?"

Mark's spirit soared. He almost nodded, but caught himself. Mamm and Daed would be upset to find out Mark liked this kind of music. They'd be even more distressed if they discovered he'd gone inside to listen.

Desire warred with his parents' teachings. Didn't God say to make a joyful noise? Unlike the slow, monotonous dragginess of *Ausbund* hymns, these lively tunes seemed more like they'd please God. If Mark were in God's place, he'd choose this more exciting music.

Mamm's and Daed's disapproving faces and the bishop's stern frown popped into Mark's mind. "I—I can't." He forced out the words even though he longed to shout *jah*.

"That's too bad." Mrs. Musselman sounded almost as sad as Mark. Her forehead creased in a frown, she glanced toward his house. "Just for a few minutes?"

The temptation was too great to resist. Too filled with excitement to answer, Mark nodded.

Mrs. Musselman led him to a side door in the garage. When she knocked and then pulled it open, the sounds flowed in, over, and around Mark, wrapping him in joy. The music crashed to a stop.

"Mom," one of the boys, dressed in a ripped black T-shirt and jeans with holes in them, glared at her. "You interrupted us."

"Sorry, guys." She flashed them a winning smile, put an arm around Mark's shoulders, and pushed him forward. "I thought you might like to meet one of your fans. He seems to know your songs by heart."

The guys glanced at each other and snickered.

"Can you play one or two songs for him before he has to leave?"

The guitar player sighed and flicked his hair. "I guess."

"Mark, you sing along," she ordered as she slipped from the garage.

Two of the guys grimaced, but they started one of Mark's favorite songs. Fascinated, he stared as fingers strummed chords, sticks tapped on drums. He was so thrilled he almost forgot to sing. Then the words burst from his lips, his feet stomped, and his hands clapped out the beat.

The band members stared at him, but continued to play. After the song thundered to a crescendo, they all focused their attention on Mark.

"Wow, kid, that's some voice," one of them said.

Mark took a step back, unsure if that was a compliment or criticism.

The teen smiled. "If you were a little older, we'd ask you to join our band."

"You—you would?" Mark couldn't believe it. Joy flooded through him from the top of his head to the tips of his toes. Him in a band?

Several heads nodded, and Mark almost floated off the ground. Then reality crashed in. His parents would never allow him to do this.

"*Danke*," he whispered, downhearted.

The drummer studied Mark. "You don't look too happy."

"I—I can't ever be in a band."

"Why not?" he asked.

Mark nibbled at his lips. "My parents wouldn't let me."

His neighbor clarified. "The Amish around here don't do music. Except hymns in church. No piano. No organ. Nothing. Just *a cappella*."

The drummer shot Mark a sympathetic look. "Whoa. That's too bad, kid. You got talent."

"Let's do one more song for him," the lead singer said. "You sing along," he told Mark.

The sadness tugging at Mark lifted at the first notes of the song. How could something that made you feel so good be bad? It didn't make sense. Music burst from deep inside him. He threw back his head and let out the notes. They bubbled and sparkled around him, and his whole body wriggled to the beat.

When it ended, Mark longed for more, but he had to go. Nobody would believe it had taken this long to feed the horses. Reluctantly, he pushed the door open.

The band members called after him to come back anytime. And Mark's feet barely touched the snow-covered ground.

Mrs. Musselman stopped him as he trudged off. "Mark, if you'd like, I'd be happy to give you music lessons."

Ach, how he wished he could agree. "We don't got the money for it." When he'd peeked in at piano and voice lessons, he'd seen kids' parents paying her.

Disappointment filled her soft brown eyes. "That's too bad. A talent like yours should be nurtured." Then she brightened. "Would you be willing to work for us in exchange for lessons?"

A *jah* almost flew from Mark's lips, but he caught it in time. "Mamm wouldn't let me take lessons. But I could do jobs for you." Maybe he'd get to hear some of the lessons while he worked.

"Wonderful." The sparkle in her eyes promised more than chores.

* * *

Eight years later, on Christmas Eve, Mark slipped over to the Musselmans' house after he'd finished his chores. Over the past weeks, he'd helped Mrs. Musselman decorate the house for Christmas. He'd cut down a blue spruce and put it up in the family room. He'd strung bulbs on the tree, hung glittering icicle lights from her eaves, tacked stockings to the mantel, inflated a balloon-like Santa and his reindeer on the front lawn, and set up a large wooden nativity scene on her wide front porch.

Everywhere Mark looked, lights twinkled, ornaments shimmered, and snow gleamed. Unlike his own plain living room, with a pine garland on the mantel and a string of Christmas cards on the wall, the Musselmans' house burst with decorations, piles of presents, and glorious music. The soaring strains of "O Holy Night" poured from the kitchen as Mrs. Musselman slid tree-shaped cookies from the oven. She and Mark warbled along.

Mark wished he could stay overnight here and wake on Christmas morning to open some of the gifts wrapped in shiny paper or dump out treats from a stocking. He'd get one or two small, practical presents from his parents, perhaps a book, a much-needed tool, or a pair of wool socks to keep his feet toasty on frigid mornings when he tended to the animals.

Mrs. Musselman interrupted Mark's thoughts. "The boys will be here soon."

She still called them boys, although they were in their twenties and married now. The oldest one even had a small boy of his own. Neither of them played in the band anymore, so their instruments and equipment sat idle in the garage. Mrs. Musselman had told Mark to use all of it whenever he wanted. She'd even encouraged him to bring his friends.

Once he'd turned sixteen, he'd taken full advantage of it. Although his parents might have disapproved if they realized he'd been the one making most of the loud music coming from the garage, he eased his conscience by using Rumspringa as an excuse for playing his heart out. All the lessons from Mrs. Musselman and her sons over the years paid off. Mark had become an accomplished musician, skilled on the electric guitar, the piano, keyboard, and drums. The Musselman family all agreed he sang like an angel. For the band, though, he'd perfected a gravelly voice with a rough edginess that everyone seemed to love.

Several of his friends joined him in the garage for jam sessions. Mark showed them what he knew, and Mrs. Musselman offered them lessons in exchange for lawn care and tree trimming. Over the past year, they'd developed a unique sound together, and in addition to popular songs, they began playing some of Mark's original compositions. Mrs. Musselman even taught him musical notation and introduced him to lyric software on the computer. She was as proud of his compositions as he was. He owed her so much. No matter how much he helped her, he could never repay all she'd done.

"Anything else you need before your sons get here?" Mark would gladly do it.

"How about sampling these cookies to make sure they taste okay?"

He grinned as he took the three kinds she held out. "I'm always glad to check out your cooking." Over the years, she'd insisted he try meals and snacks, knowing he was often hungry because, with eight children, Daed struggled to put food on the table, especially in winter when construction jobs slowed down and the garden shriveled. By Christmastime, they lived mainly on what they'd canned during the summer.

Mark chewed each cookie thoroughly, savoring every bite, and pronounced them delicious.

"Oh, good. I packed some for your family to wish them a Merry Christmas." Mrs. Musselman handed him a large tin embossed with a poinsettia.

"You didn't have to do that," Mark protested.

"I want to. I'll be giving one to all our neighbors. Even though my husband's not around this year and I have no children at home, I can't get out of the habit of baking for four."

"*Danke.*" Mark's heart went out to her. Since she'd lost her husband nine months ago, Mark had done all the household jobs Mr. Musselman used to handle. It made Mark happy to know she'd have company for Christmas. "I'd better get home. I'm sure Daed has plenty of chores to keep me busy."

"Before you go, I have a present for you."

"You've done so much for me. I can't take anything more."

"It'll be a gift for me too. Although I might be a little selfish in keeping you around here."

Mark furrowed his brow.

"I've checked with my sons, and they agree. We'd all like you to have the equipment and instruments in the garage. I know we said you could play them whenever you wanted, but as of today, they all belong to you. Merry Christmas, Mark."

"I—I can't take them. That's too much."

"If you don't, I'll give them away to someone else. But I hope you'll take them, and that you'll promise to practice in the garage. Hearing the music lifts my spirits when I'm lonely."

She'd told him that before, so Mark had spent as much time as he could playing. Not that it was a hardship. Far from it. And his friends stopped by often to join him.

"You've gotten good enough now to play some gigs. I want you to be free to take the instruments to the different venues." She reached into her pocket and pulled out a list. "I've contacted these clubs and cafés. They're all willing to give you a chance."

Dazed, Mark reached out to take the paper she held out. "My parents won't approve." He'd kept his music a secret from his family. They all believed he was doing chores for the Musselmans. He had been, of course, but only for a short time each visit.

"I can talk to them if you'd like. You're very talented. It would be a shame to hide your gifts when they could be shared with the world."

Shared with the world? She thought he was that *gut?* Pride snaked its way into Mark's heart. Maybe he did owe it to others to play his music where many people could hear it. That desire took root and couldn't be squashed.

Chapter 1

Mark kept his list secret from his family, but he pulled it out whenever he was alone. The names grew smudged from so much handling as he dreamed of playing in each of those places. And when he went downtown, he sometimes stood outside the clubs, wishing he had the courage to go inside. But his conscience held him back. No way could he defy his upbringing any more than he already had.

He and his friends met several times a week to practice together, and Mark did solo sessions, sometimes several times a day. Both his parents pressured him to join one of the conservative youth groups like his older sisters. Instead, Mark hung around with the rebellious *youngie*. Some of his friends even had cell phones, computers, or cars. Most of them still dressed Plain, but a few wore Englisch clothes when they cruised the town on Saturday nights.

One night, they passed one of the clubs on Mark's list. On impulse, he shouted to Jerry Gingerich, who was driving, "Let's stop and listen to that music."

Jerry Gingerich screeched to a halt in the middle of the

street. Cars behind him slammed on their brakes and laid on their horns.

"He meant to pull over, dude." Sam Keim cuffed Jerry on the side of his head, sending his straw hat flying.

"Why didn't you say so?" Jerry slid into a parking space as the cars he'd blocked drove around them, yelling obscenities.

He retrieved his hat, plopped it on his head, and they all tumbled from the car. Mark led the way to the door. He'd scoped out this teen club several times during the day, but he'd never been inside. His heart thumping in time to the music, he paid the cover charge, entered the dimly lit club, and led the way to a table tucked in the corner. Unlike Jerry, who strutted and preened in his Englisch clothes, Mark and Joel Wickey, their bass player, disliked drawing attention to themselves.

As they wove their way through the crowd, plenty of teen girls eyed them. Some of them giggled when they caught sight of the Amish *buwe*. Even Jerry and Sam in their jeans still had bowl-cut hair and straw hats. Jerry whipped his off and tried to hide it as he gave the Englischers flirty looks. Sam followed his lead.

They sank into chairs in the far corner, their hats in their laps, and ordered sodas. Then they all leaned back to listen.

After a while, Sam said in a low voice, "We're much better than them."

Joel nodded. "I wish we could show people here what we can do."

Mark fingered the list in his pocket. It had been almost a year since Mrs. Musselman had given it to him. Maybe they could.

When the band took a break, Mark gathered his courage and headed toward the bar. "Is the manager around?"

The server jerked a thumb toward a thirty-something man chatting with one of the band members. Mark headed toward them but stood a respectful distance away until they finished their conversation.

"Seriously, man. You've got to let us out of our contract. This hotel gig's a big deal."

"I can't find another band during the Christmas season. Everyone's already booked."

Mark approached the manager and cleared his throat. "Excuse me, but I couldn't help overhearing you. Our band would be happy to play here."

The manager snorted. "You and a million other amateurs." He studied Mark's clothing, and his lips curled. "Thought you Amish weren't allowed to play instruments."

Shame coursed through Mark. "*Neh*, we aren't, but Mrs. Musselman—"

"Adele Musselman?" The manager's face softened. "She was my piano teacher."

"Mine too. She taught me a lot of things."

"Wait. Are you the dude she told me about a while back? She did mention someone in an Amish band."

"That's us." Mark waved toward his friends in the corner.

Scowling at the performer, the manager snarled, "Looks like I found your replacement. But don't ever expect to get booked here again."

"So, what's your band's name? You got a manager I should talk to?"

Mark gulped. "I'm the manager." He'd formed the band, so he guessed that counted. "And we're called, um—" His mind went blank. Why hadn't they chosen a name? Swallowing hard, he blurted out the first thing that came to mind: "Amish Rebels."

With a sardonic smile, the manager held out a hand. "Great name. I'm Bud Reeser. You got publicity stuff—photo, posters, whatever?"

Photos? Mark tried not to cringe. Playing music was bad

enough, but pictures? With the manager waiting impatiently
for an answer, Mark fumbled out an excuse. "Not with us, but
we can drop something by on Monday."

"Guess we should make sure you're available for the dates.
Hang on."

The band had returned to the stage by the time Bud came
back. He tapped a finger on a tablet and scrolled through a list.
Mark memorized the dates Bud spat out.

"We'll be there." Mark only hoped the others would agree.

"We pay a percentage of ticket sales. Might attract a curious
crowd the first night. After that, it's up to you to get them back
with your music."

His thoughts whirling, Mark returned to the table. His
bandmates thought he was teasing, but when the truth sank in,
they all looked as dazed as he was. Then the chatter started. Joel
worked at an office supply store and could get someone to
make posters.

Tomorrow was Sunday, but first thing Monday morning,
they'd get together for a photo. Since the band name was Amish
Rebels, they'd wear their usual clothes. They'd need to find
someone with a van or a truck to transport them.

Mrs. Musselman was thrilled to help, gladly took the photo,
and enlisted one of her students who'd drive them in his cargo
van for the privilege of attending their concerts. He even had
backstage and sound experience. Everything fell together perfectly, and on Monday, Mark dropped off posters, new business cards, and publicity materials Mrs. Musselman had helped
him prep and package.

The night of their first concert, the line was out the door. At
intermission, Bud came over and shook Mark's hand. "You
guys keep playing like that, and we'll have standing-room-only
crowds. We even have a few reporters here to spread the word.
Most publicity we've ever had."

* * *

Joline Lapp pushed her nine-month-old baby sister and two-year-old brother down the sidewalk in a double stroller. When Daed had remarried three years ago, she'd been twelve, the oldest of his five children, and Nettie's four had been even younger than her siblings. Now the nine children had grown to eleven, and Joline could see endless years of baby care stretching ahead of her.

Still, she loved living at the STAR Center, where Mrs. Vandenberg had created a place to keep city kids off the streets and out of gangs by offering art, music, computers, sports, crafts, tutoring, and tons of other activities plus free food and clothes. Although Joline could attend any of the classes she wanted, she had to sneak into some of them, like music lessons and gymnastics. Her parents would be horrified to know she had a leotard, which she covered with T-shirts and sports shorts to make them a little more modest. Luckily, she did the wash, so they hadn't found out. Sadly, as much as she longed to, she'd never be able to compete or play music in public.

Her parents stayed so busy running the center and training gang members, they depended on Joline to care for all the little ones and cook meals. Most of the time, she didn't mind, but it meant she always had children chaperoning her. That was her parents' way of making sure she didn't get into trouble.

But once she dropped her siblings off at the center's activity rooms, her parents had no idea what lessons Joline took. She also used the babies' walks as an excuse to get out and explore the city of Lancaster, so different from the small country town where they'd lived before. She loved popping into little shops, getting an ice cream cone, or talking to Englisch girls her own age. Now that she'd finished school last year, she had plenty more free time. And she took advantage of it.

As she passed one of the teen clubs, she came to an abrupt stop. A poster in the window had five Amish *buwe* playing instruments. Were they really Amish? She couldn't believe it. The sign said they'd be playing that Saturday night from eight to eleven thirty. She had to come here to see.

Joline spent the next few days making plans with two of the Englisch girls she often hung out with, Amari and Elise. After her family went to bed around nine, she sneaked out, avoiding the doorman at the STAR Center, and went to Amari's apartment, where she dressed in one of her friend's sparkly dresses. When Elise arrived, already dolled up, she and Amari insisted on doing Joline's hair and makeup.

A sick feeling in her stomach, Joline removed her *kapp* and unpinned her bun.

"Wow!" Amari's eyes widened as Joline's hair fell to her waist. "Girl, don't you ever cut your hair?"

Joline shook her head. "We're not allowed to."

"You got a curling iron?" Amari asked Elise. "Maybe we can make her hair look a little shorter."

Joline fidgeted. "We're going to miss the whole thing if we don't go soon."

But Elise raced upstairs to her family's apartment and returned holding a long metal rod with a handle. When it was hot, she wound sections of Joline's hair around and around it. By the time Amari finished, Joline's hair reached far below her shoulders rather than to her waist.

"Come look at yourself, girl. You look amazing." Amari grabbed Joline's hand and pulled her toward the full-length mirror.

Joline gaped at herself. Who was this glamourous Englischer staring back at her?

"You're drop-dead gorgeous," Elise proclaimed.

Joline had to agree. She'd never spent time looking in mirrors. She could see why the Amish didn't hang them all over their houses. She could get used to gazing at herself this way. A sure path to *hochmut*. It was hard to stay humble after seeing yourself in beautiful clothes with all your best features enhanced by makeup. She flipped the curls over her shoulder.

A snake of guilt twisted inside her. This was wrong. So wrong. She should scrub her face, get back in her Plain clothes, and pray for forgiveness.

Amari jostled her arm. "Let's go, girl. Ready for your big night out?"

The sensible side of Joline vanished in the excitement. She ignored the still, small warnings of her soul, took Amari's arm, and marched toward the door with determination. Nothing, especially not nagging little voices, would spoil tonight for her.

Crowds stood around on the sidewalk, waiting to get in, stamping their feet in the slush and blowing on gloved hands to ward off the icy chill. Some stood, shivering in ragged clothing, staring longingly through the windows at the band. The frigid air vibrated to the pounding beat.

Shimmying to the music, Joline and her friends joined the line, inching slowly closer to the door. Finally, their turn came when several younger teens headed out, and Amari snagged their table. The three friends sat almost directly in front of the stage. The noise and energy reached out and grabbed Joline with its intensity. Her eyes locked on the instruments and the players. Her lips curved into a smile at the familiar Amish black broadfall pants, suspenders, blue short-sleeved shirts, and straw hats.

Her heart flipped when the lead singer's throaty voice crooned "Whenever I Dream of You," and his eyes locked with hers. Her breath caught, and she got lost in the depths of his green eyes. Was he singing this song for her?

When the last notes died down to one final guitar chord and the light *ting* of the cymbals, the audience broke into thunderous applause, cheers, and whistles. Many jumped to their feet for the standing ovation. The lead singer broke eye contact and glanced around as if dazed at the response.

The drummer stepped up to the mike. "Give it up for our own Mark Troyer, who wrote that original."

The crowd went wild.

Joline sucked air into her constricted lungs. He'd written that? Amazing. What a magical talent!

Amari leaned over. "That song was lit." She squealed. "And he's into you. Couldn't keep his eyes off you."

Others had noticed? To her, the two of them had been on an island by themselves. Everything had drifted away except for him, his words, his gaze . . . and the music pulsing between them. Joline had never experienced exhilaration like this before, and she wanted it to go on forever.

Sadly, he connected with others during his next songs, and Joline felt bereft. Still, the music was incredible, touching part of her she'd never before tapped. She'd been on a roller coaster once at Hersheypark. Like that, the music kept pulling her to peaks, then pitching her over the top to stomach-dropping thrills.

In between, the drummer, who'd turned out to be quite a joker, kept up humorous patter that made everyone laugh. She probably giggled the loudest because most of his jokes were about being Amish, so she understood the humor better than anyone else in the tightly packed audience.

A few times, Mark's eyes flitted to her, assessing, curious. He seemed to be studying her, wondering about her. She squirmed. Could he tell she was Amish? Did she want him to know?

Joline was torn. In one way, she did, but in another, she'd rather he see her as an Englischer. She hoped he couldn't tell she was only fifteen. The makeup made her look older and more sophisticated. So did the slinky dress.

The two hours flew by until Joline couldn't possibly fly any higher. She'd never been this giddy or bubbly in her life. And just when she thought she'd reached the pinnacle, the drummer stepped up to the mike again.

He announced, "Our final song of the night is another original by Mark, 'Only You.'"

Mark gazed at the spotlight around his feet as he began singing. When he lifted his gaze, their eyes met. As he sang each word of the beautiful love song right to her, Joline floated into the stratosphere. Never had she been so connected to someone else like this. Her eyes shimmered with tears.

When the song ended, she smacked her palms together as hard as she could. That had been incredible. Simply incredible.

He kept his head bowed, looking humbled at all the adulation, which made her admire him even more. Was it possible to fall in love with someone through music? Joline wasn't positive, but she thought she had.

After the crowd left, Mark focused his attention on packing up the equipment and tried to shake off the odd feeling that had come over him when his eyes met that girl's. For some reason, he couldn't look away. She was only a young girl, but his heart swelled at the yearning in her eyes. The longing of a true music lover. One who experienced the pulse of music through her whole body and deep in her soul. That girl was a kindred spirit.

He frowned. Something else had drawn him to her. She had a rebellious spirit that matched his. And if he wasn't mistaken, she appeared to be Amish, despite her makeup and sequined dress. Everything about her—the uneasiness in the way she sat, her eagerness to drink in new experiences, her wide, surprised look when her gaze lighted on unfamiliar things—all revealed her as a first timer at a teen club.

Something deep within him compelled him to pray for her. Her innocence could easily get her in trouble.

Please, Lord, keep her safe. Don't let her do anything foolish to spoil that eager, open spirit. And protect her from those who might want to do her harm.

Jerry elbowed him. "You're standing there dazed, like somebody hit you over the head. You fall in love or something?"

Mark's laugh came out shaky and hollow. "Don't be ridiculous. When would I have time to fall in love?"

That was for sure. Their lives had become a whirlwind of practices, sneaking out to gigs, and keeping up with the chores at home. And late at night, while the rest of his family slept, Mark labored over new songs—sometimes in his head, other times on a pre-charged laptop Mrs. Musselman had loaned him. He shielded it with his covers so he didn't wake his younger brothers. Mark often woke groggy-eyed and exhausted the next morning, and sleepwalked through his chores. Often, the secret knowledge of his latest creation was the only thing that fueled him during the day.

His life had become divided into slogging through the day and coming alive at night as music poured out of him. Already, after three performances, the adulation and applause had become a drug. A drug he needed to survive. Everything else faded into unimportance. Music held center stage in his life.

Chapter 2

Everything changed after their fifth gig—in good ways and bad. They were done at this club for the holiday season, but the manager had booked them for New Year's Eve and several weekends after that. The band had brought in good money because lines of eager fans wound out the door every night.

Two older men were waiting to speak to them after the club emptied that night. Mark grew antsy. He had to get home. His parents were already upset he had a "part-time job" that kept him out so late. If they knew what he was really doing, they'd explode.

He stepped forward intending to brush off the last of these lingering fans. "Thanks for coming."

The portly man with a florid face wiped his dripping forehead, then thrust out a beefy hand. "Sebastian St. James." He announced his name as if Mark should recognize it.

When no recognition dawned in any of their eyes, he registered surprise. The club manager stepped up beside him.

"Sebastian owns the largest chain of boutique hotels in the

country," Bud explained. With a grimace, he added, "He steals all my best bands."

"You guys interested in playing some gigs at my hotels? What's your availability over the next two weeks? I need to fill in for a group with a sick lead singer."

Mark could barely follow Sebastian St. James's rapid-fire delivery. "You want a singer? Or the whole band?"

"The band. Call this number. Greta will schedule you in." He handed Mark a business card, turned, and strode away.

The thin ferret-faced man behind him grinned. "Sounds like you guys need a manager, and I can help." He snatched the business card from Mark's fingers and replaced it with one of his own. "Sid Malone, at your service. I manage bands. Happy to contact Sebastian for you."

Mark felt as if he'd hopped into a buggy being yanked behind an out-of-control horse.

Sid whipped a sheaf of papers from the leather folder he held. "If you'll just sign here, I'll get you booked solid for months at a time."

"We're Amish, so we don't sign contracts. When we give our word, we keep it."

At first, Sid blinked. Then, a smarmy smile slid across his face. "Well, that's refreshing. If you want to do business without a contract, fine by me."

Sid galloped through the terms, most of which Mark struggled to understand. The main things that stood out to him were that Sid set up their gigs, arranged their travel, handled the money, paid their bills, and took thirty percent of whatever they were paid.

"Thirty percent?" Bud squawked. "That's highway robbery!"

"Seems fair to me." Sid waved to the other band members

busy with the load-out. "They're young and inexperienced, so I'll be doing tons of publicity and advance work."

"I've never heard of anyone getting more than twenty-five percent tops."

Mark's gaze ping-ponged between them. Twenty-five percent still seemed like a lot of money.

"I'm well worth it." Sid puffed out his scrawny chest. "When I negotiate their contracts, they'll get a lot more than they made here, so they won't even notice it. Plus, they'll have plenty of gigs. I can get them into places they'd never get into on their own."

Bud shrugged. "It's up to the kids here, but if you can build their careers . . ." He turned to Mark. "Don't let him charge more than twenty-five."

Sid bristled. "Okay, okay. I'll agree to that. Whadda you say, kid?"

"All right." Mark held out a hand to shake on the agreement and gave their new manager Jerry's cell number to contact them.

"You won't be sorry." Sid oozed toward the door. "I'll get good terms from St. James."

Doubt niggled at Mark as Sid slipped out into the night, but it would be good to have someone experienced handling their bookings and negotiations.

To Mark's surprise, Sid set up six dates with the hotel for a generous amount before the holidays. And he lined up several gigs after the holidays and promised to fill their schedule for the coming year. Maybe this would work well after all.

Mrs. Vandenberg stopped Joline as she was about to leave the STAR Center with the stroller. "I'm a bit concerned about you."

"Why?" Joline's response came out a little too defensive. Guilty consciences did that to you.

She tried to relax. Mrs. Vandenberg couldn't possibly know

about the club visit. Mrs. V had gone home an hour before Joline left. The guard hadn't seen her slip in or out.

"Do you think your parents would approve of what you did?" Mrs. V's eyes had a way of seeing the truth. It unnerved Joline.

Still, the elderly lady didn't know—

Mrs. Vandenberg peered through her glasses, pinning Joline with an *I know a lot more than you think* look.

Had Mrs. V read her mind? She had a habit of doing that. "A-about what?"

"Come now, Joline. Let's not talk in circles. I care about you and don't want to see anything happen to you like . . ."

Joline's mind shot back to the time she'd dashed out of the center and gotten grabbed by a man. If Nettie hadn't rescued her—

"Did you think about that when you sneaked out two nights ago?"

"H-how did you know?"

"I have my ways." When Joline's eyes flicked heavenward, Mrs. V smiled. "Yes, sometimes I get nudges from God, but this time I had an earthly helper." She waved toward the guard seated on a raised platform near the entry. "Have you ever been behind their desk?"

Joline shook her head.

"They have monitors that capture all different directions along with hallways and classrooms."

The guard didn't have to look in Joline's direction to see her? How could she have been so foolish?

"Are you going to tell Daed?" Joline couldn't even imagine what her father would do. Forbid her to leave the center? Confine her to their apartment on the top floor? If he did, she couldn't take music and gymnastics. She'd never be able to see Elise and Amari.

"I don't think that's my place."

Joline's breath whooshed out in a loud, relieved sigh.

"Seems to me you'd be the one to do that."

Neh, she could never tell Daed or . . . her stepmother, Nettie. Joline couldn't bear their disapproving gazes or losing their trust.

"It won't be easy, but I have faith you can do it."

"I—I can't."

"We've had this conversation before. You can do anything you make up your mind to do, can't you?"

Obviously, Mrs. V was referring to sneaking out. Or maybe about Joline's ability to come up with far-fetched schemes and carry them through, despite her parents' objections. Joline had a reputation as a troublemaker, a person who'd defy authority to get what she wanted.

"I'm going to trust you to tell them. I won't even dictate when, although I hope it'll be sooner rather than later."

But Joline planned to put it off as long as possible.

Mark was flying high on Second Christmas when his *daed*'s whole family gathered at the table. Following the prayer, he hummed a happy tune as he waited for the dishes to be passed.

Daed frowned. "What's that music? It's not from the *Ausbund*."

Flushing to the roots of his hair, Mark scrambled for an explanation. Before he could offer an excuse, his *onkel* cleared his throat.

"I'd been planning to discuss this after dinner, but since you brought it up . . ." Melvin addressed Mark's *daed*. "I saw something in town yesterday you should know about."

At Daed's puzzled frown, Melvin stood. "Excuse me a minute. I'll get it." He returned a minute later with a newspaper and slapped it down in front of Daed.

Daed's brows scrunched together as he read the article, then he reached the picture. His eyes flew wide. "Amish Rebels?" His voice screeched up an octave. "Amish Rebels?"

He shoved back his chair so hard it tipped over and crashed as he stood. The veins in his forehead throbbed.

"What is it?" Mamm reached for the newspaper Daed was waving in the air. As she read, her face crumpled. "*Ach*, Mark." The hurt in her voice cut Mark to the quick.

Everyone at the table turned to stare at him. His chest seized into a tight knot, cutting off his air. He couldn't meet anyone's eyes. The food he'd eaten sloshed in his stomach.

"It is Rumspringa," his *aenti* offered hesitantly.

"All three of your sisters went through Rumspringa without shaming our family." Daed jerked his chair upright and sank into it, cradling his head in his hands. "I don't believe this. I just don't believe it."

Daed sat mumbling, maybe praying. When he lifted his head, his shoulders slumped, and deep lines slashed across his forehead and around his mouth and eyes.

"I often worried," he mused as if talking to himself, "that hanging around those Englischers so much might rub off on you. I should have done something earlier."

The whole family sat frozen. Even Mark's younger brothers set down their forks to stare intently at their father.

Daed slid his chair back to the table and picked up his fork. "Let's eat now before the food gets cold." He fixed Mark with a warning glare. "We'll talk about this after dinner." Pointing his fork tines at the younger *buwe*, he warned, "Let this be a lesson to you. Never do anything this terrible."

They all nodded nervously, darting glances at Mark before focusing on their plates. Rather than shoveling in their ham and mashed potatoes, they all picked at their meals.

Mamm's teary eyes pierced him. Mark had never considered the damage he'd do to his family if anyone found out. He'd been sure nobody would ever know. If any of the Amish *youngie* came to the club and saw the band, they wouldn't risk telling anyone because they'd have to admit their own indiscretions.

Bowing his head, Mark mumbled, "I'm sorry." Not sorry for loving music, but sorry for causing his family pain, for embarrassing them, for tearing them apart.

Daed harrumphed. "That's a start," he said with satisfaction. "Giving all this up"—he smacked a hand on the paper Mamm had set face down—"will go a long way to healing the damage you've done to your reputation, your family, and your faith."

Give it up? Mark choked on a bite of green beans. *No way.*

He'd never outright defied his *daed*. Not to his face. *Jah*, he'd been sneaking around behind his father's back for years, but to talk back? Mark couldn't do it. He was supposed to honor his father and mother.

His conscience jabbed him. *Hiding your disobedience is honoring them?*

Still, he couldn't let Daed believe a lie. The band had made commitments they had to keep. Mark cleared his throat. "I can't give it up. We have gig—I mean, events scheduled for—"

"Cancel them." Daed's ultimatum cut off any argument. His word was law.

Mark shook his head. He couldn't leave the band without a lead singer. Abel Schrock, their keyboard player, and Joel, on bass, had decent voices, but neither of them had his range. "We've made agreements." Mark tried to say it softly and reasonably despite the fear and anger churning inside him. "We have to keep them."

"Any deals made with the devil can be broken."

"I'm sorry, Daed, but I can't let the guys down." Even more, he didn't want to. Maybe he shouldn't admit it, but the words tumbled out. "Besides, I love playing music."

"You love music more than your family? More than God?"

Each of Daed's words hit Mark like a blow. Did he? Had he put his music before God and his family? To his shame, he had.

But even worse, he wasn't sure he wanted to change that.

Daed's face reddened, and his words shot out, hard and hurtful. "Until you give up that music of yours, you're not welcome in this house."

Mamm laid a hand on his arm. "You don't mean that."

He shook off her gentle touch. "I most certainly do." He turned to Mark. "If you refuse to obey, get out of this house. I won't let you influence your younger brothers into your sinful lifestyle."

Mark pushed back his chair. Hesitated. Did Daed really mean that?

After one glance at his father's implacable face, Mark stood and walked out of the dining room. Without a shadow of doubt, he'd never be welcome here again.

With no idea where he'd go, Mark headed into his room, packed a bag, and left, his heart heavier than it had ever been in his life. Would he regret giving up his family for his music?

He already did. His soul ached with the loss, but he'd given his word to those clubs and hotels, and he intended to keep every one of those commitments. Maybe Daed would change his mind. Rumspringa was supposed to be his chance to try out the world.

Shivering, Mark trudged through the snow to the one place that always soothed him—the Musselmans' garage. Several cars were parked in the driveway, so he couldn't immerse himself in playing the drums or strumming the guitar. Mrs. Musselman's grandbaby might be sleeping, so Mark slumped on the floor near the instruments and cradled the guitar, air-playing chords as he fought back the lump choking his throat.

He had nowhere to go. And he already missed his family, even Daed. Grief seared through him at the thought of never seeing them again.

Picking up a pen, he poured his pain into the lyrics for "Missing You" and "Will I Ever See You Again?" which dripped word by word onto the page as he blinked back tears. He wrote fast and furiously, each phrase expressing a tiny piece of his sorrow and loss.

By the time he finished, every drop of energy had drained from him. He was exhausted and longed to sleep. For now, this garage would be his home. Although the Musselmans kept it heated, frigid air seeped in under the doors, and the cold cement floor chilled through to his bones.

Mark stood and stretched. Then he gathered the padded gigbags they used to protect their instruments while traveling. Those would have to do for a bed and covers. He curled up in his nest with his duffel bag as a pillow and drifted off into uneasy dreams.

Mrs. Musselman discovered him sleeping there several days later and invited him into the house to sleep. Her sons had departed the day before.

"You can stay here as long as you'd like," she said as she ushered him into one of her sons' bedrooms.

Then they sat in the living room, and she listened to Mark's tale, her face filled with sympathy. "Sometimes creatives have to sacrifice for their art."

The word *sacrifice* torched Mark's conscience. To him, *sacrifice* meant Christ dying on the cross. Not selfishly cutting yourself off from your family to do what you loved.

Mrs. Musselman interrupted his thoughts by jumping up from the couch. "I forgot. I meant to give this to you for your Christmas present."

"You don't have to give me anything." He had nothing for her. And after her generosity in letting him stay here and giving him the instruments, he already owed her more than he could ever repay.

She returned with a thin, gift-wrapped package not much larger than a card. He opened it and stared down at the piece of cardboard with the band's name on it and the words, *recording studio.*

Mark glanced up, puzzled. "What is it?"

"It's for your band to record a demo. Give it to your manager. He can schedule it."

"Schedule what?"

Mrs. Musselman's smile broke through like a burst of sunshine. "I keep forgetting you don't know much about the music business." She sat on the edge of the couch and leaned forward eagerly. "I've been listening to you practice. You're ready for the next step."

"Next step?" Mark felt like an echo machine.

"You go to that studio, and they'll tape your songs. Your manager can send the demos to radio stations around the country. Your band will take off."

Mark's head ached with thousands of incomprehensible thoughts. *Radio? Around the country?*

"I suggest you do mostly your original songs. They have more depth and poignancy."

Again, Mark struggled to understand. Only one thing stood out clearly in his mind. He couldn't reciprocate. "But I don't have anything for you."

"You'll never know what a thrill it is for a music teacher to watch one of her students succeed. That's the only gift I'll ever need." The glow on her face proved she meant it.

How could he ever pay her back for all she'd done for him?

Chapter 3

Joline pushed the stroller down the sidewalk, avoiding dirty slush piles. As she passed Amari and Elise's apartment building, her friends burst out the door and raced toward her.

"We've been waiting for you like forever." Amari thumped a hand against her chest as if she were having a heart attack. "Where you been, girl?"

"Wait 'til you see what we have," Elise said breathlessly.

"All day? You didn't go to school?"

"It's Christmas vacation. We don't go back until January third."

Joline stared at them. "Amish schools only get off Christmas Day and Second Christmas." Why did the Englisch schools give scholars so much time off? It made no sense.

"Anyway, you gotta hear this." Amari clamped a hand on Joline's arm.

Joline yelped. In Amari's excitement, her painted fingernails pinched Joline's skin like crab claws.

Amari didn't seem to notice, she just dragged Joline into the building and toward the rickety elevator. "You're gonna die when you hear this."

Elise bent to lift the front of the stroller over the gap in the floor, and the three of them squeezed into the elevator around the sleeping babies.

Her friends chattered excitedly and talked over each other so that Joline could barely figure out what they were saying. But neither of them would tell her their secret. When they reached Amari's room, Elise parked the stroller in a corner and motioned for Joline to sit on the floor.

"Now close your eyes," Elise commanded.

Joline did, half expecting them to play a prank. A button clicked and strains of music filled the air. And then a voice she recognized sang the first words of a song.

Her eyes flew open. "Where did you get that?"

"Hush, girl. I'll start it again. Just listen."

This time, Joline kept her eyes shut and let the sound flow over her as she pictured the Amish Rebels on stage, the lead singer's eyes fixed on her. That feeling he'd been singing directly to her washed over her. When the second song ended, she leaned her head back against the wall, lost in a dream.

Then the next tune began. Instead of expressing heartfelt love, the lyrics overflowed with longing and loneliness. The last strains of "Missing You" died away, leaving tears trickling down Joline's face. By the time "Will I Ever See You Again?" ended, all she wanted to do was find Mark Troyer and wrap her arms around him to comfort him. She dashed away her tears.

Amari stared at her with tenderness. "You think he wrote those about you?"

Joline sucked in a breath. She'd wondered—and hoped—as the lyrics wound their way deep into her heart. But her friends had sensed it too. She had to see him again.

"I wish I could hear those again, but I need to get back."

Elise's brows drew together. "We've spent the past several

days listening to the radio for his songs to come on, and we made you a playlist, but how can we get it to you?"

"Playlist?"

Amari rolled her eyes. "I don't believe you, girl. What you just heard was a playlist. But unless you have a phone or computer or something, we can't share it."

"They have computers at the STAR Center, don't they? Get someone to set you up an account." Elise jotted something on a piece of paper and handed it to Joline. "Just hand them this so they know what you want."

"Once you have it, email us." Amari sighed. "Wish you had a phone so we could text."

"After you have this playlist," Elise explained, "you can listen whenever you want."

Joline clutched the paper to her chest. She could listen to those songs anytime? It seemed too good to be true.

But her friends weren't done with their surprises. "Guess who's gonna be at the teen club on New Year's Eve?"

"He is?" Joline squealed. She had to find a way to go.

Sid had been shocked and impressed when Mark handed him Mrs. Musselman's gift. "With friends willing to invest in you like this, you guys are gonna go far. By the way, you see that great press I got you in the newspaper?"

Mark winced. He sure had. It had cost him his family.

"Two national TV channels picked it up. Once the demo goes out, you'll be in demand by every TV station and media outlet in the country."

His parents would never know about the TV, but if the papers printed more stories . . . "Could we keep it out of the local papers?"

"You're kidding, right?"

"It's just that our parents don't approve." That stopped Mark short. Had Daed told anyone else's parents? None of them had mentioned it.

"They better get used to it, kid. You guys are going to be stars. Big stars."

Sid had been right. Radio stations began playing their songs, and requests flooded in from around the country. Mark still couldn't believe it. They'd be playing in the Lancaster area until mid-January, but after that, Sid had set up a tour in the Southern states, then out West. Mark would be going to states he'd only heard of in school—Texas, New Mexico, California. Who knew where they'd go from there?

Amari and Elise schemed with Joline for ways to see the Amish Rebels. But in the end, Mrs. Vandenberg made it easy by setting up a huge New Year's Eve's party that would last long after midnight. She intended to keep kids off the streets that night. Joline begged her parents to let her attend the whole event so she could watch the star drop in STAR Center lobby.

Daed frowned over her request. "I don't think that's wise. You can enjoy the party in the early evening like the rest of us."

"It will be too hard to get up in the morning," Nettie added.

Joline's teeth clenched at her stepmother's statement. She wanted to snap, *Why am I always stuck watching your children?* But she stopped herself before the words left her lips. If she disrespected Nettie, Joline would lose any chance of going to the event at all.

She swallowed hard to rein in her temper. "But my friends will be there, and they'll be staying the whole time." She didn't mention those friends were Englisch.

Daed gave her a disappointed look. "That's between them and their parents." He'd often lectured her about doing things because everyone else was doing them.

Backtracking quickly, she said, "I just meant I didn't want to leave them alone."

"Sounds like they'll have each other if they all stay."

Why did he have to be so logical? Joline switched to a different tack. "But I've never, ever seen a star—or anything—go down at midnight. It sounds like so much fun."

Daed stroked his beard. Maybe she was making progress.

"I promise to wake up early the next morning to take care of the babies."

"You know, Stephen, Joline works really hard watching the little ones and cooking," Nettie said. "Maybe we should let her do this."

Joline couldn't believe her stepmother was standing up for her. She felt like flinging her arms around Nettie and hugging her.

"You think so?" Daed looked thoughtful.

Nettie smiled at him. "*Jah.* I don't think one late night will hurt."

"You're probably right." He turned to Joline. "All right, but you need to be upstairs here and in bed two minutes after the star drops."

"*Danke, danke, danke,* Daed!" She flashed Nettie a grateful smile. "*Danke,* Mamm!"

Nettie beamed at Joline's use of *Mamm,* but a sharp pain flickered in Daed's eyes. He could tell it wasn't genuine. For years now, he'd been trying to get Joline to call Nettie *Mamm,* but Joline avoided addressing her stepmother most of the time, except when she wanted something. Daed had called it manipulative. From time to time, a genuine and unexpected *Mamm* popped out of Joline's mouth, but those were rare.

Still, right now, Joline was so thrilled about getting permission to stay up until midnight, she felt generous enough to give Nettie a real smile. A smile her stepmother returned tenfold.

Nettie's sincere pleasure sparked guilt in Joline. She should be kinder to her stepmother. Nettie had been unfailingly caring and nice from the first day they'd met. And Joline rarely reciprocated. She did her chores, often grudgingly, but gave no more than the bare minimum when Nettie was watching.

In secret, Joline lavished the babies with love, and she'd grown to love her little stepbrothers and stepsisters. But she tried to hide that from Nettie. Joline wanted Nettie to feel the resentment that still simmered inside Joline's heart because Nettie had come between her and Daed. Tonight, though, Nettie had turned out to be Joline's champion. She'd gotten Daed to say *jah*.

A worm of guilt wriggled through Joline. Neither of them would have agreed if they'd known her real plan.

On New Year's Eve, Joline stayed close to her family until they were ready to take the little ones up to bed. Amari and Elise had arrived an hour before, but they kept their distance until Joline was alone. Then, as they'd plotted earlier, the three of them moved near the door, waiting for a large group to exit.

A big family headed their way. Joline knew their six-year-old daughter and bent to talk to her. Elise and Amari moved in to shield Joline from the security cameras. Keeping her head down, Joline walked beside the little girl as the family ambled outside. She continued with the group to their parking spot down the street before waving goodbye.

"We did it." Elise giggled when the family pulled away. "Now let's get you ready."

Laughing and chattering, they jogged to the apartment building. Half an hour later, three glammed-up girls headed for the teen club.

"Wish you didn't have a curfew," Amari said. "My parents are spending the night at their party. They think I'm sleeping over at Elise's."

"And my mom thinks I'm staying with you, which I am." With a snide smile, Elise confided, "Mom doesn't know Amari's parents are away. Me and Amari do stuff like this all the time. Our parents haven't caught on yet."

That shocked Joline. She couldn't imagine lying to—

Wait a minute. It sounded so awful when Elise and Amari admitted it, but Joline had done the same thing. Her parents thought she was at the center. And she'd used other people to slip out of the building secretly.

She couldn't blame her behavior on friends' influence, because she'd deceived her parents first. Her stomach roiled. If Mrs. V found out, would she tell Daed? She might.

Joline shoved down those thoughts as they crossed the street to the club. The music and anticipation of seeing Mark Troyer again squashed her guilt. She was here now, and she intended to enjoy herself.

She'd worry about getting back into the building later. Like the Englisch fairy tale of Cinderella, Joline had to be back before midnight.

Mrs. Musselman had been ecstatic about Mark's songs playing on the radio and the band's upcoming road trip, but she insisted she'd miss Mark when he left. She enjoyed having his company, and he was grateful for her generosity and friendship.

Being next door to his family, but not able to visit them, had been tearing at Mark's soul. He wanted to say goodbye to his sisters and brothers before he left. He'd have to find a time when Mamm and Daed weren't around.

"Be sure to make a New Year's wish when the ball falls at midnight," Mrs. Musselman told him as he'd headed out the door for his gig. "I'll be here watching it on TV and will make a special wish for you and for my family."

Mark had been taught to pray rather than wish, but since he'd disobeyed his parents, he wasn't sure if God would answer his prayers. That night, though, when he played "Missing

You," he closed his eyes and sang it for his family. Inside, he wished and prayed for a chance to say goodbye.

When he lifted his lids as the last note faded away, that Amish girl was walking through the door. His eyes widened at her beauty. Tonight, she'd put her hair up in a ponytail, and her curls fell over her shoulders. She had something sparkly on her head. A tiara maybe. And her dress glittered, sending off waves of rainbows as she passed under the small recessed lights near the door.

Abel cleared his throat, reminding Mark they had a program to put on. Jerry jumped in to tell a few jokes, while Mark regained his composure. Mark couldn't help wondering what that girl's parents were thinking to let her out so late at night. She looked too young to be going through Rumspringa. Even if she were, what family would allow their daughter this much freedom?

That thought stabbed right through him. If his parents had their way, he'd be home in bed right now. Maybe she was defying her parents the way he'd rebelled against his. For some reason, that thought made him sad. For her and her parents.

"And now," Jerry announced, "if we can get our lead singer back from his daydreaming, we'll sing 'One More Time.' Mark, you ready?"

Mark jerked back to the present, to the stage, and to the program as Jerry tickled the skins and Joel riffed on the bass. Sam strummed the electric guitar, and Mark melded his whole being into the beat, waiting for his cue. When Abel's keys swung into Mark's intro, he avoided looking in the Amish girl's direction. He didn't need to get distracted again. He did his best to avoid looking at her through the next few songs. When he began "Only You," he accidentally glanced her way.

Her whole face alight with pleasure, her eager eyes met his, and Mark lost all sense of time and space. His mouth reacted to the music behind him, and he sang, but he wasn't conscious of the words. Just her eyes drinking in every syllable.

He shut his eyes at the end to break the connection. If he didn't, he'd never be able to concentrate on the next song. He made it through the set and slipped out the back door into the alley to gulp in some fresh air and clear his mind.

When he came back inside, he faced the tables far to her right. But just before their final song, "Will I Ever See You Again?" she and her friends rose and rushed for the door. His lyrics floated out the open door, and she turned, her eyes glimmering with tears as if she thought he was singing it for her.

He wanted to correct her mistake and tell her he'd written it for his family. But as she hurried down the sidewalk after her friends, he wondered if he'd also sung it for her.

Bud had asked them to end with "Auld Lang Syne" after midnight, so Jerry filled in the few minutes before the ball drop with some patter and jokes. Then everyone grew quiet as the large screens around the room reflected New York City, and the crowd counted down.

Why had that girl left early? Where was she doing the countdown?

He shook off his thoughts as the crowd counted down to *one*. People blew noisemakers. Cheers rang out, couples kissed, and Abel started "Auld Lang Syne." Some of the audience joined in.

Mark made his wishes and said several prayers, including one for that girl.

The new year had begun, and for the first time in his life, he had no idea where he'd spend his next New Year's Eve.

Chapter 4

Amari squealed as they raced down the sidewalk. "We cut that too close. But that song, girl? I think he's into you."

Joline wasn't a squealer, but for once, Amari's screech and breathless words echoed Joline's inner feelings. The cracked sidewalk tripped her up. Elise reached out and caught Joline's arm before she fell.

How did Englisch girls manage to get around in these shoes? Her feet ached from being at such an unnatural angle, and she teetered on the spindly spiked heels.

"Take them off," Elise urged, when they reached the apartment lobby.

Relieved, Joline complied. She was most comfortable going barefoot at home, but she wore sneakers in the city to protect her feet from sharp objects. The down-to-earth feeling of her soles against the ground contrasted with the glitziness of her slinky dress. She pulled the glittery tiara from her head.

Earlier tonight, she'd joined her friends' laughter and primping; now it made her ill. She couldn't wait to get out of these clothes. Never had she been so eager to pull her hair back into a bun, to slip on Plain clothes. Sneaking around like this wasn't worth it.

Except for one thing.

As the elevator creaked upward, Joline closed her eyes, and everything disappeared except Mark Troyer's eyes focused on her—and her alone. She sucked in a rapturous breath. And had he directed that last song to her? When would she ever see him again?

At the last chords of the band's final song, the crowd sprang to their feet for a standing ovation. Shouts of "Encore!" rippled through the room, then swelled to a booming demand.

Bud, who'd been planning to keep the club open until one, nodded. Sid, out for a buck, as always, wove through the crowd with his straw hat, collecting donations. Sid had taken to wearing Plain clothes for most of their gigs.

"People respect me more," he insisted.

That grated on Mark. He imagined the bishop's disapproval of an Englischer pretending to be Amish. But who was Mark to judge? He was doing the reverse—acting like he was Englisch.

Mark drew his attention back to the music. People were waiting for more songs.

After the band finished a series of encores and the hat overflowed with bills, Bud brought the impromptu set to an end. Once all the fans had collected their coveted autographs and snapped photos with their favorite band members, Bud ushered the crowds to the door.

"Guess this is the last time I'll see you guys," he said morosely. "Sid tells me you're headed out on the road trip of a lifetime."

Mark wanted to promise to return, but he had no idea when they could. Sid had already booked them well into the following year. Still, they owed Bud so much. He'd given them their start.

"Next time we're in this area," Mark assured him, "we'll definitely play here."

Behind Bud's back, Sid made a cutting motion across his throat and shook his head.

Mark defied him. "Put Bud on the schedule when we're near Lancaster."

Sid grimaced. "You're the boss."

It sure didn't seem like it. Sid had taken over everything. He told them where to go, what time to get up in the mornings, when to practice, and when to rest. He even took all the money and paid all the bills. Other than a small bit of pocket money Sid doled out weekly, they depended on him for every purchase. Whenever resentment reared its ugly head, Mark replaced it with gratitude for all the details Sid handled.

Tonight, as they prepared to leave, Sid was busy smoothing out and counting the money in his hat. "Several hundreds in here," he gloated. "People must be flush with Christmas cash."

At the word *Christmas*, sadness swirled through Mark. Had it only been five days since he'd left his family on Second Christmas? Six, now that they were two hours into the first day of the year.

Nostalgia filled him. Would he ever see any of them again once the tour officially started in mid-January? The final song of the night strummed at his heartstrings. In addition to his family, the girl standing in the doorway haunted him.

Jerry sidled up to him. "That girl really got to you."

Mark shook off the memories. "I was trying to figure out if she's Amish."

His friend raised his eyebrows. "She sure don't look it."

"Not what she was wearing, but her openness and innocence."

Sid strode over. "She's into you, but you can't get involved with these groupies. No distractions. I seen too many bands break up over relationships. Love 'em and leave 'em, I always say."

Indignation surged through Mark. That girl deserved better. Did she go see other music groups? What if one of the band members thought like Sid did? Mark wanted to protect her from something like that. But how could he? With no idea of who she was or where she lived, he couldn't warn her parents, although he'd like to. And what right did he have to criticize her when he wasn't honoring his own parents?

As soon as they reached the apartment, Joline tore off the clothes and washed off the makeup. Once she had her dress and apron adjusted, she breathed a little easier. With rapid movements, she twisted and tucked her hair into a tight bun and fixed her prayer *kapp*. Thrusting her arms into her coat sleeves, she urged her friends to hurry.

Elise laughed as she dusted more glitter on her eyelids. "Relax, Cinderella. We'll get you there before your coach becomes a pumpkin and your ball gown turns into rags."

Amari laughed. "Looks like that already happened."

Joline's lips tightened. Usually, she ignored her friends' mocking comments about her Plain clothes. Tonight, they grated on her. Or maybe her annoyance with herself was spilling out onto them.

"Let's go. We don't have long." Amari opened the door and waved them through.

As each second went by, Joline willed the elevator to go faster.

Her pulse, which had pounded with exhilaration from the music, now banged with fear. If she didn't get back by midnight or they couldn't find a group to sneak in with . . .

When they arrived at the STAR Center, five teens stood

226 / Rachel J. Good

outside watching through the window as songs floated out. Joline wasn't so sure they'd provide the right cover, but Amari marched over to them.

"You going in?" she asked.

One boy looked her up and down. "Why? You want someone to kiss at midnight?"

"We need to sneak our friend inside." Amari waved at Joline, who could have died when all eyes turned to her.

Joline squirmed under their assessing glances.

"Whoa. You a bad girl?" one asked.

Another sneered. "What you gonna give us?"

Elise gulped. "They have food and stuff inside."

A tall, skinny teen snickered. "That ain't what we had in mind."

One of his buddies elbowed him. "Maybe doing a good deed will give us luck in the new year. Plus, it's cold out here."

A few of them made faces, but they formed a circle around Joline. All of them pressed so close, they made her uncomfortable. The clanking chains, tattoos, and strange sweetish smoke brought back memories of being grabbed in the alley by that man with a knife. She swallowed the waves of fright washing over her. Tensing her body, she worried about protecting herself if they tried anything. She'd never have Nettie's skills, but people here would come to her rescue if these guys overpowered her.

With Amari and Elise leading the way, they entered the building in a tight knot. The teens waited until Joline had slipped into the massive crowd gathered to watch the star drop and then raced upstairs for refreshments.

Joline wanted to thank God she'd gotten inside safely, but should she be grateful she'd gotten away with disobedience? Somehow that didn't seem right.

A hush fell over the crowd as the star flickered on. Then the countdown began. Shivering with anticipation, Joline yelled the numbers with the crowd, and the giant sparkling star descended from the third floor overhead into the first floor lobby.

She'd never seen anything this beautiful outside of nature. The star glided lower and lower. *Three! Two! One!*

Happy New Year!

The crowd burst into thunderous applause. Music blasted from above, and people started singing words that sounded nothing like *Englisch*. After a quick wave to her friends who were singing along, Joline snaked swiftly through the press of people. She had to get upstairs.

If she broke her promise, *Daed* and Nettie wouldn't trust her to stay up late again. Even worse, if they ever found out what she'd done tonight, they'd never let her out of their sight.

The next few weeks flew by for Mark, and then the band loaded up Sid's van with their equipment, instruments, and duffel bags. Giddy with excitement, they headed off for their first professional gig.

During the winter months, they played in Southern and Western states. Once spring arrived, they headed for the East Coast. After a while, traveling grew old. All the cheap hotel rooms smelled of sweat and mildew and stale cigarette smoke. The venues blurred together. So did the songs.

The only thing that kept Mark going was writing new songs. The band performed on some local TV shows, then went national. Their songs got radio play time across the country, and newspapers in many locations interviewed them. Sid did a great job of getting advance publicity, and he scheduled the tour to take advantage of the weather. They relied on him for everything as the first year rolled into the second, and then the third. After four years on the road, they were all exhausted.

So Sid scheduled a Thanksgiving Eve gig at Bud's club in Lancaster. Sid hadn't given them their usual weekly pocket money the past two weeks, but he'd promised them a big Christmas bonus and a whole week off after tonight. That lifted everyone's spirits, and they threw themselves into this final performance before their break.

When the concert ended, Mark searched for Sid. He usually slipped out as they played their final numbers to bring the van around for the instruments and equipment. Mark had seen Sid leave, but the van was nowhere in sight. They couldn't call him because he always held on to their phones while they played. They'd all purchased phones with their first earnings so they could plan gigs, but Sid didn't want to chance one accidentally interrupting a song. He stored them in a special bag he kept in the van trunk.

After a half hour of waiting, Bud approached them. "Listen, guys, it's almost two a.m. I really need to get home. I have to get some shut-eye before morning."

"But what about our—" Mark gestured toward the stage.

"Leave your equipment here for now. My place will be closed tomorrow, but you can pick it up the day after Thanksgiving. You don't have any gigs that day, right?"

Jerry nodded. "We have the week off."

Bud herded them to the door and thanked them again. Then he waved and locked up.

They shivered in the frigid weather. They hadn't dressed warmly because they'd only rushed from the van into the venue. Normally, they had a crew of two who handled all the equipment, but Sid had given those guys time off, and both of them had traveled to their homes in Maryland and Virginia for the holidays.

Mark worried the van had broken down or Sid had been in an accident. "We should walk around to see if we can find where he parked." At Mark's insistence, they walked several blocks in every direction.

"Let's just go to the hotel and get warmed up." Jerry stamped his feet in the slush. "My toes are already frozen."

"Yeah," Abel agreed. "Maybe he drove somewhere to get something to drink. That's what he did two years ago in Georgia when we took a few days off."

Jerry blew on his fingers. "But that time he waited until we had everything in the van, and he dropped us at the hotel first."

"Maybe he thought he'd get back before we ended, but he got caught in traffic," Mark suggested.

"If so," Jerry said, "when he sees we're not at Bud's, he'll know to come to the hotel."

They all trudged toward the hotel, but when they headed inside, the desk clerk stopped them before they got in the elevator. "Your manager refused to pay the bill for your rooms for the rest of the week, so we've rented them out. He said you had other accommodations." He gestured to their duffels piled in a corner near the counter.

While they all stood there shell-shocked, trying to make sense of that, the man bustled over to the desk and returned with an envelope. Mark took it from him and opened it.

> "Well, guys, it's been fun, but I have bigger fish to fry. I found the next big star, and I've booked her in Vegas next week. I switched all your venues for next year to her band. Sorry to leave you hanging, but you're in your hometown, so you all have family. And don't bother coming after me for money. You didn't have a contract, so you have no leg to stand on. Good luck, Sid"

"What?" Jerry shrieked. "He took off with all our money?"

In disbelief, Mark reread the note. As it sank in, sickness filled him. Most likely, his bandmates could return home, but he couldn't. Mrs. Musselman had more grandchildren now, and they always stayed with her during Thanksgiving and Christmas weeks. She'd have no room for him.

He had no money, no job, and no place to live. What was he going to do?

Chapter 5

Abel dug in his pockets. "I have $2.17. Maybe if we pool our money, we can get a room for the night. We can't call our Englisch neighbors at three in the morning."

That plan made sense. They each pulled out what they had left. Between them, they had $17.28. Not nearly enough to pay for a room.

The other desk clerk, a sweet-faced Mennonite woman, beckoned Mark over and held out a piece of paper. "Here's the address of the STAR Center. In the building next door, they house people who want to get off the streets. It's free."

"Sounds good," Jerry said. "Let's go."

None of them wanted to venture out into the bitter cold again, but the tiny thread of hope for a warm bed kept them going. When they reached the STAR Center, the neon BE A STAR sign taunted Mark.

"We already are stars," he mumbled. "Or at least we were." Would they ever be stars again?

They filed into the building beside it, which looked like an old warehouse. To their surprise, the inside appeared clean and bright. A hulk of a man with tattooed forearms sat at a desk, dozing. He snapped to attention when they walked in.

"Can I help you?" His eyebrows rose as he took in their Amish clothing. "First time we ever got an Amish gang in here."

"Gang?" Mark was taken aback.

"We usually house young adults trying to get out of gangs."

The band edged backward toward the door. "Maybe we came to the wrong address."

"I was just kidding about you being a gang. Everyone's welcome here."

Still wary, Mark shrugged. "Someone told us we could sleep here tonight, but I think she misdirected us."

"Naw, she didn't. Usually, we have room. Unfortunately, our beds fill up fast this time of year. We don't have any left."

Jerry groaned. "We walked all this way for nothing?"

The guy smiled. "Actually, Mrs. Vandenberg, the owner, must have been expecting you. She had five cots and bedding delivered yesterday. If you don't mind cots, you're welcome to them."

"Right now, a cot sounds *wunderbar*." Sam swayed on his feet.

"Welcome, then. I'm Victor Rivera. Let's get you settled."

They helped Victor set up the cots, then tumbled onto them gratefully. When they woke the next morning, he directed them to the showers and free breakfast.

Mark didn't like taking things for free, so after they'd eaten, he asked if they could do chores to pay for their lodging. Surely a place as large as this could use help cleaning, washing dishes, sweeping, whatever. A kitchen worker suggested they check with one of the offices upstairs. The band trooped up there, and Mark tapped on the office door marked MRS. VANDENBERG.

"Come in, come in," a slightly wavering voice called out.

Mark pushed open the door to find an ancient woman seated

behind an enormous mahogany desk. "Happy Thanksgiving," she chirped.

Thanksgiving? Mark had almost forgotten it was today. For the past four years, Thanksgiving and Christmas had meant a much-needed day off. At the word *Christmas*, old memories flashed through his brain. Mark always avoided thinking of those painful holidays of the past.

She beamed at him. "Well, this should be the start of many happier Thanksgivings and Christmases for you from now on."

Mark fidgeted. She didn't just say *Thanksgiving*, she'd also added *Christmas*, as if she read his mind. Impossible. She knew nothing about him or his life. She'd probably figured out the band was down on their luck, and she hoped to cheer them up.

"I'm so glad you're here," she said to Mark. "I've been waiting for you."

She must have mistaken him for someone else. He shifted uncomfortably. As he struggled to explain who he was and that he wanted to work, she held up a hand.

"First, let's take care of your friends here. I'm sure they'd like to go home and spend Thanksgiving with their relatives."

In short order, she'd arranged for a car to take them all home. Wistfully, he wished them goodbye, happy they could return to make peace with their families, even though he had no hope of reconciling with his parents. Even if he gave up his music, which deep in his heart, Mark knew he couldn't ever do, his *daed* would never forgive him.

Once again, the elderly woman surprised him. "Your family might be ready to forgive and forget too, maybe even sooner than you think."

Mark shook his head. She had no idea how stubborn his *daed* could be, but how had she known what was bothering him?

Mrs. Vandenberg rose from her chair. "I know you want to work, and I have the perfect place for you, but let me introduce you to the CEOs first." She led him a short way down the hall to another office and tapped on the door.

When someone called for them to come in, Mark was astonished. He couldn't believe these people were working on Thanksgiving Day.

"We don't usually work on holidays." Mrs. Vandenberg turned the knob and motioned for Mark to enter first. "But I knew you'd be coming today."

Dumbfounded, Mark stared at her. "How?"

A secretive smile lifted the corners of her lips. "God gives me nudges from time to time."

A man inside the room laughed. "Make that all the time."

As Mark walked through the open doorway, a man and woman sat at side-by-side desks. In an open area nearby, a beautiful Amish girl played with several young children. Mark's heart flipped over. He was pretty sure she was the Amish girl who'd attended their concerts four years ago. She was even more beautiful than he remembered, and he wondered if any of the children were hers.

He barely heard the introductions to Nettie and Stephen Lapp. Although Mark tried not to gawk, his gaze kept straying to the *maedel*. Was it possible?

"We need somebody to teach music to beginners," Stephen said.

At the word *music*, Mark's head snapped back to the man behind the desk.

"What?" He must have misheard.

Mrs. Vandenberg laughed. "Thought that might get your attention."

Her peal of laughter attracted the girl's attention. She turned to stare, then gasped. "You're Mark Troyer, lead singer for the Amish Rebels." She appeared starstruck. "Where's your band? Are they with you?"

Stephen and Nettie, on the other hand, looked horrified. "Joline," Stephen thundered, "how did you know that?"

She hung her head. "I, um . . ."

Mrs. Vandenberg interrupted. "Mark is an answer to prayer. Stephen, why don't you ask what instruments he can play?"

Too preoccupied staring at Joline to answer, Mark tried to form a coherent response to the question he'd soon be asked, but her sparkling eyes mesmerized him. She was the same girl, but now she wore a *kapp* and an Amish dress. He swallowed hard, remembering her hair flowing over her shoulders and her slinky dresses. If he had to choose, he'd say she looked even lovelier now.

Frowning, Stephen studied Mark. "You play instruments?"

Reluctantly, Mark dragged his eyes from Joline. "Piano, electric guitar, and drums."

"He's also the lead singer," Joline added. "He has the best voice." At her father's glare, she shrugged. "Well, he does."

He snapped, "Later, you can explain how you know that."

Nettie's gaze flew back and forth between Joline and Mark. "I don't know, Stephen. Maybe this isn't a good idea."

He shot her a grateful glance. "I think you're right."

Mrs. Vandenberg intervened and turned to Mark. "Would you be willing to teach piano classes?"

"Teach? I'm not sure . . ." He could play, but how would he explain his techniques to others?

"You can do it," Mrs. Vandenberg assured him. "The students will be beginners. Teach them what your piano teacher taught you."

Mark stared at her. It almost sounded as if she knew Mrs. Musselman. He could share his early lessons—doing that would be like sitting on the piano bench next to her when he was small. The idea flooded him with happy memories.

Maybe instructing others could be a tribute to the woman who'd introduced him to music.

He wished he could visit her. Maybe after her family went home, she'd welcome him back, but first he needed to make money. He never wanted to stay at her house again unless he could pay his way. He owed her that.

As if Mrs. Vandenberg had tapped into his thoughts, she said, "Of course, we'll pay you." She named a figure that seemed way more than a piano teacher would ever make.

Mark shook his head. "I'm not worth that. Could I do it in exchange for room and board?"

"Room and board is included. I have a policy of paying people fairly. I find they do much better work when I do that."

"I can't accept pay too." He planned to re-form his band once he could line up some gigs. Most places would be booked until spring, so it might be a while. For now, though, he'd have a roof over his head and work to keep him busy.

Mrs. Vandenberg waved off his protest. "Now, what about your equipment? I could send a crew to pick it up and bring it here. You're welcome to set it up in one of the practice rooms."

"I can't let you do that."

Nettie laughed. "Telling Mrs. V *no* is pointless. She'll do what she thinks is best. The good thing is she always seems to be right."

"I have a better idea." Mrs. Vandenberg beamed. "What if you organize a Christmas concert here? Some of the former gang members used to play in bands. I'm sure I can get you some decent musicians."

"I could sing," Joline burst out. "I know the words to all your songs."

The rapturous look on her face took Mark's breath away. How did she know his songs?

From the expression on her *daed*'s face, he was wondering the same thing. His sharp "*Joline*" cut through her exhilaration.

Deflated, she turned away. "Sorry," she muttered. Shoulders slumped, she hurried over to separate two squabbling toddlers.

"I meant a sing-along with Christmas carols," Mrs. Vandenberg clarified.

Mark pulled his attention back to the chirpy elderly woman who was waiting for an answer. He had no idea how he'd pull together a concert in a few short weeks. "Could I use my band for this performance? They're all in the area." He hoped his friends would agree to play Christmas carols.

"What a marvelous idea! I'm sure that would draw a large audience—exactly the kind of kids we'd like to bring in to the center."

"I'm also happy to work with some of your residents to get them ready for a future show."

Mrs. Vandenberg's eyes twinkled. "What about for New Year's Eve? Maybe we could have the amateurs as the opening acts before your band."

When Mark nodded, she turned toward Joline's scowling father. "Isn't this wonderful, Stephen?"

"I don't think—"

Mrs. Vandenberg cut him off. "Exactly. Don't think, just pray." With that, she turned and exited. "Come along, Mark, let's get everything set up."

With one last curious glance in Joline's direction, Mark followed. Joline hadn't turned around since her *daed*'s rebuke, and Mark missed her eager eyes on him.

He'd followed Sid's advice and brushed off all the groupies. It hadn't been hard, because every time he looked at the women and girls flocking around him, all he could see was that Amish girl's innocent, but thrilled, eyes, and her hair flowing down around her shoulders in soft curls.

Now, she was right here in front of him, but judging from her dress, she shouldn't have anything to do with a wayward rebel like him. But from her expression, she just might be interested.

The only problem was her *daed*. Mark needed this job until he could get the band back together. He couldn't take a chance of getting fired. No matter how tempting Joline was, he intended to keep his distance.

Chapter 6

Joline couldn't believe her luck. She'd had a crush on Mark Troyer since the first night she'd first seen him play. Elise and Amari had kept her updated on all his new hits, and she'd listened to his songs whenever she could sneak into the computer room. Joline couldn't wait to let her friends know Mark was staying here at the center.

She hadn't told anyone, not even her best friends, she'd been taking singing lessons along with piano lessons. After the music teacher had discovered Joline's passion for Amish Rebels' music, Letitia had encouraged Joline to harmonize with their songs. Eyes closed, Joline imagined herself on stage with Mark. Whenever she did that, she sang her heart out.

Her parents would have forbidden music lessons had they known, but Joline excused her disobedience because, even though she'd turned nineteen, she planned to enjoy that freedom of Rumspringa for a while longer. Daed and Nettie kept pressuring her to take baptismal classes, and she'd agreed to start this spring. Now, she was glad she hadn't talked to the bishop and made that commitment yet. Although her dream might never come true, she longed to convince Mark to let her sing with his band.

Joline had avoided telling her parents she'd sneaked out to see the Amish Rebels twice, four years ago. Because her guilty conscience and fear of getting caught had kept her from going to more concerts, she'd ignored Mrs. V's instructions to confess. That meant her parents never knew she'd attended Mark's concerts.

She gulped. *Until now.* She'd given away her secret by fangirling over Mark.

His face frozen in stern lines, Daed sat, arms crossed, waiting for an explanation.

Why hadn't she controlled her excitement? She could have looked for Mark later, spent time with him without alarming her parents. He seemed as interested in her as she was in him. After Daed discovered what she'd done, though, he'd probably forbid her to hang around Mark. All her joy and excitement over seeing the Amish Rebels in person fizzled.

She kept her back turned as she bent to pick up the baby. Maybe if she busied herself with a diaper change, she could avoid a confrontation with her parents.

"Joline, come here!"

At Daed's barked command, her stomach plummeted. No matter how upset Daed got with her, he'd never spoken to her in such a harsh tone before. She was afraid to turn around. Afraid of what her punishment would be. Afraid she'd be forbidden to spend time with Mark.

"*Jah?*" she said meekly. "Should I change Irene's diaper first?"

"Katie can do it." As usual, Nettie supported Daed. "Katie, please drop everyone at their activities. Then you can take the little ones for their morning walk."

"Sure, Mamm."

Sweet as pie, Katie pointed up Joline's rebellious spirit without saying a word. Joline gritted her teeth. Living with a saintly stepsister only made Joline's actions appear more sinful. Ever since grade school, when Joline had let a pig out to scare Katie, her stepsister had gone out of her way to make Joline look bad. Not that it was hard to do. Joline was honest enough to admit that to herself, even if she tried to pretend otherwise around others.

Joline helped dress the babies in snowsuits. "I could take everyone to their activities." Perhaps that would give Daed a little time to calm down.

"Absolutely not. You stay here." Daed didn't sound like he'd soften in the least.

Katie shot Joline a sickeningly honeyed smile, but her eyes gloated.

After Katie pushed the stroller out the door and herded the young ones in front of her, Mrs. Vandenberg poked her head in. "Stephen, I forgot to remind you that God sometimes works in mysterious ways—ways we may fear or judge as wrong— but if you trust Him, He'll bring about beautiful results in the end. Be sure to pray long and hard about your decisions."

At her words, Daed's clenched jaw relaxed a little. "Thanks for the advice."

Joline flashed Mrs. V a relieved and thankful smile.

But Mrs. V wasn't done. "Time to come clean, Joline, like I told you years ago."

Heat crept into Joline's face. Mrs. V hadn't forgotten. Joline couldn't meet the older woman's eyes. Instead, she turned around and picked up a few toys scattered on the floor.

"That's enough," Daed said the minute Mrs. Vandenberg exited. "We want answers. And we want them now."

Her insides quavering, Joline slow-walked to their desks for a scolding and her punishment. Head bowed, she stood in front of Daed and Nettie. Daed waved for her to sit down. He must be planning a lengthy lecture.

"Explain." That one simple word sliced through Joline like a lash.

"Well," she mumbled, struggling for words, "um, what did you want me to explain?" She didn't want to tell any more than she had to.

"Start at the beginning. How did you meet this Mark? And how do you know anything about his music?" Daed had other questions in his eyes, but he pursed his lips into a thin line as if reining in his anger.

Joline prayed he wouldn't ask those other questions. "My, um, friends saw a poster for the Amish Rebels . . ."

Dad's mouth tightened even more when she mentioned the band name. "First of all, what friends are we talking about?"

Kneading her hands in her lap, Joline answered reluctantly. "Elise and Amari."

With a loud sigh, he turned to Nettie. "I was concerned about her hanging around with those Englischers, and you said I shouldn't worry."

Nettie gave him a sympathetic smile. "It shouldn't be a problem if the heart is in the right place."

"But temptation—" Daed sounded anguished.

"I trusted Joline to act wisely in the face of temptation."

Nettie didn't add, *Obviously, I was wrong*, but Joline was positive her stepmother was thinking it.

"I'm sorry," Joline began.

Daed put her on the spot. "For what?"

Hanging her head so she didn't have to meet his eyes, Joline mumbled, "One night, I went to see the band."

"Where?"

She'd hoped he wouldn't ask. "At a teen club."

Nettie frowned. "Don't those open later in the evening?"

"*Jah.*"

"What does that mean?" Daed glanced from Joline to Nettie.

"It means Joline must have sneaked out after we went to bed."

"What?" He turned to face Joline. "Is that true?"

Her *jah* was barely audible.

"You went downtown after we went to sleep?" Daed looked incredulous. "I can't believe this." He lowered his head into his hands. "This is all my fault. I gave you too much freedom when you were younger. And I allowed too much rebellious behavior."

Joline bit her lip. She should confess about New Year's Eve too, but Daed seemed overwhelmed.

Nettie moved the conversation in a different direction. "I doubt you'd have learned the words to all his songs from attending one performance."

Daed sucked in a breath. "How—?"

Would this grilling never end? With each revelation, Joline's shame grew. "I had a playlist." Before they could ask, she added, "From Elise and Amari."

"They encouraged you in this disobedience?"

Joline couldn't let her friends take the blame for her bad behavior. "It's not their fault. I'm the one who wanted to see the band. They didn't know I shouldn't listen to music."

"But how did you play the music? Do you have a hidden phone or something?" Nettie persisted.

Leave it to Nettie to home in on the practical. Joline wished her stepmother hadn't grown up non-Amish. She understood what a playlist was. Daed would have no idea, so Joline might have skated by.

When Joline didn't answer right away, Nettie persisted. "Joline?"

With a heavy sigh, Joline admitted, "I listened to it on the computers downstairs."

Daed shook his head. "I can't believe this. I thought you were getting ready to take baptismal classes this spring." He

sounded old and defeated, though he was only in his early for-
ties.

"I—I was." She didn't want to say she'd been thinking about
waiting again. With classes held every other year, she'd have
two years before the next ones began. Rumspringa would provide an excuse for following her dreams. Maybe in those two
years, she and Mark . . .

Her father interrupted her musing. "Nettie and I need to
talk over the consequences of your behavior, and we'll both
pray about it. For now, you're forbidden to use the computers.
And I'm sure you know to stay away from Mark's music
lessons."

Joline breathed out a small sigh of relief. Daed hadn't said
she had to stay away from Mark or his studio. Just his lessons.
Her conscience warned her Daed had intended to include all of
that, but she twisted his words to mean she could talk to Mark
anytime except during his lessons.

Before she could dash off after Mark, Daed stopped her.
"Until we decide what we're going to do, you must stay upstairs here in our apartment at all times. I don't want you going
anywhere."

She'd be grounded indefinitely? They had a huge apart-
ment/office complex here on the top floor of the STAR Center,
with plenty of games, books, art supplies, and chores to keep
her busy. She filed paperwork for STAR and cared for her
youngest siblings, but losing her freedom and missing classes
irritated Joline.

Though she longed to protest, she couldn't take that chance.
Whenever she'd complained about restrictions in the past,
Daed had added to the punishment. Better to stay quiet and
wait.

She was dying to tell Elise and Amari, but Joline couldn't
even email. If only she had a phone, she could call them and
break the news. She couldn't wait to hear their squeals of de-

light. They'd be over here like a shot, haunting the halls for a glimpse of Mark. And they could take Joline's messages to him. But no phone and no computer access meant no way to communicate with Mark or her friends.

Until she learned what Daed planned for her, Joline vowed not to grumble about her confinement, hoping her father would go easier on her. Who knew how long these restrictions would last or what other consequences Daed might add if she griped.

How could she bear knowing Mark was only one floor below her, but she wasn't able to see or hear him? Or get to know him. Or ask him about the desire burning in her heart.

Mark called Sam's Englisch neighbor and left a message about reuniting the band for a Christmas concert. Now that none of them had their phones, getting in contact would be a challenge. After using modern conveniences, they'd all find it difficult to go back to the Amish way of life.

To his surprise, Mark enjoyed teaching the children who came for lessons. Although he planned to get the band back together, he wondered if he might find it hard to leave when the time came. These kids had so little to look forward to except a life of poverty. If he could add brightness to their rough days or teach them a skill to earn money, he could start them on a path to a brighter future.

In his spare time, Mark called all the clubs and hotels nearby to set up gigs. None had openings until late spring. He took whatever dates the venues offered in May and June, but the money the band made from those scattered concerts wouldn't be enough to go on tour. They'd also need a van, which they couldn't afford.

Mark could try to book places farther away, but after a few days, his music students had already wormed their way into his heart. If he went out of state, he'd miss their lessons. He didn't want to let these kids down.

He also enjoyed jam sessions with various ex-gang members who were training for careers at the center. When people in the area discovered a member of the Amish Rebels was teaching there, the crowds of afterschool kids increased tremendously. Many of them just wanted to be around a celebrity, but Mark encouraged them to stay and take classes. He was glad he could help promote the center and repay Mrs. Vandenberg for giving him room and board when he'd been so desperate.

She seemed to take a special interest in him, stopping by to chat and make sure he was happy. One of those times, he mentioned Sid's betrayal, and she questioned Mark about it.

"I didn't sign a contract," he explained, "but even if I had, I wouldn't know where to find our ex-manager. Besides, I'd never sue him. We lost everything we earned, but I learned a painful lesson."

"What lesson was that?" Mrs. Vandenberg studied him, her eyes bright with curiosity.

Mark discarded his first thought: *Never trust anyone.* He scrambled to come up with a better answer. "To take care of everything myself."

"Hmm. Is that the best choice? Sounds like you learned not to trust others."

How did she do that? He hadn't mentioned not trusting people.

Before he could answer, her eyes bored into him, and she snapped out another question. "How can you get married if you don't trust?"

Married?! What put that in her head? That was the farthest thing from his mind. Or was it? For some odd reason, Joline popped into his thoughts.

Mrs. Vandenberg smiled and nodded as if she could tell. "You might be surprised what your future holds."

Mark wouldn't mind a bit if it meant time with Joline, but he could never marry her. Not when he never intended to join the church. Despite that, he threw in one other comment he thought Mrs. Vandenberg would like, even if he didn't quite believe it himself anymore. "This thing with Sid happened for a reason, so we just have to trust God knows best."

"Of course," she said. "Once *you* believe that too, you'll find He's been leading you every step of the way."

Mark squirmed. How did she know he didn't believe it?

She turned, and her cane clicked across the floor as she headed for the door.

He couldn't let her go without expressing his gratitude. "Thank you for this job," he said for the millionth time since he'd arrived.

"I'm the one who should thank you," she insisted. "You're bringing in so many teens who've avoided coming in here. I'm grateful for that. And God has a wonderful plan for your life. It makes me happy to play a small part in your future. I'll be playing a much bigger part later on."

Mark stared after her as she disappeared down the hall. What in the world did she mean by that?

Chapter 7

Joline fumed inwardly as she waited for her punishment. Her parents took three whole days before they decided what to do. They consulted Mrs. Vandenberg and spent a lot of time in prayer. Then they waited until all the children had gone to school and Katie had taken the little ones out for their daily walk.

Joline watched her stepsister with envy. She'd give anything to switch places with Katie. Instead, she followed Nettie into the living room of their apartment.

The large room had enough seating space to accommodate all fourteen children, two parents, and several guests. Since Daed and Nettie's marriage, they'd added five more children to the family.

Daed had chosen a cozy corner and pulled two chairs close to his. Nettie took the chair beside him, so she and Daed formed a unit. The two of them faced Joline, making her feel isolated, alone, and condemned.

Nettie began the conversation. "After much prayer, we've decided it's time for you to take responsibility for your life."

Daed examined Joline with a searching gaze. "We can't follow you around to make sure you're obeying rules and doing what God wants you to do. Since you'll be joining the church this spring, that decision must come from your heart."

Like they were part of a tag team, Nettie picked up where Daed left off. "I, um, took baptismal classes for the wrong reason." She stared down at her hands clasped in her lap. "I did it to marry someone I had my eye on. We're praying you'll only join when your heart is right with the Lord."

Joline scrunched her brows together. She understood what they were saying, but they still hadn't mentioned her punishment. That's all she cared about at the moment. How long would she have to wait to see Mark again?

"Mrs. Vandenberg thinks we shouldn't interfere with God's plans for your life. She said you'll face your lessons and consequences soon enough."

"We both"—Nettie waved a hand to encompass her and Daed—"disagreed with Mrs. V's advice, but after praying about it, God led us in that direction."

Would they ever get to the point? Joline didn't care how they arrived at their decision. She just wanted to know what her punishment would be. All this buildup must be leading to some major restrictions.

"We've been trying to direct your steps, but if obedience to God's laws doesn't come from your heart, it's not genuine. So, we've decided to give you your freedom."

Joline couldn't have heard Daed right. "What does that mean?"

Nettie's eyes softened. "We expect you to pray and follow God's leading, but we're going to trust you completely. You are free to choose what to do and how to act. And only you can decide when you're ready to join the church."

There had to be a catch. They couldn't possibly mean she was free to do whatever she wanted.

Daed's face turned grave. "We hope you won't take this as a license to sin. We're praying you won't do anything to bring dishonor to God. Or to the STAR Center. Or to our family. Or to yourself."

"The only condition we're giving you is to pray about everything before you do it." Nettie glanced off into the distance. "I wish I'd done that when I was your age. I might have saved myself years of pain."

Daed reached for her hand. "But you got through it, and He's blessed you since then."

"He certainly has. He's given me much more than I deserve after what I did." Nettie gave Daed a tender smile, then she focused on Joline. "I pray you won't have to learn your lessons the hard way like I did."

But Joline had already tuned her stepmother out. A glorious future stretched out ahead. Getting to know Mark. Joining his band. Becoming a star. She could hardly wait.

Mark hadn't seen Joline for days. He'd wondered if her parents had forbidden her to hang around him. Then suddenly, she started following him everywhere. He'd open the door after a piano lesson, and she'd be standing outside. Ditto when he and the ex-gang members finished a jam session or the rare times his Amish Rebel bandmates got together to practice carols for the Christmas concert.

Her eagerness to listen to music reminded Mark of how he used to hide outside the Musselmans' house to hear their band. Joline had that same hungry look in her eyes. His heart ached for her. He remembered how crushing the Amish prohibitions against instrumental music had been to his spirit. He'd been like a bird with his wings clipped, fluttering helplessly to escape a cage.

After the fifteenth time—not that he was counting—she'd scurried away after he'd opened the door, he debated about

talking to her. As he stood there, staring after her, Mrs. Vandenberg came up behind him and set a hand on his shoulder.

Mark jumped. He hadn't heard her approaching. He'd been
so lost in thought he'd missed the click of her cane on the
linoleum.

"She is a lot like you, isn't she?"

Mrs. Vandenberg's observation matched what Mark had been
mulling over. By now, he'd become accustomed to her reading
his mind.

He nodded. Joline definitely had the same love for music.

With a teasing note in her voice, Mrs. Vandenberg said, "I've
noticed her following you around like a lovesick puppy."

A lovesick puppy? Was she implying Joline had a crush on
him? He'd had that sense the few times their eyes met, but
with the way she'd been running away, Mark assumed she'd
been avoiding him because she was more interested in music
than in him.

He needed to set Mrs. Vandenberg straight. "I think Joline's
starved for music the way I was when I went to the Musselmans' house." He'd already confided his whole history to
Mrs. Vandenberg, so she'd know what he meant.

"I believe you're right. However, I suspect she's interested
in more than your music."

Heat crept up Mark's neck and splashed onto his cheeks.
He'd never talked to anyone about his inner feelings about
girls. It certainly didn't seem appropriate to discuss something
so private with an elderly woman, especially one who owned
the business and who'd hired him.

Mrs. Vandenberg laughed. "I've had plenty of experience
with young love. I had a fairy-tale love story of my own, and
I've matched many couples. God has given me quite a few
nudges about bringing couples together."

Startled, Mark stared at her.

"If you don't believe me, check out the quilt hanging in the lobby. I brought together every one of the couples on those one hundred squares."

Mark had seen the impressive quilt and wondered about the embroidered names and dates.

"God chose to pair those couples. I just followed his guidance to prod them along."

"I see." Mark wasn't sure where this conversation was going. Unless . . .

Visions of his name and Joline's added to the quilt supplanted the image of Joline's awestruck eyes gazing into his.

"I've come to talk to you about Joline, but don't get ahead of yourself," Mrs. Vandenberg warned. "Now is *not* the time for a relationship."

Could his face burn any hotter? Mark jerked his imagination away from the quilt and Joline's sweet face, hoping Mrs. Vandenberg couldn't read all his thoughts. Besides, Joline looked so demure in her Plain clothes. Most likely, she'd joined the church, a commitment he wouldn't make because he'd have to give up his music.

"Mark?" Mrs. Vandenberg drew him back from his musing. "I'm concerned about Joline."

That snapped him to attention. "Why?" He hoped she didn't have an incurable disease or . . .

Mrs. Vandenberg sighed. "Joline has a wonderful life ahead of her as a wife and mother, but . . ."

His spirits nosedived. She was married. He should have guessed.

"Oh, my." Mrs. Vandenberg studied his slumped shoulders and disappointed expression. "I didn't mean to mislead you. Joline hasn't joined the church yet."

Mark's heart leapt at the possibilities. Maybe they could be together after all.

Mrs. Vandenberg gave him a sharp glance. "Joline's promised to start baptismal classes in the spring, but I'm concerned about her behavior from now until then. She's taken quite a shine to you, so I hope you'll influence her to stay on the straight and narrow."

A bitter laugh escaped Mark's lips before he could stop it. "Me? My *daed* kicked me out of the house because I—

"Exactly." Mrs. Vandenberg beamed at him. "You know how painful that can be. I'm sure you wouldn't want Joline to lose her family or end up getting in trouble."

Neh, he'd never want her to face the seediness he'd endured in so many cities, the pressure to perform even when he was sick or down, the loneliness of holidays without family . . .

Mrs. Vandenberg's chirpy voice interrupted Mark's dark memories. "I knew you'd understand."

He nodded. "I'd never want someone as innocent as Joline to go through troubles or heartbreak."

Then, Mrs. Vandenberg shocked him. "You might be surprised to hear she has a rebellious spirit like yours. I figured you'd know how to deal with that. And, even more importantly, you know the principles and morals she should live by from the Bible and Ordnung."

Mark gulped. *Jah*, he did, even if he hadn't been following all of them himself. He couldn't meet Mrs. Vandenberg's eyes. "I'm not a good example of that."

"Sometimes people who've broken the rules are the best teachers because they've experienced the consequences."

She waited a moment to let that sink in before changing the subject. "What would you think of advertising more drumming and electric guitar lessons? I bet we could draw in younger gang members, hangers-on, and street kids if you're willing to accept additional responsibility."

Mark jumped at the chance to fill his lonely hours. "Of course."

"Wonderful. I'll also put posters around town for the Christmas Eve and Christmas Day dinners. With the free meals plus your concerts, I'm expecting a large crowd. I can't thank you enough for all you've done to attract teens who were hesitant to come inside."

"I'm glad I could help. I can never repay you for everything you've done for me."

"You don't owe me anything. If you want to repay anyone, repay God."

Repay God? How could he possibly do that?

Only one idea came to mind: surrendering his heart and soul to the Lord. But Mark wasn't ready to do that, and he wasn't sure he'd ever be.

Her heart pounding, Joline ducked behind a column when Mark's band exited from their practice room. Mark had almost caught her listening in several times. She tried to stride away nonchalantly as if she'd only been passing the room on her way to a new destination. She hoped she'd fooled him.

Every time she'd come this way, she'd never been brave enough to approach him and ask the question burning inside her. Time and time again, her nerve failed her. People who knew her as bold and rebellious would never believe she'd be too scared to ask anyone anything. But this was the first time she'd ever been attracted to a man, let alone a man who had the power to make her dreams come true.

Frowning, Mark's bandmate Jerry exited the room but turned in the doorway. "I don't believe you guys. How can you give up what we worked so hard for?"

Joel followed him out. "Life on the road is rough. My family's glad to have me home, and I plan to join the church."

Jerry's loud sigh carried down the hall to Joline. "So, you're breaking up the band? What about the rest of us?"

"He's not the only one." Abel squeezed past Jerry. "I'll do this Christmas Eve gig, but after that I'm done."

"You can't quit until after New Year's Eve," Jerry insisted.

"Sorry, but I promised my parents I'd give up my music as a Christmas gift to them and, most importantly, for God."

"Where are we going to find a backup singer who can play keyboard?" Jerry practically screeched.

Joline's thumping pulse galloped faster. She could sing and play keyboard. Was it possible? Knowing this might give her the courage she needed to approach Mark.

With a regretful apology, Abel hurried away. He seemed eager to avoid his bandmates' pressure. Sam and Mark headed into the hallway, talking in low murmurs.

Jerry stopped them. "What'll we do? Abel's quitting before New Year's Eve, and Joel's not staying with the band after that."

Sam shrugged. "Maybe it's for the best. Time we all grew up."

"You're not gonna let us down too?" Jerry turned to Sam with a stricken expression.

"I'll do Christmas Eve and New Year's Eve, but I'm not going back on the road."

Mark tapped his chin with a knuckle. "I booked some gigs in May and June. I'll have to cancel if we lose all three of you."

"Rumspringa shouldn't last forever," Sam said solemnly. "It's time we all started baptismal classes."

Jerry brushed that off. "I'm not ready yet."

Joline peeked around the column to study Mark's face. He shifted from foot to foot uncomfortably. Was he feeling guilty about not joining the church? She hoped he wouldn't give up the band before she had a chance to sing with them.

Mark gazed in her direction. She ducked back. Had he seen her? If so, he'd think she was a fool. She doubted he'd want anything to do with her if he realized she'd been spying and eavesdropping.

Jerry stayed for a while, slouching against the doorjamb and moaning about the group breaking up. Joline wished he'd head home so she could talk to Mark before he found someone else to take Abel's place.

Finally, Jerry took off. When Mark returned to the room, Joline hurried after him. No way could she pass up this opportunity.

As Mark walked into the practice room, he was torn about the future. Although he wanted to keep the band together, he was reluctant to take time away from his young, eager students. He didn't want to let them down. And if he were honest, he'd miss being with them and seeing them progress. Now he understood what Mrs. Musselman meant when she said it gave her joy to see her pupils succeed.

It seemed his friends had made his decision easier. Losing three of them meant he'd have to cancel the gigs he'd booked. He also needed to find a singer and keyboard player for New Year's Eve.

"Mark, wait," someone said behind him.

He recognized her voice instantly. Joline.

"I want to ask you something."

Her soft words strummed a place in his heart that, until now, had remained untouched. The exquisite music stirred unfulfilled longings and desires.

He turned to face her. She lifted long lashes to look up at him, and his breath caught in his throat. He drowned in her beautiful, pleading eyes. For several long, delicious moments, they gazed into each other's eyes and souls.

Whatever she asked, his answer could only be *jah*.

"I—I, um, overheard Abel saying he wouldn't be playing with the band at New Year's."

Mark had caught glimpses of her hiding behind the pillar listening as he and his friends talked. Still stunned by her beauty, he managed to nod.

Her words came out in such a rush, they squished into each

other. "Could I take Abel's place? I can play keyboard and sing. Plus, I know all your songs."

She stared at him expectantly.

What? Mark couldn't process her request. It made no sense.

Joline clasped her hands together by her heart. The longing on her face almost did him in.

Mark had to be honest with her. Many fans knew all his songs, but that didn't mean they could sing well or perform in public. Some even played keyboard, but that didn't mean they could keep up with the band's tempo and rhythm. But how could he say *neh* to those imploring eyes?

He had to find a way to explain that performing was an art. Instead, he did the same thing Mrs. Musselman had done—invited her to watch the band practice.

Joline's face shone as if lit from within. A breathless *ach* filled with wonder escaped her bow-shaped lips. "*Danke, danke, danke.*"

Her eager response made Mark glad he'd extended the invitation. With his bandmates there to help him make a solid decision, he could let her down gently. He'd let everyone else in the band vote first. Then he wouldn't need to weigh in at all. And he wouldn't be the one who rejected her.

Chapter 8

Joline couldn't believe Mark had invited her to band practice. She probably sounded like a fool by thanking him so many times, but those *dankes* barely expressed all the joy in her heart. Even if he said *neh* to her joining the band, she'd have the experience of a lifetime.

Her enthusiasm bubbled over. "I'll see you tomorrow at four."

His eyebrows rose. He must think she was a creeper. First, she spied on the band from behind the column. Now she knew his practice schedule. He'd be shocked if he found out she stood outside most of his practices and lessons, listening through the door. And how would he feel if he knew he'd starred in all her romantic daydreams from the first night she'd attended his concert?

Up and down the hall, instructors opened their doors, and students streamed out. *Ach!* Katie would come to collect the little ones from their classes. Joline had to leave before her stepsister saw her, but she was reluctant to break eye contact.

Mark blinked first. "I have a keyboard student coming."

Joline ached as if she'd been cut adrift on a lonely sea. She stared after him until he disappeared from view.

A young boy bounced past her and into the room. The door banged closed with a loud, final click, shutting her off from Mark. Still, Joline didn't move until Katie called to her.

"Instead of just standing there, why don't you help me get everyone? Or you could go up and start dinner."

The reminder of daily chores shattered Joline's fantasies. She moved away from Mark's door, hoping Katie didn't realize who'd absorbed all her attention, because her stepsister would be sure to report it to her *mamm*.

Despite Daed and Nettie granting Joline her freedom, they kept a constant eye on her. She feared if they suspected her plans to join the Amish Rebels, they might step in and revoke their hands-off policy.

Mark still couldn't believe he'd invited that distracting beauty to listen to their practice. When his friends arrived ten minutes before the start of practice the next day, he explained about a visitor coming to listen.

"What?" Jerry's voice rose in disbelief. "Since when do you invite anyone to watch us?"

Abel looked relieved. "Have you found someone to take my place?"

"I doubt it, although our guest did claim to play keyboard and sing."

"Claim to?" Joel asked.

"*Jah*, supposedly this singer knows all our songs."

Joel groaned. "*Ach*, one of those fans who think they're ready to be stars? Why didn't you say *neh*?"

"I couldn't. I'm counting on all of you to vote against—"

"Mark?"

The lilting question stopped his bandmates in their tracks. Everyone turned to stare at Joline.

"This is the guest?" Jerry's gaze zigzagged from Joline to Mark and then to the other bandmates, who were all gaping at her.

Joel elbowed Mark as he walked past. "I can see why you couldn't say *neh*," he whispered.

Mark struggled to regain his composure, but she'd thrown him so off balance, he wasn't sure he'd succeed. "Come in, Joline. Meet the band." One by one, he managed to introduce them without stumbling too much.

She stood there, starry-eyed. He waved her to a chair he'd set in the corner of the room, and she walked toward it in a daze. She reminded him of himself the day Mrs. Musselman encouraged him to listen to her sons' band, so he extended the same opportunity his mentor had.

"Feel free to sing along." His invitation earned him glares from all his bandmates.

Joline shrank back the same way Mark had when the Musselman boys frowned at him. As intimidated as she looked, Joline probably wouldn't sing very loud. Maybe the instruments would drown out any off-key squawking. At least he hoped they would. If she messed up their practice, he'd take a lot of ribbing.

As they started the first song, she proved him right. She only mouthed the words, and the guys relaxed. The tension eased, and his friends grew more animated. Mark didn't. He froze up and missed his cues.

Jerry crashed to a stop. "If you can't keep your mind on the music, Mark, maybe we should go."

Mark forced himself to concentrate. "Let's start again from the top."

This time a faint, melodious harmony drifted over Mark's

words. Everyone kept playing, but they all stared at Joline. She'd squeezed her eyes shut, so she had no idea she'd become the center of attention. Her voice soared to a crescendo as the song ended.

"Whoa!" Jerry stilled his tinkling cymbals. "Bring that girl up here and hand her a mike."

Joline's eyes popped open. "I—I don't think . . ."

Her protest trailed off when Abel beckoned to her and held out his mike.

"Me?" she squeaked.

He nodded. "Let's do a softer one. You know 'Missing You'?"

Joline's eyes brimmed with tears. "*Jah.*"

"Come on then," Abel encouraged.

She sought Mark's approval. When he bobbed his head up and down once, she hopped up from her seat and hurried toward Abel.

Glad Joline was behind him onstage, Mark focused on her empty chair to keep from turning to watch her. As the instrumentals began, he swayed slightly to the beat and steeled himself.

Joline stuttered through the first few bars, but once she got into the song, her notes blended perfectly with his. She grew softer when he did and increased her volume when he emphasized phrases. Even Abel, after all their years of practicing together, had never anticipated his every move like that.

When the song ended, Abel fixed an awed gaze on Joline. "We've found my replacement."

Everyone else applauded. Everyone but Mark. He couldn't move. He barely heard his bandmates congratulating her. Chills had gone up his spine at the magnificence of Joline's melody and their perfect unity.

* * *

Joline couldn't believe it. The guys in the band crowded around her, complimenting her singing, insisting she'd be the perfect addition to the band. They welcomed her as one of them. All except Mark. And his was the only opinion that counted.

Maybe he didn't like her singing. Or had she annoyed him by adding those final trills? It had changed the ending a little and drew more attention to her rather than him. He might not appreciate being upstaged like that.

She stole a quick glance in his direction. His furrowed brow, his distracted air didn't bode well. This was his band, after all, and he'd have the final say.

"Mark?"

Jerry's sharp voice seemed to pierce through Mark's musing, and he snapped to attention, turned in their direction, and stared at Joline as if she were a stranger.

She shivered. He was acting as if he'd never seen her before. That couldn't be a good sign.

"So . . . what do you think?" Jerry asked Mark.

He blinked several times. "I don't know what to say."

"Say *you're in*," Abel coaxed. "I won't feel as bad leaving you if you have a replacement like this." He motioned toward Joline.

Mark nodded, but his frown deepened. "Did you say you play keyboard?" He avoided looking in her direction.

She swallowed because he didn't look overjoyed at the prospect. "I've been taking lessons."

His long-suffering sigh told her he didn't really want to hear her play, but the other guys crowded around the keyboard. Abel stood and indicated she should sit.

Reluctantly, she sank onto the bench. What if Mark hated her playing as much as he disliked her singing? She couldn't bear his rejection. She didn't care if she ever got to play in the band if he'd just smile at her again.

"Go on," Jerry commanded, "play something."

Joline sat and ran her fingers over the keys. Should she play one of their songs? Or would that upset Mark more?

"Do you know any of our other songs?" Abel asked.

"*Jah*," she whispered, unwilling to disturb Mark.

"Show us."

At Jerry's order, she stiffened her back and willed her fingers to remember the notes. Usually, music flooded through her and flowed into her fingers. She found the notes automatically. Today, anxiety interrupted that smoothness. Her opening notes came out choppy.

"Relax," Abel said. "Maybe we should stop crowding her. Let's give her a little space."

Everyone moved toward their instruments. Only Mark stood nearby, clutching his suspenders as if he wanted to wring someone's neck. Most likely hers.

She'd never be able to play if she concentrated on him. She blocked out everything except the familiar white and black pattern of the keys. This time her fingers moved of their own accord. The first notes of "Will I Ever See You Again?" tripped out softly, but gradually Joline's confidence grew. As it did, Jerry tapped the rhythm softly on the drums. Then Joel strummed a few chords. Soon, they upped their volume to the usual levels, following Joline's lead.

"You're good," Abel said as she finished. He turned toward Mark. "I'll work with her on the timing, but I think she can pick it up quickly."

When Mark didn't respond, Abel elbowed him. "What do you think?"

"I agree." His words came out strangled.

Jerry's sticks crashed down. "That sounded real enthusiastic. What's the matter with you, man?"

Joline's heart sank. She'd already guessed the problem. Mark

264 / Rachel J. Good

didn't want her in the band, but no way could he tell her *neh*, not with his bandmates' enthusiasm.

Mark swallowed several times to clear the lump in his throat and held on to his suspenders for dear life. If he let go, he'd sweep Joline into his arms and kiss her. He'd never felt this depth of connectedness with another person, let alone a woman. He had no idea how to handle the waves of longing washing over him.

He had to do something, say something. His friends pinned him with searching looks, trying to figure out what was wrong with him. Joline had blindsided him in more ways than just her music, but he couldn't let anyone know.

He growled, "Let's run through a few of our New Year's songs. Abel, you help her." He hadn't meant to sound so demeaning by saying *her*, but Mark couldn't bring himself to say her beautiful name. He worried it would come out as lyrical as a love poem and give away his feelings.

Jerry clanged his cymbals. "You ready?" he snarked. "Or do you plan to glare at that chair for the rest of our practice?"

With an effort, Mark smoothed his face and even managed a half smile. "Let's do the first four tunes. We'll stop in between for Abel to give instructions."

Joline tripped up a few times, and they had to restart three times after Abel made suggestions for improvement. She proved to be a fast learner, though, and didn't make the same mistakes twice. In fact, the only one who messed up was Mark. He croaked his way through the first song.

"You coming down with a cold?" Jerry asked him.

Mark shook his head, unsure if he could trust himself to speak. He cleared his throat several times, but it didn't help. Every time he thought of her, he choked up. It had been years since he'd prayed, but he was desperate.

Lord, I know I don't deserve to ask for any favors from You, but Mrs. Vandenberg does. I want to do my best for her. Please help me concentrate on the music instead of Joline.

Afterwards, he felt more peace than he had since he'd first formed the band. He missed praying and depending on God's help when he faced difficulties. He yearned to go back to those days of simple, uncomplicated faith. A deep desire to reconnect with the Lord surged through him. For a moment, he considered leaving the band, returning to his family and the church, and committing his life to God.

Behind him, Abel patiently went over a section with Joline. Abel had made that choice. So had Joel. But Mark couldn't break up the band. And he could never, ever give up his music.

If he couldn't get his attraction to Joline under control, though, the band might split up over his inability to sing whenever she was around. Yet, what could he do with all these feelings swirling through him? Music had always carried him away, transported him. Joline did all that and more. Much, much more.

He made it through all four numbers by focusing on the posters hanging on the wall across from him and avoiding glancing back at the keyboard. Not that Joline needed his assistance. All the other guys crowded around her to help and gawk. Envy ate away at Mark, but he kept himself centered on his own music.

Every time Abel instructed Joline, Mark closed his eyes and kept composing a new song in his head. He might never have the courage to share it with the group, but it channeled his thoughts. His bandmates muttered to each other, but Mark drifted on a creative wave.

"Don't mind him," Joel said. "He gets like that when he writes music. Pretty soon he'll have a new composition for us to try."

Mark tried to hold on to the strains floating through his mind, but Joel's words stopped the flow.

To cover up his inner turmoil, Mark rasped, "I think we've done enough New Year's prep for today. Time to work on Christmas Eve."

"You can stay to listen if you want, Joline," Jerry invited.

Mark gritted his teeth. He'd meant for her to leave so he could relax. He could feel her eyes on him, and he tensed up more.

"I'd better go." She sounded uncertain and reluctant.

"Come back tomorrow," Abel said. "We'll get you up to speed."

Mark pretended to be fiddling with his mike as Joline crossed the room. Once she walked out the door, he breathed easier.

She needed daily practice with the band to get ready to take Abel's place, but Mark had no idea how he'd cope. Every time she sang, his spirit melded with hers. For the first time in his life, he understood the meaning of *soul mates*.

He'd found his, but Mrs. Vandenberg had warned him away from Joline.

What had Mrs. Vandenberg said? Something about it being the wrong time for a relationship. Did that mean he'd never have one with Joline?

That thought made everything in him ache with loss.

Joline had gotten her heart's desire—a chance to play with the Amish Rebels. But her victory had fallen flat. She'd pictured exchanging secret looks with Mark as the songs ended, but he'd barely tolerated her. And he'd seemed relieved when she'd headed out the door.

Maybe she'd made too much of their eye contact at his concerts. For all she knew, he did that with any random girl in the audience. She'd imagined a romance that didn't exist. It would be hard to practice with the group when her crush refused to look her way and acted like he could barely endure her presence.

As much as she'd enjoyed playing and singing with the band, maybe she should forget her desires. Trying to force herself into a group where she wasn't wanted had been a terrible mistake.

Chapter 9

Joline continued attending band practices, and they all—well, all but Mark—assured her she was doing well, but he still avoided her. She would have plunged into despair if Mrs. Vandenberg hadn't asked her to organize the yearly nativity play. Making costumes and helping the youngsters rehearse took up a lot of her time in the weeks leading up to Christmas Eve.

The play would be onstage first, followed by the Amish Rebels. The band needed most of the stage behind the curtain, so Joline had the children perform the nativity in front of the curtain to allow the band to set up.

For the dress rehearsal, she'd set up the stable backdrops and manger before the band carted their instruments backstage. Only a curtain separated her from Mark, but from the way he'd been treating her, he must wish they had an ocean between them.

The play went smoothly until the star didn't descend for the Wise Men. The rope must have gotten stuck. Joline dashed behind the curtain to tug it free and smashed into a hard chest.

Mark? She melted against him as he wrapped his arms around her to keep her from falling.

"Are you all right?" His deep voice sent her pulse skittering.

Joline never wanted to leave his arms. She tilted her head to look up, up, up into his eyes. The message in his gaze left her breathless. She froze and couldn't answer.

"Joline?" The rest of Mark's question hung in the air between them, unexpressed.

"*Jah?*" Could it be? Was he really looking at her like he had at the concerts?

Sparks of passion in his eyes lit an answering fire in her own.

He groaned. "We shouldn't be doing this."

"Why?" *Please don't let go*, she begged silently.

"Because I'm not with the church."

"Neither am I."

"You're not? But you will be."

Joline shook her head. "I want to go on tour with you." She glanced down, unwilling to see him recoil.

Mark sucked in a breath. "You can't."

Her words wobbled. "I figured you'd say that. You don't like me."

"Not like you?" His Adam's apple bobbed up and down. "I—I can't think of anything but you."

Jerry and Sam banged through the door with the drum set.

Mark jumped back and dropped his arms to his side. "Talk to you tomorrow?"

Joline nodded, then floated through the rehearsal, forgetting all about the star.

His insides whirling like a blender, Mark took a seat as close to the stage as he could for Joline's nativity play the next day. He couldn't take his eyes off her as she organized the children.

She adjusted costumes, soothed nerves, and whispered encouragement to the shy ones.

She was a natural with little ones. He'd seen her with her siblings. She'd make a wonderful mother . . . *and wife.*

Where had that come from? He barely knew her. But deep inside, the idea had a rightness to it. He'd found his future partner.

Mrs. Vandenberg tottered to the seat next to him. "I see you've ignored my advice."

"Huh?" Reluctantly, Mark turned toward her.

"Do you remember my warning? Now is not the time." She tut-tutted. "Until the time is right, you're setting yourself up for heartbreak."

With longing burning inside him, Mark chose not to listen. After all, what did an old lady know of young love? She claimed to have matched all those couples, but it might have been coincidence. Besides, Mark didn't need a matchmaker. He trusted his heart.

As the play began, the Bible story of Christ's birth touched him. The past four Christmases had been lonely and devoid of God, family, and love. Now he had love—if Joline felt the same way about him as he did about her. And his soul drank in the truth of God's gift to the world. And to him.

Even the glitches, when a small shepherd tripped over his robe or Joseph poked Mary with his staff or Joline raced behind the curtain to lower the star, all made him smile with joy. Never had he paid this much attention to the truth behind the Christmas story. This small, imperfect nativity scene reminded Mark that God loved him enough to send His Son to earth.

By the time the play ended and Mark led the crowd in rousing renditions of Christmas carols, his spirit overflowed. High above all the other voices in the audience, he could pick out one angel's voice as it rang out in amazing beauty.

Mark wished he hadn't committed to playing with the band tonight. He wanted to enjoy the rest of the evening with Joline by his side. Since he couldn't have his wish, he'd play all out for her. Afterwards, they could talk.

His cheerful mood deflated when her parents stood and ushered all the children out before the band took their places for the rock concert part. With a flick of his wrist, her *daed* indicated she had to accompany them. Just before she exited, she gave Mark a sad, apologetic look, one that held yearning and promises.

He'd miss her tonight, but she'd be at the Christmas dinner tomorrow. Maybe they could sneak some time together.

The next day, the band assembled for a concert of Christmas carols in the cafeteria before dinner. A huge crowd filled the many tables around the room. Joline came in late, flanked by her family, her mouth set in disappointed lines. Were her parents keeping her away from him?

With this being Abel's last concert, the cheerful hymns contrasted with the bittersweet ending of their band. As they played the last notes of "Joy to the World," Mark pined over losing Abel, but his pulse leapt a little as he imagined his future, singing with Joline. And he belted out the final refrain with gusto.

After the music ended, everyone enjoyed a delicious dinner. Mark sat at the table Mrs. Vandenberg had reserved for the band, disappointed he had his back to Joline. As he ate, several former gang members went up to the stage to tell their stories of finding God and how it turned their life around.

Each story needled Mark with guilt. How far he'd come from his childhood trust in the Lord. He'd turned his back on God. His rebellious heart had no room for spiritual things. Even worse, he'd made music his idol.

He'd broken the first commandment—*Thou shalt have no*

other gods before me—along with the fifth when he didn't honor his parents. Mark *rutsched* in his chair as he faced all the ways he'd ignored the Lord's directives.

Then Joline's *mamm*, a sweet, demure Amish woman, holding a small baby, with several children clinging to her skirts, told about her childhood growing up in the city and joining a gang. Mark's jaw dropped as she talked about the rough life she'd lived. Everyone there, including Mark, remained spellbound as she recounted coming back to the Amish and faking her faith before finally surrendering to the Lord. Her poignant story, the testimonies of the former gang members, and the simple innocence of last night's nativity play reminded Mark of his childhood, his early beliefs, and the precious gift of the Christ Child.

He bowed his head when Mrs. Vandenberg led everyone in prayer at the end, and he didn't lift it after she said *amen*. Deep inside, he knew what he had to do—ask for forgiveness for turning his back on God. By the time he'd finished his prayer of repentance, most of the people had departed, including his bandmates and Joline.

Now Mark knew his future path with certainty. He'd turned his life over to the Lord, and he intended to join the church, even if it meant giving up his plans for restarting the band. Even if it meant giving up Joline.

Joline railed about sitting with her family on Christmas Eve and Christmas Day. Her parents, ignoring their promise of her freedom, insisted the whole family must celebrate the holiday together. They left before Mark's concert on Christmas Eve, ushered the children out immediately after Christmas dinner the next day, and invited relatives to their apartment for Second Christmas, leaving Joline no chance to speak with Mark.

She could hardly wait to see him again. Until then, she lived in delicious anticipation. Maybe he'd offer her a permanent spot in the Amish Rebels. She had one more wish—a larger, more important one. She hoped he'd ask to court her.

The next time she saw Mark was at band practice. Instead of staring at her with longing, he'd gone back to avoiding her. Perhaps he needed to do that to concentrate on his music. She'd have to get used to it. To ease her hurt, she threw herself into practicing all the new songs for New Year's Eve and comforted herself by remembering the way he'd looked at her when they were alone.

"I can't believe how well you fit into this band," Jerry remarked near the end of practice. "I miss Abel like crazy, but I'm so glad we found you. Don't you agree, Mark?"

Mark's only reply was a noncommittal *um-hmm*. He seemed very preoccupied. When the session ended, he held up a hand. "I have something to say to everyone."

They all faced him expectantly. Joline clasped her hands together. Would he announce she was going on tour with them?

Keeping his eyes on the floor, he said, "I've had a change of heart. The Christmas program reminded me of what God has done for us. I spent some time in prayer and surrendered my life to the Lord. I'm sorry if I'm letting you all down, but I can't continue with the band. I'll keep my promise to Mrs. Vandenberg to play on New Year's Eve. That'll be my last concert, and I'll start baptismal classes this spring."

Joel hurried over and clapped Mark on the shoulder. "I'm so glad. We can take classes together."

Sam joined them. "I'll be doing the same."

"Looks like I'm the only one who's not joining you." Jerry turned and left in a huff.

Joline stood there, stunned. Mark planned to break up the Amish Rebels before she had a chance to travel with them. She waited until everyone had gone, then she approached him.

She desperately wanted to go out on the road with the band. "Can you wait a year or two before joining the church? It will give us time for a band tour before we settle down to baptismal classes."

Mark shook his head. "*Neh*, I'm eager to live my life for God."

"But what about me?" Joline regretted her whiny tone. "I really wanted—"

"I'm sorry." Mark's words rang with finality. "I'm giving up everything for the Lord."

Everything? He didn't mean her, did he? "You said you wanted to talk? About what?" *Please say you still want to be with me.*

As much as she loved music, Joline longed to be with Mark even more. She'd give up her dreams for a chance to date him.

Mark struggled to turn away from the pleading in Joline's lovely eyes and focus his full attention on his newfound faith.

Lord, please give me the strength to resist temptation.

"Joline, I can't deny I'm attracted to you, but it was a mistake to fall for you."

"A mistake?" Her words held pain and disbelief.

He could hardly believe it himself. Two days ago, thoughts of Joline had consumed him so much he could barely sing. Now he had to give her up.

"I'm joining the church, so I won't date until after I'm baptized."

She looked as if she had to face one of the horrible tortures in the *Martyrs Mirror* his parents used to read to him.

"I already told my parents I'd start baptismal classes this spring," she said. "We can do it together."

"I'm not in the same *g'may* as you."

That stopped her short, but only for a minute. "We can

study together. That would give us something to do, just the two of us."

That sounded so enticing. Mark would love nothing better, but his conscience warned him not to give in. Joline had made her infatuation with him plain from the beginning, and he didn't want her to do this just to be together.

"Look, Joline, as much as I'd love to spend time with you, I don't want you to join the church to be with me."

"I'm not," she protested, but her words sounded hollow. "You can ask my family. I really did say I'd do it this spring."

"You asked me to put off classes so you could go on tour with the band. I'm not trying to judge, but it seems your heart isn't ready to make that commitment."

"It is," she insisted.

Lord, help me, Mark begged. It would be so easy to encourage her to join with him, but then something Nettie had said on Christmas Day flashed through his mind.

"Remember your stepmom's story? How she joined the church only because she wanted to get a date with a certain man? I worry you might be doing the same thing."

Rebellion flickered in Joline's eyes, and her lips tightened. Mark had seen that same glint whenever she spent time around Nettie.

"I'm not anything like my stepmother," Joline seethed.

Mark adopted a conciliatory tone. "I just meant you both faced a similar situation."

The anger on Joline's face signaled him to change the subject. But what he had to say wouldn't make her any happier. He cleared his throat and forced himself to speak the truth God had laid on his heart. "Whether or not you choose to join the church can't depend on me."

"It doesn't."

"The only way I'll ever know that for sure is to end our relationship for good."

"But we haven't even started yet."

"You're right. And we never will. I'm sorry, Joline, but I care about you too much to ever consider courting you. Not now. And not in the future after we've both joined the church." Despite his pain and regret, his breakup speech came out with a finality that convinced even him of its truth.

Chapter 10

Joline whirled around and stalked off before the tears burning behind her eyes trickled out. How dare he compare her to Nettie? How dare he reject her?

I'll show him. I'll join the church and prove I meant to do it.

But even as she thought it, her commitment felt as hollow as her heart did without Mark. Once again, he'd cut her adrift and opened a vast gulf between them. Only this time, he'd made it permanent.

She rushed down the steps to the first floor and bolted out of the STAR Center. Her escape resembled the night she'd fled from Nettie and Daed's budding relationship. Then, too, she'd been filled with fury. Daed had betrayed her, replacing her in his life with a new love. Now Mark had done the same. Only his new love was not another woman, but God.

Why did everyone she loved reject her? Abandon her? Mamm had died, leaving Joline alone and grieving. Then Daed had chosen a new bride over his oldest daughter, who'd spent years caring for him. Now Mark had rejected her, leaving her crushed and heartbroken.

As she had so many years ago, she ran heedlessly down the sidewalk with no aim in mind but to escape the pain. When she finally stopped, out of breath, she stood in front of the teen club where she'd first seen Mark. Its windows were dark and empty, as dark and empty as her life.

Joline leaned her cheek against the rough brick wall and let tears run down her face. With fifteen-year-old fervor, she'd fallen head over heels for Mark inside this building. Her crush had grown into full-blown love once she'd seen him again. And now?

She'd die an *alt maedel* because she could never love anyone else the way she loved Mark. If she had to live her life alone, she would. But first, she'd prove to him she meant what she said. She'd take those baptismal classes just to show him.

Mrs. Vandenberg had warned Mark about getting entangled with Joline, saying it would lead to heartbreak. And it had. His spirit lay shattered.

Although he loved Joline with all his heart, he could never date her, because he'd always wonder if her commitment to her faith had been genuine. Despite knowing he'd done the right thing, Mark hadn't anticipated the pain of being around Joline as they prepared for the New Year's Eve concert.

It didn't matter if he looked anywhere but at her. He sensed her presence all around him. Every note she sang pierced his heart.

Even worse, he hated himself for crushing Joline's spirit. Instead of her usual bubbly exuberance, she appeared glum. It took all his willpower and constant prayer to keep his feet planted rather than giving in to the temptation to pull her close and comfort her.

After the New Year's concert, Mark intended to go somewhere else and find a different job, but Mrs. Vandenberg asked him to stay on for another year.

"I'm joining the church," he explained. "I'm sure the bishop wouldn't approve of me giving music lessons."

"Let's talk to him together. You're doing so much to bring in kids who'd otherwise be getting in trouble or joining gangs, perhaps that will weigh into his decision."

Mark doubted it, but he rode with her to talk to his bishop, who agreed to pray about the decision and encouraged Mark to do likewise.

Until now, Mark hadn't prayed about his future. When he did, God gave him peace about staying at the center and reassurance he'd made the correct decision about Joline.

Mrs. Vandenberg reinforced both choices on the way home. "I know it isn't easy to stick to your plan. But someday, Joline will be grateful for your strength. If she were in a relationship, she'd focus her attention on you rather than on the Lord."

"I had a feeling that she'd only join the church to please me."

"Unfortunately, you're correct. Joline has so much potential, but until she puts aside her rebellion and follows God's will, she'll never be able to channel her talents the way He has planned for her."

"You think us breaking up will help her do that?"

"It definitely will. You're sailing in the right direction. Don't let Joline's gales blow you off course." Mrs. Vandenberg patted Mark's hand. "Keep praying for her. God has something special in mind for her."

Mark's heart swelled with both joy and sorrow. Joy that he could play a small part in the Lord's plan for her life. Sorrow that he wouldn't be around to see it.

Mrs. Vandenberg's car pulled into the parking garage at the STAR Center, and they both took the elevator upstairs. Just before they parted in the hallway, she said, "Remember, 'joy cometh in the morning.' God will reward you greatly for this sacrifice."

The talk with Mrs. Vandenberg helped Mark stay the course

as they had their final practice the afternoon of New Year's Eve. Tonight, he'd say goodbye to his bandmates. Several months from now, most of them would be applicants in the same baptismal class. All except Jerry and Joline.

Mark prayed God would guide both of them back to the faith. Mrs. Vandenberg's reassurance that Joline had a special future ahead kept Mark from going back on his plan.

An hour later, Mrs. Vandenberg brought news from the bishop, who said God had given Mark a talent and he should use it to help others. Mark had gotten the same confirmation through prayer, so he accepted the position at the STAR Center, even though it meant seeing Joline and living with a constant reminder of his loss.

That night, he gave his music everything he had in him. So did the others. Joline's voice soared over his in spine-chilling beauty. Yet, as they stopped playing to watch the star descend to the STAR Center lobby floor to ring in the New Year, it seemed each band member's heart sank with it. None of them joined the raucous cheers celebrating a fresh start because they were only one song away from telling each other goodbye. After that, the Amish Rebels would cease to exist.

Never had Joline been as thrilled as she was tonight. Being onstage with the Amish Rebels and belting out their lyrics was a dream come true. But she'd lost Mark, so this performance proved bittersweet. She poured all her heartache over him into the music.

Amari and Elise sat in the front row, gazing at Joline in admiration. The three of them had never imagined she'd meet the Amish Rebels in person, let alone sing with them. But here she was onstage as part of their band, and music flowed from all of them like honey.

Because Joline's parents had given her the freedom to make her own decisions, she planned to stay until midnight, see the star drop, and play "Auld Lang Syne." Then she'd stay out until the wee hours of the New Year talking to her friends.

Elise and Amari had comforted Joline when she'd confided in them. They held out hope she and Mark would work out their differences, but Joline sensed Mark's deep core of inner strength, a trait she admired in him, a trait that would keep him from caving in to pressure. And she respected him too much to try to sway him from his principles.

Joline always sang with her eyes closed, so she didn't notice someone had slipped into the room to listen. When she lifted her lashes, she sucked in a breath.

Right behind Elise and Amari sat Katie, glowering as Joline tinkled the keys for the next song. Her parents had ushered her siblings upstairs long before the concert started. Joline never expected anyone in her family to know about this. Somehow, she managed to keep moving smoothly through the intro. But her mouth was so dry, she wasn't sure she'd be able to sing.

Luckily, Mark always sang alone on the first verse, and she joined him for the chorus. Then, she had a solo in the second verse. Joline closed her eyes as soon as Mark began, though she usually focused on him. She had to shut out her stepsister's disdain. Katie's disapproval had thrown her so much, Joline almost missed her cue.

She came in one beat too late, but quickly matched her tempo to Mark's until they blended beautifully. The poignancy of this piece fit her mood, and she poured all her sadness and loneliness into the music. When they finished together, the crowd went wild. Whoops and hollers and a standing ovation.

Katie slipped from the room, no doubt going to tattle. What would their parents do when they found out?

Joline had agreed to pray about her choices, but she hadn't. Not even once. She'd done whatever she wanted with no regard for God's will. Maybe that's why her relationship with Mark had ended. But Joline couldn't pray that Mark would go on tour again and take her along. That desire definitely hadn't come from the Lord.

With Katie gone, Joline let the music transport her, take her to new heights. She even improvised. She got so into the tunes, she forgot her sorrow and exuded pure joy as the final song reached its crescendo.

The band had planned a break to watch the star drop at midnight. Then, they'd close with "Auld Lang Syne." A ripple of anticipation swelled through the crowd as everyone surged toward the lobby.

Joline stopped short. Standing in the doorway, grim-faced, stood Daed and Nettie. How long had they been there?

They didn't say a word because they didn't have to. Disapproval radiated off them. They kept a sharp eye on her as the star dropped. Though she longed to cheer with the crowd, knowing her parents were judging her every move kept her silent.

The exhilaration running through her as the crowd applauded had eased some of Joline's pain over Mark, but the loss throbbed like a toothache. And playing one final song, a tearjerker, would bring up all the agony of losing him.

Her parents trailed the crowd back into the auditorium and stood like sentinels by the exit. Joline closed her eyes and poured her sorrow into every note. She'd gotten so involved in the melody, she shut out everything except the haunting tune.

As the last note died away, Joline kept her eyes shut, hoping to hang on to the magic a little longer. But Elise and Amari rushed to the stage, embraced her, and squealed.

"I can't believe how good you were!" Amari jumped up and down in excitement.

Elise just shook her head. "You were up there onstage with those dreamboats. Lucky you!"

"I never could have done it without you." Joline had to give them credit. "If you hadn't recorded all the band's songs, I never would have known them well enough to do this."

The three of them hugged again.

"Let's do something to celebrate," Joline suggested. "First, let me introduce you to the band."

But as she turned to lead the way, the immovable wall of two angry parents blocked her way.

"Upstairs, Joline, now," Daed ordered.

She sent her friends a silent apology and headed for the elevator.

When they reached the apartment, Daed waved her toward the bedroom she shared with Katie. "We all need our sleep. We'll talk about this tomorrow."

Joline tossed and turned all night, dreading her punishment.

The next morning, when she rose, Daed said, "Pack your things. You're going to stay with Aenti Betty and Onkel Amos. You can help with your cousins and work at the farmer's market. We've arranged with their bishop for you to take baptismal classes there."

"But I don't know anyone in their *g'may*."

"All the better. Maybe that will give you time to concentrate on reading the articles of the Dordrecht Confession and prepare for baptism."

All the walls seemed to close in around Joline, cutting off her escape. Her *aenti* and *onkel* were stricter than Daed, and her cousins were young. She'd have no one to talk to, no one to confide in.

"Wait!" Joline pleaded. "This isn't fair. You gave me my freedom. I shouldn't be sent away because of it."

Daed's voice was low and sorrowful. "Look me in the eye, Joline, and tell me you prayed about singing in that band."

Joline couldn't do that.

One hour later, she was in Mrs. Vandenberg's Bentley, being driven to her *aenti* and *onkel's* house in Mount Joy. She'd had no chance to say goodbye to the band members, Mark, Elise, or Amari before she was whisked away.

Ever since New Year's Eve, Mark had not seen Joline. Though he missed her terribly, it was for the best. He could breathe easier. But he couldn't help wondering where she was.

He was unprepared for the emptiness inside when Mrs. Vandenberg informed him Joline had gone to stay with her *aenti* and *onkel*. Mark's throat closed up, and he couldn't ask his most pressing questions: Would she choose to take baptismal classes? If she did, would she mean it? Would he ever see her again?

Chapter 11

As the loneliness of winter budded into spring, Joline dreaded starting baptismal classes. All she wanted to do was run away. Maybe she could find Jerry, and the two of them could restart the Amish Rebels. But each time she fantasized about it, deep inside she knew joining a band would never make her happy. Not if Mark wasn't in it.

By now, he'd be starting his own baptismal classes. And at harvest time, he'd join the church. Then, no doubt, he'd find a lovely girl to date, one with a deep, abiding faith. Joline pictured the type of *maedel* he'd choose—sweet, docile, gentle, spiritual, kind—the exact opposite of her. But Mark deserved that kind of wife.

Joline's restless spirit rebelled at the thought of making a lifetime commitment to God and the Amish faith. She didn't want to follow rules or do the right thing.

Betty and Amos insisted she attend the singings, but Joline made no friends. Most of the *youngie* were several years younger than her, and she'd never be able to talk over her prob-

286 / Rachel J. Good

lems and doubts with anyone. None of them would understand her love of music, her stint with a rock band.

She also stayed aloof from the plodding farm *buwe* who showed an interest. No one could compare with Mark. And she could never give her heart to anyone but him.

Alone at night, Joline had nothing to do but pine for Mark and study the Dordrecht Confession. Though she didn't really understand the High German, she plodded through, struggling to find meaning in each article. And she said tentative prayers for her family's health and that Mark would find happiness, despite being unsure if God would listen to someone who was faking her faith.

The first day of baptismal classes, Joline squirmed on the bench. She longed to be anywhere but here. The bishop gave them all an opportunity to leave if they didn't want to commit their lives to God and the church.

Here was her chance. She could stand up and flee. But where would she go? And what hope did she have for a future outside the church? Besides, she'd vowed to show Mark she'd joined the church.

Miserable, Joline stayed, knowing she didn't belong.

The bishop directed his question to the first applicant. "Do you have anything to say? What is your desire?"

The *bu* answered as he'd been taught, "My desire is to renounce the devil and all the world, accept Jesus Christ and this church, and this church to pray for me."

One by one, each of the *buwe* answered in turn, "That is my desire too."

Joline *rutsched* in her seat, and her stomach clenched. She couldn't lie.

Suddenly, the gravity of what she was doing came into sharp focus. If she said these words, she'd be committing to accepting Jesus, to living for God her whole lifetime. It meant an end to her rebellion, to her self-centered life. She'd need to seek God's will and follow it no matter how difficult. Could she do that?

She tuned out the bishop's question as he looked at the other *buwe*, and instead she examined her own heart.

Guilt and grief overwhelmed her as she recalled all the cruel, hurtful things she'd done, all the times she'd defied her parents and God, all the times she'd shown off. Her pride in her looks, her voice, her abilities. The catalog of her faults stretched so long and so far, Joline didn't see how anyone, even God, could pardon her.

Amidst her despair, a still, small voice echoed inside. "Whatever you've done, I will always love you and forgive you."

It didn't seem possible when she was drowning in sin, but Joline grasped for that lifeline. With overwhelming gratitude, she accepted God's gift of grace.

As the bishop turned to the *maedels*, Joline was ready. "That is my desire too," she declared.

A burden lifted from her soul. She'd turned her life over to God. With her tendency for rebellion, it wouldn't be easy living for Him, and she'd need a lot more forgiveness, but today she'd made a commitment she intended to keep.

As fall leaves fluttered to the ground, Mark sent a letter to his parents telling them of his baptism and letting them know he'd be teaching music at the STAR Center. He wasn't surprised when they didn't answer.

It looked to be a lonely Christmas. He prepared his students to present music for the STAR Center's annual holiday meal. This year, though, he did it with a heavy heart because he had to do it without Joline. He'd never realized how much her enthusiasm and energy meant to him until it was missing.

Mrs. Vandenberg stopped him in the hall a few weeks before Christmas. "I've decided to set up a drama program and hired a lovely Amish woman to oversee it. Would you be willing to work with her on music for the nativity play?"

His heart aching, Mark squeezed his eyes shut for a few moments. Last year, as she'd prepared for the nativity performance, Joline had bumped into him, and he'd held her in his arms. Longing overwhelmed him. Would he ever get over her?

But Mrs. Vandenberg was waiting for an answer. Mark swallowed hard. "I'll do my best." He prayed she wasn't planning to match him with another Amish *maedel*. His heart belonged to Joline and always would. He only hoped his sacrifice had brought her to the Lord. He prayed every day that God would protect her and lead her to do His will.

"Awesome. She's waiting in my office." Mrs. Vandenberg's cane tapped a jaunty rhythm to the elevator, and upstairs she opened her door and motioned for Mark to precede her.

He stepped inside and came face-to-face with Joline.

"Mark? I didn't know you'd still be here." Her eyes burned with love for him.

Mrs. Vandenberg smiled. "I leave you two to your planning." She exited and shut the door behind her with a snap.

Words tumbled over each other as they caught up on what they'd been doing. Tears filled Joline's eyes as she recounted the day she'd turned her life over to the Lord.

"It's all thanks to you," she said in a shaky voice. "And God, of course. But if you hadn't broken up with me, I would have gone through with the classes just to be with you. I never would have faced my failures and sins. Or asked God for forgiveness."

Mark's heart swelled until his ribs ached from the pressure. He couldn't believe it. God had brought the one woman he'd always loved back into his life. And now, they'd be working together.

He reached for her hand. "Joline, I want to be partners in

the performances here in the center, but I'd also like us to be partners in life."

Before he could even ask whether she'd consider him, Joline jumped in with her usual exuberance. "I do too."

Mark laughed. His joy overflowed. He loved her spirit and enthusiasm, her zest for life, her bubbly personality, her . . . Actually, his list could go on forever. And that's how long he prayed their union would last. Forever.

Epilogue

One year later...

Mark had thought last Christmas had been the happiest holiday ever. He and Joline had worked together on the Christmas program, being sure all the music and drama centered on the Lord. And there hadn't been a dry eye in the room at the end.

Mrs. Vandenberg had seated Mark at a table near the stage, but the surrounding chairs stayed empty, pointing up his aloneness—except for the smiles Joline flashed his way as she raced around taking care of last-minute costume and prop emergencies. Those smiles meant the world to him.

When he rose to direct the musicians and singers, he turned his back to the room and put all his energy into making this the best program ever. When the show ended, Mark and Joline's eyes met, and they shared a special love-filled glance before he turned around to face the audience, who continued to applaud the children's performance. He hoped the enthusiastic response would help these street kids gain confidence and keep going with their music and acting.

His gaze drifted to his previously empty table, now filled with people. To his shock, every seat, but two, was filled with his extended family. Their eyes were all shining, and they were clapping enthusiastically for the children.

As the young performers scampered off to join their own families, Joline came up beside him. "Surprised?" she asked. "Mrs. Vandenberg contacted your *daed* and arranged transportation for everyone."

Mark couldn't believe it. "She's something else. I wish we could do something for her."

"I think we already have." Joline tilted her chin toward the table where Mrs. Vandenberg was still applauding. "She told me matching up couples is her greatest joy in life."

Mark glanced down tenderly at the woman he loved most in the world. "She does an excellent job."

"I agree."

Mark enjoyed introducing Joline to his family and spending time with hers on Second Christmas. And thanks to Mrs. Vandenberg's intervention, both families became friends and attended Mark and Joline's spring wedding. So did Mrs. Vandenberg—as an honored guest.

They presented her with a gift, but not to be outdone, her wedding gift to them was a large apartment and office combination like the one Joline's parents occupied, but at the opposite end of the STAR building.

Throughout the rest of the year, Joline and Mark organized shows that glorified God and brought His Word to the community, loving every minute of their work and life together.

After the curtains closed on this year's Christmas performance and the children had returned to their seats, Mark stayed backstage and drew Joline into a dark corner, where he kissed her thoroughly.

"I thought last Christmas was my happiest ever," he said. "I'd reunited with you and my family, but I had no idea this year would be so much better. I'm so blessed to have you as my wife."

"I'm blessed too." Joline stood on tiptoe to kiss him again. "I have a Christmas surprise for you that might make this year even more special."

He waited expectantly for his gift, but he never could have guessed the gift she had for him.

Joline looked down shyly. "You're going to be a father this summer."

Mark sucked in a breath. "You mean . . . ?" He choked up and couldn't get any more words out.

When she nodded, he embraced her, cradling her head against his heart. "I'm so grateful for all God's given us."

After so many years of lonely holidays, Mark had a feeling each Christmas gathering from now on would be better than the one before. They'd not only have their extended families with them to celebrate the Lord's birth, they'd have their own little ones.

"*Danke*, Lord, for all your wonderful gifts," Mark said, "and especially for the birth of Your Son."

"Amen," Joline said softly, her eyes alight with joy, before their lips met in a holy, heartfelt holiday kiss.

Read more Amish Christmas romance by Shelley Shepard
Gray and Rachel J. Good in
CHRISTMAS AT THE AMISH BAKESHOP

As the most joyful holiday draws near, three couples discover
the recipe for love includes faith, hope, and the sweetest blessings . . .

A CHRISTMAS CAKE FOR REBECCA
New York Times bestselling author Shelley Shepard Gray

When carpenter Aden returns to Lancaster after twenty years
away, bakeshop owner Rebecca is dismayed to find he's still as
handsome and kind as ever. He broke her heart when he left the
community back then. Will a holiday emergency provide a second chance at love, this time forever?

BEST CHRISTMAS PRESENT EVER
USA Today bestselling author Rachel J. Good

When a lonely widower with an ailing daughter meets a new
cake decorator at the bakeshop, they discover they were once
childhood playmates. But as each of them helps the other care
for family, their neighborly kindness inspires a gift that only
love could make possible . . .

THE CHRISTMAS CUPCAKE
USA Today bestselling author Loree Lough

A builder who never learned to read believes he must hide his
fond feelings for a kind schoolteacher. But after they run into
each other at the bakeshop, she offers to teach him—and as
Christmas approaches, each of them learns a lesson about the
great gift of love . . .

Visit us at kensingtonbooks.com

Visit our website at
KensingtonBooks.com
to sign up for our newsletters, read
more from your favorite authors, see
books by series, view reading group
guides, and more!

Become a Part of Our
Between the Chapters Book Club
Community and Join the Conversation